Del

Bodymore Murderland

A Novel By:

Delmont M. Player

Dedication

This book is dedicated to my heart, my first love, my wife, and my REFLECTION, Chanae Angela Temple. Engraved on my arm, written across my heart. I love you more than you will ever know, and I am so PROUD and HONORED to tell the world that you are mines! I often think about when I first laid eyes on you more than twenty three years ago, and I swear that I never thought I could love you more. Than A'myiah's birth forced me to fall DEEPER IN LOVE with you.

So I said this has to be it, but then Darrien and Ahmad came and taught me just how UNBEARABLE and BEAUTIFUL diamond love was as I continued to fall deeper in love with you baby. You have held me up when I was down, pushed me forward when I wanted to back out, and still manage to remain strong under all the weight the world laid on you. And that's a fate not many women can stand under and survive. You are one of the 'RARE' women who not only 'talk the talk', but 'walk the walk', especially when it counts.

That's why I can't wait to legally make you my WIFE! I promise that when 'OUR STORY' is all said and done. It's gonna be a Best Seller because N.E.I.W.W.A., and you are more beautiful, irresistible, and thorough today than you were when I first fell in love with you. You are my past, present, and future Chanae. Your love has proven to be unconditional, unforgettable, and MORE POWERFUL than time, distance, and pain. I love you Beautiful, and I ain't EVER LETTING YOU GO! You will always be my No.1 Cat, and I'll Always be your biggest fan!

4

Acknowledgments

Off the T-O-P I have to thank God/ Allah for giving me a gift to write and blessing me with a strong mother (you know I love you LP), an amazing wife (you know what it's hitting for), and a beautiful family (you know who you are) who has never given up on me.

Next up is **MY RIBS**! Latonya 'Thuglife', Victoria, De'bre'anna, Ta'nyah, A'Myiah C.J., Jasmine, Jadah, J'nai, Delmonte, Falynn, Darrien, Little Detauwn, Jordan-Antauwan, and Ahmad. I can't think of a better team to carry the family torch and break the 'CYCLE' we created. I love you all to pieces. THERE'S NOTHING Y'ALL CAN'T DO! Winning is in your blood. Each one of you were born with what it takes. You don't have to try hard to fit in, because you were born to stand out. Love each other, respect one another, and ALWAYS remember that no matter what y'all may go through, at the end of the day y'all are family, and that alone 'OVERRIDES' everything.

What can I say when it comes to my Idols? How can I truly salute my brothers Detauwn and Antauwn and show my appreciation? I can't so I'll just say this, 'Thank you both for teaching me what real honor, loyalty, respect, and MANHOOD was.

HOLD UP! Let me slow down and give some much deserved love and overdue admiration to a few rare 'caliber' of women, who know what it's like to struggle against time, distance, and pain. Y'all didn't always win, but y'all always fought! And for that, I am forever GRATEFUL!

Saprina Edwards, Tineeka, Tiffany, Yo-Yo, Missy, Trina, Trease, Little Missy, Keisha & Kia, Leslie, Michelle,

Shalane, Aunt Elester, Aunt Maxcine, Sis. Re-Re Spriggs, Ann, Sis. Roberta, Ms. Bunny, Sis. Keisha, Sis. Rachel & Raqual, Emoni, Emma, Sis. Simone, Thompson, Tinika, Dania, 'Moose Trap' Midget, Ni'ziah, Zi'ariah, Erika, 'Pea' Brown, Danielle Ownes, Ebony, 2nd Mother Shawnell Alexander, Sis. Shaneesha, Sis. Muffin, Sha'Nyiah, Ma-Ma, Nikki, Sis. Lashaun, Booty, Ms. Jane, Tisha, Mom Jacqueline Shakir, Susan Kerin, Momma Mary Moore, Aunt Heidi, Ms. Sarah, Dorrene, the Mckinnon family, Mrs. O, Helen King, Tasha & Paulette, Socoria, Lakeria, Sabrina, Beama, Lil' Blvd Shannon, Park Heights Octavia, Sanlo, Silvia, China, Janell, Jasmine, Tiphani, Lenuar, Angie, Paula, Tish, Robin, Karla Wingate, Shaneeka, Keisha Paylor, Cassandra, Annie, Victoria, Zee, Ayana .J, the 38 Posse, and South Baltimore's own 'T.A.B.U.' Click.

Y'all have rode with me through a lot of the madness. Y'all have kept me strong and on my toes at one time or another, and made sure that 'OTHERS' OVERSTOOD that there were still real, principled, 'mentally conscious and spiritually unbreakable' Man behind the walls. Everybody not Rats, Rapist, Cowards, Game Runners, and/or undercover Homo Thugs. Thanks for all the extra love, support, prayers, lessons, letters of encouragement, phone conversations, and time. YOU ARE APPRECIATED!

A special acknowledgement to all of my fallen loved ones on the other side of the clouds watching over me...My Pops 'Timothy Player', My Aunt Priscilla, My Aunt Barbara, Grandma Lily, Aunt Janie-Maye, Dottie, Mrs. Dorothy Alexander, Debre Leach, Creole Truesdale, Ms. Fuzzy, Donnett, Ms. Sandra, Tiffany, Roofy, my niece Journey S., and all the rest. A hole the size of your heart was left in the world when God called you home, but you will NEVER BE FORGOTTEN!

Much respect to all my Menemies who kept it 100 no matter what, a middle finger to all my SO-CALLED men who didn't. You know exactly WHO YOU ARE. Only rock with a nigga when he's in the streets or able to help you out. Big ups to Park Heights, North & Long, Black Pigtown, and all the other hoods I ran through, corners held me down, Men I rolled with, and the Gangsters & Gentlemen who took the time to lace my boots and guide me through on both sides of the fences.

Now I said that I wasn't going to mention no dudes, 'family, friends, or foes', for one reason or another, but I wouldn't be keeping it 100 if I didn't pay homage and tip my hat off to my man Anthony 'Bucky' Fields, Southeast D.C.'s finest for respecting my pen game, and believing in my vision when nobody else did or would. Especially since he has a 'sick' pen game himself. And for the record, My wife and Me, are the real life *'Ameen & Shawnay'* from *The Ultimate Sacrifice series.* Thanks for giving me a chance Slim. I won't let you down; I got this! Now sit back and let me show you how we put it in down 'N DA STREETS' of Baltimore for real!

To all the GOOD MEN & THOROUGH WOMEN still standin' and Carryin' Their Weight, I salute you because you kept your vows to the game and stayed strong through all its ups and downs. THAT MAKES YOU A WINNER! Believe that. The losers went out sitting down, pointing fingers, dropping names, and signing statements, wishing they had the 'Balls & Clits', to Stand Up when it counted the most. RAT BASTARD! And finally, shoot outs to Stacey Lee Mouzon, the fat, funny-built, female dog that testiLied at my May 25th –thru-June 11th 1999, Murder Trial. The State

of Maryland called you a Star, so I just made you famous.
SAY CHEESE!!!!!

Summer 2012

"Baltimore City Police Department. What's your emergency?"

"Hello! Hello!" What sounded like an older woman's voice came through the headset in an excited whisper.

"Baltimore City Police Department. How may I help you, ma'am?

"Please send someone! We need help! Somebody's been shot and oh God he's bleeding to death. They shot him for no reason. Why would they just shoot him for no reason?"

"Okay, ma'am, I am going to need you to try and calm down and tell me where you are." The dispatcher was already tracing the call, but she was trained to keep the caller calm and gather any additional information she could. "Ma'am, can you tell me where you are?"

"Locked inside of some vault in the basement of the old Federal Bank across from the shopping mall on Reisterstown Road. These guys…they…they just stormed in demanding money and shot the cop. They—

"Ma'am," The dispatcher cut her off. "Is the officer with you still alive?"

"Yes, but he's bleeding to death for God sake. I don't think he's gonna make it and I don't know what to do. I don't think I can do this. Why is this—hold on, I think I hear someone coming. Oh God! One of them is coming back! Please help us!"

"Ma'am! Ma'am!" The dispatcher repeated but only managed to hear what sounded like a brief struggle before the phone went dead. *"All units! All units! We have an Officer down and a possible robbery in progress in the…!"*

Bodymore Murderland

"A'ight, look these niggas ain't no different than any other niggas we done hit. So, everybody already knows the routine. When we get up in here, any of them niggas get to faking, slump 'em'. We ain't got no time to be bullshitting. Any questions?" Black asked before tossing the burner phone out the passenger side window and looking around. "Good."

Black zipped up his navy-blue windbreaker with the word Police emblazed across the back in bold yellow letters. Then he pulled down his ski-mask and adjusted the Baltimore City Police badge that hung around his neck on a silver ball-link chain. "Let's get in here, handle our business, and bounce. No fuck ups."

"And, yo, whatever y'all do, make sure y'all get the nigga behind the counter first. Y'all can't let him hit that button under the counter because it will deadlock the employee's door from the inside and set off the silent alarm they got hooked up in the back.

"Man, we got this! Lil' Dray barked grilling Card. He didn't really like the nigga and he damn sure ain't trust him. To him, Card was another pussy stuntin' like he was cut like that. "We have been over this shit a hundred times. You just worry about keeping this motherfucker running and ready to go when we come out."

"Yeah, dug, this what we do," Black assured Card just as several police cars came flying by to report to the police involved shooting and possible armed robbery in progress that didn't exist. It was simply a trick out of the old gangster handbook to open a window of time for the type of move they were about to pull on these so-called 'TreeTop Piru Blood' niggas.

"A'ight. That's us right there." Black looked over his shoulder. "Everybody double check their shit! We about to move."

Present were Lil' Dray and Mumbles, two of Black's partners in crime, his baby mother's cousin Card and Peacock, another Lexington Terrace homeboy that they were forced to bring along due to their other crime partner catching a dumb ass domestic violence charge a few days before the lick.

"Let's get it then." Mumbles said cocking his chrome Mossberg pump shotgun. Lil' Dray slid over and put his hand on the sliding door handle so he could snatch it open as soon as they pulled up in front of the spot.

Black nodded to Card, and he pulled out into traffic and floored the gas of the gold Dodge Grand Caravan. Quickly eating up the 4600 block of Park Heights Avenue and damn near crashing as he came flying into the 'Red Maple' parking lot. Black, Lil' Dray', Mumbles and Peacock were out of the caravan rushing through the double glass doors of the 'Red Maple' with their guns drawn before Card even brought it to a complete stop.

"Baltimore city police department nigga! You better not move!" Mumbles ordered jumping across the countertop, slapping a man to the floor with the back of the Mossberg. "Stay your young bitch ass down, or I'm gonna push your whole shit back!" He added pressing the business-end of the Mossberg up against the gang member's brow.

"Hold it down!" Black fired continuing to move towards the Employees Only' door.

"I got this." Mumbles replied never taking his eyes or aim off the Blood nigga.

Black pulled the 'Employees Only' door and led Lil' Dray and Peacock into the narrow, dimly lit hallway. They already knew that at least three more Blood gang members were inside because they had been casing the store all morning waiting for B-Rock to show up.

"They should be in there. Lil' Dray whispered to Black over the sound of hip hop music. He pointed to the only closed door in sight that appeared to have light coming underneath as they continued to ease down the hallway.

Black used his hand to signal for Peacock to kick the door in so he and Lil' Dray could rush in and do their thing. Peacock nodded, stepped forward and kicked the door open with all his might. Black and Lil' Dray immediately ran in and went straight to work. They were all over B-Rock and his crew before they even had a chance to react. Black covered B-Rock and the man to his right. Lil' Dray' quickly closed the distance between himself, the 'Red Maple' store owner and a tall, skinny dude that looked like the rapper Snoop Dogg. He slammed the business-end of a four-fifth into the store owner's face. "You bitches know what time it is."

"Blood, you know who you fucking with?" The *Snoop Dogg* looking nigga who had arrived in the red Maserati with B-Rock earlier bucked trying to get up. Blood, y'all got us fuck—

Black slammed his face into the desk, slung him to the floor and blew his brains all over the place without a moment's hesitation to show B-Rock and the others, that they were fucking with real killers.

"Look, man; I got zero tolerance for bullshit and tough niggas. We already know y'all niggas moving weight up out this bitch! We been clocking the spot all week, so don't play no fucking games. We want the money y'all got up in this bitch. And the gym bag you came in with." Black aimed his gun at B-Rock's head. "Now what's it gone be? You, niggas going to play fair, or y'all wanna be tough guys too?"

"B-Rock calmly put his hands up in a sign of surrender before kicking the gym bag he carried in out from under the desk." Take it, blood. You got it."

"The bag is cool, but we came for everything, not just that bag. Where the rest of the money at?" When no one spoke, Black nodded at Lil Dray. "They think we bullshittin', dug."

Without a word, Lil Dray upped his gun and shot the man closest to B-Rock. Then he pointed the gun at the store owner. "You're next."

"It's a small safe behind that photo right there on the wall." The store owner said quickly, visibly afraid.

"Come on. Get your ass up and open it, nigga!" Lil' Dray demanded snatching the scared motherfucker up outta his chair, pressing the gun firmly up against his temple. "And you better not try nothing stupid."

Lil' Dray watched closely as the store owner removed the photo from the wall and tried to enter the six digits safe combination twice before he said something.

"Stop shaking nigga and take your time."

The Blood nigga took a deep breath and exhaled before trying again. This time Lil' Dray heard the magic sound and- couldn't help but smile when the chump cracked the safe open, and he saw all the stacks of cash.

"Bingo! Lil' Dray said pushing the store owner back into his seat and gesturing for Peacock to clean out the safe.

"Nah, I got it," Black said, not really wanting Peacock to do too much. It wasn't that he didn't trust Peacock, Black was just used to handling his business with his men only. "Come over here and watch him." He nodded towards B-Rock.

Black snatched the gym bag up off the floor and made his way around the desk to the safe while Lil' Dray' relieved the store owner of his jewels by roughly ripping them from his neck. Black opened the gym bag and peeped inside. Sweet, he thought. At least ten strong smelling, well compressed pounds of weed. Black nodded and quickly swept all the money out of the safe into the gym bag.

"On Blood, Y'all niggas got me fucked up!" B-Rock yelled and shot Peacock in the shoulder. Black spent and shot him in the face. B-Rock's body dropped and lay sprawled at Peacock's feet. But not before he got off another shot that tore across Peacock's forearm.

"Didn't I tell your stupid ass to watch him?" Black barked grabbing the gym bag. It was a good thing that the store was inside the old Shell Gas Station because the building had been designed to minimize an explosion, so the sound of gunfire probably didn't travel too far.

"I told you to watch the nigga!"

Black sized up Peacock's wound as he came around the desk. His shoulder wasn't so bad, but his forearm was bleeding all over the place.

"He caught me off guard," Peacock said in his defense trying to hold his banana-split looking forearm closed as blood seeped through his fingers.

"If you would've watched him like I said, your ass wouldn't be shot. Damn man! Fuck! Let's bounce." He surveyed the scene one last time and hissed, "What are you waiting for, Dray. Crush that nigga and let's get outta here."

Lil' Dray didn't need to be told twice. He shot the last remaining Blood gang member, the store owner in the back of the head and watched him fall forward, slumped over the desk before running out the office to catch up with Black and Peacock.

"Damn, yo, what the fuck happened?!" Mumbles questioned as soon as Black and them emerged from the back of the store and he saw all the blood on Peacock.

"I'll catch you up on the ride. Let's go." Black replied still moving for the doors behind Peacock knowing that now wasn't the time to discuss Peacock's fuck up.

Mumbles knew exactly what time it was. No more needed to be said. He brought the barrel of the Mossberg down and blew the head off the dude that he held captive.

******

On the way to Lincoln Park, Lil' Dray' and Black kept cutting their eyes at each other as they removed their fake Baltimore City Police equipment and tried to stop Peacock from bleeding to death. They both knew what had to be done.

Peacock was a soldier and all, but his DNA was all over the crime scene. So, when Card finally pulled into the little opening of the Lincoln Park woods, Black shot Peacock in the side of the head and threw an old rug in the back of the Caravan over top of his body and climbed out.

"Damn shorty, y'all some cold niggas." Card said looking inside the back of the Caravan.

"Man, just go get the car." Lil' Dray' ordered as Mumbles and Black grabbed the two jugs of gasoline and started pouring it all over the inside of the Caravan.

"Pull the rug back and get that nigga's body too," Black said knowing that it was the only sure option to ensure that nothing traced back to them.

"You got the money and shit Dug?" Mumbles looked at Lil' Dray' jumping out of the back of the Caravan, and he nodded and held up the gym bag as Card pulled up in his black, tinted window Vigor. "A'ight nigga, fire that shit up."

Black pulled the sliding door all the way closed and tossed a match through the side window and watched as the Caravan turned into a huge fireball while Lil' Dray and Mumbles went and hopped in the car.

"Nigga, if you don't bring your ass on!" Mumbles stuck his head out the car window and yelled at Black when he realized he hadn't move. "You, standing there looking all crazy and shit! Get your dumb ass in this car."

Black took one more look at the flame engulfed Caravan and climbed into the car with Mumbles and them. "I just wanted to make sure everything went up."

"We good." Lil' Dray' assured him looking in the passenger side rear-view mirror before opening the gym bag and tossing a pound of weed back into Mumbles lap as Card slowly pulled off. "Let's blow something for that nigga Peacock."

"Damn, that shit strong as a motherfucker." Mumbles said tearing into the plastic, picking up a big ass sticky bud.

"Yeah, that's that fire." Lil' Dray retorted messing with the radio until he located an old ass club song on 92.Q. "Yo, after we break down and take care of D.W.'s bail. I'm trying to go out. We can hit the China Room or something. "Shid, I'm down." Mumbles replied splitting a blunt and dumping the tobacco all over Card's floor as Lil' Dray turned the music up on the bullshit as factory system and started to sing along.

Hey! You knuckleheads! Hey! You knuckleheads. Walking down the avenue, walking down the avenue… A few more streets and we'll be through…

As the club music echoed through the Vigor with an off ass base, Black fell back into his 'Mental Roller Decks 'trying to figure out who they could sell the weed too. Getting rid of the guns wouldn't be a problem. All they had to do was trade 'em' off with some niggas down the buildings or something. *'Sandtown, North and P, Park Heights, R and G, Whitelock, Cherry Hill, North and Long, and Dopefield…'*

Player Delmont M. Player

Chapter 1

"Yeah, baby!" Anthony 'Billy Lo' Izzard hugged his girlfriend Lakeria Stanback the second he exited the prison walls and stepped on free ground. "Daddy's home." Billy Lo had met Lakeria almost two years ago through an Internet Pen Pal service, and she'd been riding ever since.

"Mmmmh." Lakeria squeezed him tight. "I am so glad; you're finally home baby." Lakeria started kissing all over him. In her mind, she had met Anthony at the perfect time because she had all but given up on men. They were all dogs in her book. At least the leftover ones were. All the good ones seemed to be locked-up, taken, or dick-chasing. But, the thirty-eight-year-old, thick peanut butter brown beauty, had lucked up and found herself one of the last real niggas still standin'.

"Me too baby. It's my turn" Billy Lo looked back at the Maryland House of Correction, or *The Cut*' as they called it with a bitter smirk. He had just brought a fifteen-year bid to the door for these peoples. fourteen years and nine months to be exact. And he stood like a man the whole fucking way. But still, after his parents died in a car accident everybody had turned their backs on him. And that was when he needed them the most.

Billy Lo had almost lost it. His parents were everything to him. Especially his mother. So, after her death, he started running wild. Robbing and stabbing niggas, running his bid up, but he didn't care. *He was hurt.* Plus, it was his only way to survive after motherfuckers started disappearing. It was like he was a fucked-up nigga or something like he hadn't played fair when he was out there or kept his mouth shut when shit hit the fan. First niggas let his *'first love'* and gangster bitch Lotti get murked, then they fucked his *'so-called'* main girl, and finally, if that wasn't enough, they turned around, took what little bread he had left and left him for dead. But, it was all good because he hadn't forgotten and he damn sure hadn't forgiven. It wasn't until he met his man Diamond and Lakeria that he began to care again.

"Come on baby, let's get away from this hell hole" Billy Lo grabbed her hand gently and led her towards the car.

As they drove in silence. Billy Lo enjoyed the scenery, so much had changed since the fall of '98'. The game was fucked up. Truly in a state of flagrant disaster. From what he could see from the inside and from what Diamond had gathered from the outside. It was almost sad.

The game Billy Lo once knew and loved was all but dead. It was no longer about morals and principles. No longer about honor and respect. Now, it was all about money and manpower. Known suckers and rats were controlling the streets of Baltimore and money had some of the City's grimiest killers behind them. The *'Golden'* days were over and whoever had the gold made the rules. There were gangs and everything running around the City now. Shit! Even the music was fucked up. Niggas weren't rapping about shit! But, Billy Lo was a three-three-year-old, egg head, 5'5'slim, brown-skin Park Heights nigga, cut from that old-school cloth. He had been suited and booted by legendary enforcers and notorious gangsters like Warren Stuckey and Rudy Williams. Men who played the game by all its rules.

Today, niggas didn't respect shit or honor nothing, but money. Then so many old niggas talked about that *'Old School'* game, but they too were playing the new one. Billy Lo knew that it cost so much to be a man with the price of being a follower so cheap, but in the fall of 2013, he knew that he might just be the most real thing to hit the streets since AIDS.

Delmont M. Player

"Here we are baby" Lakeria pulled up outside of an apartment building in Essex Maryland. "Home, sweet home."

Billy Lo looked around and took a few mental notes. Even the County Boys ain't seem like County Boys no more with their iced out jewels, souped up ears, and mean mugs. Billy Lo smiled. He guessed they still couldn't sense danger though. Living in Essex didn't seem like it would be too bad because it would allow Billy Lo to do heavy dirt in the City and sleep comfortably in the County.

"Baby, come on," Lakeria said anxiously snapping Billy Lo out of his thoughts. "The apartment up here."

"Oh, my bad baby" Billy Lo locked the car door. He could see the lust in Lakeria's eyes and knew it was time to put in some much-needed work and get his dick out of the dirt. The business he had to take care of for Diamond would have to wait a few days. Lead the way.

Billy Lo admired Lakeria's big ole' ass as he followed her to the apartment building. He could not wait to get up in that pussy and blow her back out. It had been a long time. Too long.

"I love you, Anthony!" Lakeria spoke over her shoulder opening the apartment building door.

"I love you too baby girl!" Billy Lo replied sincerely.

He would never cross her. Lakeria was his baby. She had been there when nobody else cared. Held him down when nobody else would and for that, he would always be grateful. Billy Lo never planned to repay loyalty with betrayal ever again. He had made that mistake once by leaving Lotti, back then he hadn't known any better, but he was focused now. And just like he would never repay loyalty with betrayal, he would never reward those who had betrayed him with loyalty.

"And I'ma about to show you just how much" Billy Lo added slapping Lakeria on her ass as he followed her into the apartment.

Chapter 2

"Well, it won't be much longer now Ock," William 'Shabazz' Taylor said to Diamond as they jogged the penitentiary yard like they did every morning for exercise and meetings of the minds. Prison, especially 'The Cut' was no place to be out of shape. Mentally or physically.

"Yeah, I know" Diamond replied. "It's been a long time. And you earned it."

Yusef 'Diamond' Brinkley was a handsome, light-skin, bald-headed Sunni Muslim with an Osama Bin Laden beard from West Baltimore's Murphy Homes Projects. Who'd been in prison since '1989' when the sudden cooperation of his then right-hand man had threatened to bury him in prison forever and forced him to accept a thirty-five-year plea agreement.

"Yeah, that's what they tell me."

With good time and a few more programs, Diamond was looking to see the front doors in a couple of months. It wasn't so bad that he couldn't say the same thing for his former running partner's snitching ass. The sucker had saved him a lot of trouble by going back in the streets and getting his wig split by some young kid trying to make a name for himself.

"I know the game ain't what it used to be, but it's still money out there. A nigga just got to know what's he's doing." Diamond added as they neared their twelfth lap as if going straight wasn't even an option.

"That's the easy part, Ock. Your problem is going to be, trying to keep a leash on them youngsters of yours." Shabazz said knowing from experience how undisciplined guys could fuck up a good thing. The old Southside, gray hair gangsta had been serving time since men started choosing profit over principle.

"Oh, I got them little niggas" Diamond assured him. He had already sent Billy Lo out there to bring some law and order to the messes his little cousin and them were making. And he knew Billy Lo would follow through because his word and his honor meant everything to him. That was one of the main reasons why Diamond fell in love with his character when they had first met after he came out of the Baltimore City Supermax 4 years ago. "Billy Lo gonna hold it down until I get there."

"Diamond!" Shabazz only called his name when he really needed him to listen closely and understand exactly what it was that he was about to say. "Whatever you do don't lose focus out there. And don't lose control. You gotta keep your head in the game at all times, and maintain control of everything and everyone around you or your going to lose. Now I know them young boys ready to fall for you, but that stuff they got going; not going to last. *Blood and business never does.*"

"You got to think, Ock." Shabazz's words came out slow, as if after great thought. "Like I told you. I've spoken very highly of you to my nephew. He knows that you're a real solid dude with a good business head. So, everything is gonna be taken care of. The only thing you gotta do is get out there and control them kids."

"And that's it, huh?" Diamond smiled looking into the steady penetrating eyes of the flat-nose mobster.

"*That's it,*" Shabazz replied with a sinister look in his eyes that always amazed Diamond. For the life of him, he couldn't understand how an old, clean cut, smooth face guy with an angelic look could give off an aura of power so strong that it could not be denied. Maybe it was the fact that he would square off against anybody, at any time. "Like an old buddy of mines used to say. Loyalty is admirable in a follower. In a leader it shows weakness."

"He ain't never lied." Diamond said shaking his head in agreement as Shabazz's words begin to register. He knew that Shabazz was a Man's Man through and through. His case was legendary, and you could read about all the work he had put in back in the day on any number of computers in the legal library. The onetime hitman and former friend of Stringer Bell had refused to roll over and become a 'Rat Bastard' like those before him when an FBI Agent got killed, and the Feds started rounding gangstas all across the city up.

"That's fifteen," Shabazz said winded coming to a stop near the gate.

"I thought you said twenty?" Diamond looked at him still running in place.

"Yeah, but I gotta make a run and take care of something," Shabazz replied looking towards the gym. "I'll get my other five when I get back."

"A'ight, that'll work." Diamond nodded and jogged off with his thoughts. Him and Billy Lo had a master plan. And with patience, discipline, and commitment nobody would be able to stop them. If shit went right, Diamond would be walking out of prison just after the 'New Year' to a team of young wolves ready to take Baltimore by storm. All Billy Lo had to do was handle his business, and everything else would fall into play just like they had discussed.

******

"DAMN!" Black barked slamming the phone.

"What's up nigga?" Lil' Dray questioned waiting on the update from the streets. "What Peanut say? Your cousin's man ain't call yet."

"Nah," Black replied taking a deep breath as Lil' Dray shook his head. He knew that he wouldn't like the sound of that. "Man, I wish we never got moved off Killer-K."

"Yeah, I know." Lil' Dray thought about all the shit they had lost. Phones, Oxy, uptown streets, knives, and the C.O. bitch they were both fucking. "But them niggas jumped out there."

Black knew that Lil' Dray was right. The Blood niggas had already been trying their hand, but once they found out that Black and Lil' Dray were over the jail for spanking a few of their homies, they came for retribution. "Yeah that was dumb." Black said thinking about how the Tree Top Niggas tried to pull them a move while they were together. "I guess they figured cause they were deep and had a fake ass stronghold, niggas were gonna bitch up or something."

"I bet they don't think that anymore." Lil' Dray said remembering how they had jumped out on the Bloods. Before making reference to a few other West Baltimore dummies. Who had peeped the move and rolled with them when they got to rocking.

"I know one thing though before we leave this jail. I'ma get that nigga with them bricks and black hyena tattoos, and if I can't when we get up town I'ma make a house call."

'What you know that nigga or something?"

"Nah, but that Lil' Bitch stabbed me while I had the cuffs on and I heard him talk about being from the Avenue, so I know he's right there where the rest of them Blood niggas be. They're all Tree Top Piurs." Black said and Lil' Dray knew that he was serious. "That's why I hope this nigga call."

"Nah, that's why I hope this nigga not one of them dudes that be talking all that shit while they're locked up, then come home stuntin'." Lil' Dray said.

"Yeah, you and me both," Black replied knowing that they had everything riding on this nigga. "Like I said. I don't really know the nigga or nothing. I mean, I talked to him a few times and saw him once when I went down Family Day with Diamond, but that's it."

"A'ight, but you don't think your cousin just gonna say Yo, going to take care of shit if he, not right?" Lil' Dray asked.

"Nah, my cousin ain't gonna do no shit like that," Black assured him. "But Dug, I ain't gonna lie. I wish D.W. weren't on that dumb ass box so he could handle that shit."

"That nigga can't move a muscle though. Then Mumbles on the run. Man shit crazy. I wish we would've just caught that bitch ass nigga Card before he bailed out. I swear to God, I would've torn the fur off his hot ass myself."

"Shid! Not if I would've gotten to him first."

Lil' Dray and Black could pass for brothers. They both had that rough 'I been in so many streets fights' and 'I dare a nigga to step out there 'look. The pair had become friends after too many knuckle fights during their Harlem Park Middle school days when their neighborhoods (a small up and coming Southwest Baltimore spot and a major project in the heart of West Baltimore) beefed on sight. After they squashed their beef, sealed their friendship and brought their crews together, it was a wrap! And everybody from the school to the hood knew that 'if you fucked with one, you fucked with them all.' Not a week went by where they weren't in some shit. Stomping some niggas or rumbling a crew. Still, by the end of eighth grade, it was only Lil' Dray, D.W., Black, and his sandbox brother Mumbles that became inseparable.

"Well, let's just hope this nigga come through for us." Lil' Dray said hopefully. "He probably just getting some pussy. I know if I just came home that's what the fuck I would be doing." Lil' Dray added moving his body in a sexual manner. "I'd be like…"

Black knew he was just trying to lighten the mood because Lil' Dray knew how impatient he could be at times.

"…plus, we got a good week before trial supposed to start anyway. And you know them bitches gonna probably try to postpone that shit most likely."

"You right Dug, I'ma chill and give Yo a few days." Black nodded. "If Yo call, Peanut already got all the information he needs. A nigga just ready to hit the bricks."

"You know I feel you on that." Lil' Dray was tired of sitting in the jail too. But he didn't want to rush this nigga into fucking up or backing out. "I'ma call Tina real quick and see if she heard anything."

"Yeah Dug, do that. And find out if Mumbles dropped some money off yet before I press one of these bitch ass niggas out over here. Because we need to get another phone."

******

"I am so tired of babysitting this piece of shit!" Detective Bruce 'Bunchy' Baker barked in frustration. "I don't see why we just don't stop playing all these *'cat and mouse'* games with this little wannabe gangster. Let's just run him in, take him up in one of them dry-cells and go old school on his ass. I'll bet he tells us what we want to know then!"

"Now that's wishful thinking, but we can't afford another lawsuit." Detective Lashaun Gibson said reminding her partner of what happened the last time they went all N.Y.P.D. on a suspect. "And besides it's only a couple more days until the trial begins anyway."

Det. Baker still felt like they were wasting their time focusing on White when Pair was the one still at large. "Yeah, well, they could've given someone else this babysitting detail. I mean come on, do you honestly believe that this little piece of shit is going to cut The Home Monitor off his leg and run out in the streets to commit cold-blooded murder? Even he can't be that stupid, right?"

"You would be surprised," Gibson replied. But honestly, she knew Baker was right. They needed to be concentrating on protecting the State's Key Witness and finding Pair because if anything he would be the one to pull the trigger on this. Be it before or after the trial. But the Captain's Orders were the Captain's Orders, and Gibson had no plans of challenging them. At least not this time. "I'll tell you one thing though. I pray that he try's it on our watch."

Bodymore Murderland

"Now who's doing the wishful thinking?" Baker cracked a slight smile as thoughts of finally nailing 'one of the four wannabe gangsters' the proper way crossed his mind.

******

"Them bitches still out there?" Mumbles asked D.W.'s girl Tiara as she peeped out the window showing him nothing but her long legs and barely covered ass.

"Yup." She replied still looking. "It looks like they're talking."

"A'ight. You can close the fucking curtain now, damn!" D.W. barked shaking his head wishing like hell that his grandmother would've had a phone so that he could've done his Home Monitor time over at her spot because Tiara was getting on his last nerve. "Or you want them to know we know they out there?"

"Whatever Donald." Tiara rolled her eyes letting the curtain fall back into place. She knew Donald was just trying to show off like always. But she didn't trip because she knew that as soon as Mumbles left he would be all up in her ass apologizing and shit. "I'ma go ahead and go back upstairs and finish watching TV before I end up cursing your black ass out."

"Yeah, why don't you do that?" D.W. fired wanting to get up and slap the shit out of her. "And put some fucking clothes on while you're at it too."

"Bye Mumbles." Tiara ignored D.W. and headed for the steps. "And don't forget to tell Cat I said hi."

"I got you Yo." Mumbles stole one more look at her ass as she made her way up the stairs with an extra twist in her hips.

"Dumb ass bitch!" D.W. tried to mumble under his breath, but Mumbles heard him.

"Yo, you crazy as shit." Mumbles shook his head. "Keep carrying shorty like that if you want to. That shit gonna come back on you one day."

"Yeah, a'ight." D.W. retorted like that was the least of his worries. "I swear this bitch driving me crazy though Dug. I can't wait to get up off this box so I can cut her dumb ass off."

"Ah, nigga. You act like you got a lot of options. I got more than you." D.W. fired smiling.

"Let you tell it." Mumbles couldn't help but laugh. His sense of humor alone got him more play then D.W. But it was his bedroom brown eyes, dimples and confidence that drove all the hood-rats insane and kept Cat ready to put her foot in somebody's ass. "Nigga, you know my shit tight. I got a wife and bitches still be trying to jeopardize their life."

"A'ight *D-M-X*," D.W. said honestly knowing that Cat probably would kill someone over Mumbles funny looking ass.

"Nah, but seriously though." Mumbles looked at D.W. "I thought you suppose to have been got that shit cut off last week."

"I was but somehow that bitch Gibson got a body attachment order to hold me until Dug and them finish the trial." D.W. got up. "My P-O said that shit legal too. I'm telling you Dug, that bitch ain't gonna stop until we all dead or caged up."

"Man, fuck that bitch!" Mumbles said after pondering on D.W.'s word for a moment. "All a nigga gotta do is make sure Card bitch ass get touched."

"I still can't believe that nigga nutted up like that. Especially after all that old-school gangster shit, he talked."

"You?" Mumbles repeated shaking his head like he really couldn't believe. "I can't believe Yo, did that shit to his own cousin's baby father. I mean fuck me, and Lil' Dray, but Black like his family."

"Yeah, that's definitely some sour ass shit. It's cool though. He gonna eat the same poison all the rest of the rats ate."

"Yeah, lead." D.W. laughed.

"Yo, you dumb as shit." Mumbles gave D.W. a pound and brotherly hug. "Look, I'ma about to jet. I got to drop this bread off for Black and Lil' Dray so them niggas can stop crying."

"Check on that other thing too Yo, see if them niggas heard anything from the dude."

"Man, you know I'm on that shit." Mumbles assured. "I'ma make sure that shit straight before me and Cat bounce."

"Y'all still going down Texas?"

"Yeah, her crazy ass aunt Pooh, got a spot out there." Mumbles replied. "That's the best alibi I can think of right now. But like I said before. If shit ain't in order. I'ma hit this nigga head myself. Fuck that! I ain't letting my Dugs go down like that."

D.W. nodded. It went without saying that he would do the same thing. "Shit gonna be good though. So, you just go ahead and enjoy yourself while you down there."

"Oh, without a doubt." Mumbles gave D.W. some more love and headed for the back door to go take care of business. "One."

"One," D.W. repeated following him to make sure the door was locked.

Chapter 3

"Mmmh... Anthony baby! Right there. Shit baby, that's my spot." Lakeria was bent up in some half looking alphabet while Billy Lo slammed 10 1/2 inches of dick into her tight, wet pussy. "Mmmmh…"

"Hmmm." Billy Lo, moaned as Lakeria's lava-like pussy gripped his dick like a vice-grip. Billy Lo looked down and saw his wet dick sliding in and out of Lakeria's pussy and put his back into it. He loved having her in the buck because she couldn't run. He started thinking about all the shit she used to talk about being nasty and fucking his brains out when he was locked down and picked up the pace. "Who's pussy is this huh? Come on, talk to me!"

"Ahhh…baby it's…it's yours, all yours!" Lakeria pushed on Billy Lo's six-pack to keep him from digging so deep. "Ohhh…God! Baby… mmmh…!"

Billy Lo had been home for two days now getting his dick out of the dirt. And every time he and Lakeria had sex it felt even better. No more phone sex. No more jerking off to letters and photos and no more bullshitting about the nasty shit he was going to do to her. "It better be." Billy Lo, leaned back and held Lakeria's legs up by the ankles with one hand, and slapped her firmly across the ass as his mind flashed to all the sex he and Lakeria had been having over the last forty-eight hours. He knew she was about to cum so he slowly long stroked her until he saw her thick cum started to cake-up around his dick.

"Ant…Anthony, baby…baby, I'm…oh my god! I'm Cumming!" Lakeria's face flushed and her eyes rolled back into her head as she bit her bottom lip. "Oh, my God! Umph…umph…umph!" Lakeria laughed shaking her head after

Bodymore Murderland

Billy Lo pulled out and fell back on the pillows with his head propped up. "Damn!"

"Yeah, I know." Billy Lo smiled as Lakeria slide down his sweaty body and started sucking his dick like a pro. She cleaned all the cum and nut off his dick real good before hitting his balls for good measures. Unlike in her few past relationships, Lakeria knew how to keep her man happy (food, sex, and love) because he had told her how. So, she continued to rub his nuts, suck his dick, and make loud slurping sounds; until Billy Lo grunted and nutted down her throat.

Billy Lo couldn't help but laugh because all that 'I don't do this, I don't do that' bullshit went right out the window when he got home and started hitting that *G-spot.* "I told you."

"Boy, shut up." Lakeria popped him upside the head knowing exactly what he was referring to. He had been making that statement for two days now. Every time she did something that he used to say only 'Good Girls' did. You make me sick. Lakeria added getting up to get ready for her first day back to work.

"I told you, I'ma make you a freak." Billy Lo said slapping her on the ass and watching it jiggle.

"Anthony stop! You play too much." Lakeria said loving every minute of it as she floated to the bathroom feeling like a million bucks. She blushed at the thought of the things Billy Lo had talked her into doing. Swallowing, taking it in the butt, and some more shit. It was true what her mother used to say, "The key to figuring out if you got a good man, is by figuring out how far you're willing to go to please him."

Billy Lo hopped in the shower with Lakeria and ate her pussy again before she got ready and left for work. She had to show some new clients some property out in White Marsh, Maryland, so he knew she would be out for a minute.

Billy Lo hit the button on the CD-Player after walking out of the bathroom and fighting to do a couple of push-ups. Lakeria had gotten all the CD's he had told her to get, so his little collection consisted of nothing but that real throwback gangster shit. *Tupac, Nas, Wu-Tang Clan* and *Biggie*. Billy Lo let the *'All Eyez On Me'* bump while he got dressed and went through his prison bag looking for the number Diamond had given him the night before he left.

After finding the number and grabbing a couple hard earned prison dollars, Billy Lo was out the door. Nobody knew where he was laying his head at and he planned to keep it that way. During the last few years on his bid Billy Lo had made Lakeria start using his last name on letters and everything. And once she moved he made her get a P.O. Box and would not allow her to put no other return address on his mail. Billy Lo didn't trust nobody. As far as he was concerned Diamond and Lakeria were the only family he had. So, when it was time for him to go out and get his revenge anybody could get it. Everybody that faked, and all the mother fuckers that was down with it.

As Billy Lo, exited the apartment complex, he reached into his pocket, pulled out his burner phone, and made his call. He heard a female's voice answer the phone after the third ring and got straight to business.

"Yeah. Hello, can I speak to Peanut? Oh, how are you doing? This Billy Lo, Diamond's homeboy… Right… Good. I can't call it. I'm just trying to take it one day at a time you know?" Billy Lo chopped it up with Peanut for a few minutes then got down to the business at hand.

"…nah, I'ma just give you my P.O. Box Number. You can drop everything off there. You got a pen? A'ight. The number is…" Billy Lo gave Peanut the P.O. Box information and directions to the Post Office then hung up and headed towards the shopping mall to pick up a few things for himself and the apartment. He decided that he would call Diamond later that night after he picked up everything. For now, he would just hit the mall and shoot back to the crib to relax until Lakeria got home.

Bodymore Murderland

******

"Yo! It's on!" Black fired walking up on Lil' Dray in the dayroom after getting off the phone with his daughter's mother. "I just talked to Peanut. She said all is well. Yo, grabbed that last night."

"That's what I'm talking about." Lil' Dray's day instantly brightened. And he needed that because Tina was stressing him the fuck out. On top of that, he heard shit about her dealing with some clown from down 'The Hill.' "That's what a nigga needed to hear Dug."

"Man, from now on, if a nigga ain't on the team we're not fucking with him period. I don't care who peoples he is." Black knew that they were playing a dangerous game, and the only way to win was to play for keeps. "I should've let you slump that nigga when he clammed up about that other shit." Black added. Coming up all he ever wanted to be was a respectable, stand-up gangster. That's it. Nothing else really mattered. "You was right the whole time."

"I told you that nigga was soft Dug, I felt it." Lil' Dray replied thinking about the move Card tried to pull last year after a robbery. "Now his bitch ass playing with a nigga's freedom."

"You was definitely on point. But I'll bet you this. That shit won't happen again. I don't even give a fuck if a nigga ain't on the team. If he shows any signs of bitch and got anything to do with our business. I'm cracking his shit off the muscle. Straight like that!" Black fired hoping that Billy Lo came through for them. He seemed straight up. And Diamond always tooted his horn. But Black knew that that didn't mean a nigga was about that gun smoke. "Anyway Yo, I'ma bout to go jump back on this horn and call Peanut back."

"Bet. Give her my love too." Lil' Dray looked at Black wishing Tina was as thorough as Peanut. Peanut was a real live gangster bitch. Tried, tested, and proven. One of them crazy bitches a nigga wanted by his side when shit went south. "You a lucky ass nigga Dug."

"I heard that." Black smiled and made his way out of the dayroom. His mind was on getting back on the streets and leaving the smell of blood, sweat, and shit to the niggas who enjoyed it.

******

"Hold on baby." Diamond left his wife on hold and clicked over. "Hello!"

"What's up Diamond in the rough?"

"Oh, shit! What's good my nigga?" Diamond smiled recognizing Billy Lo's voice and signature nickname. As a matter of fact, hold on. "I got my wife on the other line." Diamond clicked back over on the cell phone. "Hello... Yeah, baby. I'ma call you back in a few minutes... Nah, I got Anthony on the phone... Yeah, I love you too baby." Diamond hung up and clicked back over. "Billy the Kid. What's up?"

"Ain't too much. Slow motion. You know me."

"Slow motion, better than no motion." Diamond said then got focused for the curve ball he knew Billy Lo was about the throw at him. "So, what's the business?"

"I just picked up my paycheck today, so I should be able to send you some bread soon. Give me a day or two." Billy Lo replied.

"I appreciate that man." Diamond caught the hidden message. "My money funny as shit right now too, so a nigga can definitely use a few dollars."

"That shit ain't nothing slim. We family and I know that you'd do the same thing for me." Billy Lo looked at his watch and knew he had to get back to the apartment before Lakeria got out of the shower, so he didn't have to explain what he was up to. "But, look Yo, I'm not going to hold you up. I just wanted to touch bases with you and let you know that I'm on shit out here."

"Come on nigga; you ain't got to do that. I know what's up." Diamond assured him. "But be safe and take care out there shorty, and tell Lakeria I said hi."

"Will do." Billy Lo said "One."

"One." Diamond ended the call and strolled down his numbers until he saw his wife's name before hitting the send button. "Hey gorgeous, I'm back."

Diamond laid back on the bunk to get comfortable as his wife went back to talking about the latest book she was reading.

******

"Baby, get back in bed." Cat rolled over half asleep when Mumbles took his arms from around her and crawled from beneath the covers naked.

"Hold up baby." Mumbles whispered, quickly removing the heat from his pants pocket, on the floor next to the bed, and creeping over to peek out the window. "I swear I heard something."

"Ain't nothing out there. You know I would've heard it." Cat assured. She knew how paranoid he'd become lately. Always thinking that the police were on the other side of the door or just around the next corner. He was so lucky that she loved his black ass so much. "You just hearing shit."

Mumbles knew Cat was probably right. She slept light enough to hear paper burning, but he still looked around the parking lot. Tomorrow couldn't come quick enough. He could not wait to get on the road and head down south.

Ever since Card's punk ass had dropped his name in the 'Red Maple murders.' Mumbles had been jumping from motel to motel and hiding out with the only woman in the world that he trusted with everything from his life to his liberty. Cat was his world. His rib and soulmate. He couldn't imagine being without her. Even on the run. The bond they had was unbreakable. Plus, she was a rider, and everybody knew that when it came to Mumbles, it wasn't nothing she wouldn't do and that went both ways.

"What are you doing now?" Cat asked when she saw Mumbles picking up his jeans and *Oakland Raiders* Jersey.

"I'ma go take a look outside."

"No, you ain't." Cat fired throwing the sheets back. She decided to ease his mind because if he went snooping around the motel in the middle of the night, somebody was bound to call the police. "I got something else I need you to take a look at."

Mumbles looked back towards the bed and saw Cat laying there in nothing, but her sexy little high heels with that signature 'lip biting' look, and couldn't help but lick his lips. Cat was a chocolate dime piece. The perfect combination of rapper *Foxy Brown* and Porn Star Cutie *Jade Fire*. With all the women Mumbles had ran through. He could not think of one that came close to being anything like Cat in no shape, form, or fashion.

"You gonna have to look a lot closer than that baby." Cat smiled.

"Why you gotta be so nasty?" Mumbled questioned, thinking that even without her make-up, she would be a *Top Model Finalist*.

"Because I know how much you love it."

Mumbles dropped everything and shot over to the bed, as his dick got harder than a lead-pipe. He wrapped Cat up in his arms and aggressively started kissing her. Then he cupped her full, Hersey-Kiss nipple breasts, and started making his way down south. Mumbles never got tired of making love to Cat and worshiping her temple. Everything about her drove him insane and straight liquefied him. Her touch, her taste, her love, her smell, and the comfort that never failed to calm him and ease his mind, when he needed it most. It was just something about knowing that she always had his back no matter what.

"Mmmmm." Cat moaned and rolled her hips as Mumbles sucked, licked, and kissed his way across her body. Cat looked

Bodymore Murderland

down, brought her legs back as far as she could, grabbed Mumbles by the back of his head, and offered him a taste of power.

Mumbles took his time, carefully using his long, thick tongue to drive Cat wild; because he wanted to make her cum over and over again. Pausing to look at her pretty little pussy as it opened, throbbed, and closed shut like it had a mind of its own. Mumbles smiled to himself because he knew that no other nigga could make Cat's pussy talk like that.

Mumbles tenderly sucked one of Cat's pretty little soft black pussy lips into his mouth, and that was all it took. From that moment on nothing else in the world mattered. Not Card, not the police, not Black, and not Lil' Dray. The only thing that mattered was tasting Cat's delicious pussy and fucking her brains out.

Cat arched her back and moaned the instant Mumbles tongue contacted her clit. "Mmm...baby!" Cat started shaking her head from side to side, breathing all crazy. "Ssssshit! Eat that pussy Daddy!"

"I got you, baby." Mumbles paused to kiss her pussy softly and went right back to work. Tomorrow could wait.

Chapter 4

After making toe curling love to Lakeria, Billy Lo slipped out of bed, peeped at the clock on the nightstand, and saw that it was duck hunting time. He waited for Lakeria to stir, roll over hugging her pillow, and dose back off; before grabbing her car keys, and tip-toeing out of the room. In the living room, he got the gear he'd purchased earlier from behind the couch and started getting ready. He knew that once he hit-the-door. It would not take him no time to get to the P.O. Box and pick up the package Diamond's folks had left.

When Billy Lo picked up the information and stuff from the Post Office, he was kind of surprised to see a picture of Card. He thought everybody knew that nigga was a rat. His chump ass had pulled the same shit back in the mid 90's when they were all over the jail fighting cases. Billy Lo quickly tucked the twin Glocks and got rid of the photo and address. He didn't need it. Card had particularly raised him. So, locating him wouldn't even be an issue. All he had to do was swing pass Africa's house, or if all else failed post up outside of Card's mother's bar down South Baltimore

Billy Lo pulled over at the next Gas Station and gave Africa a call. He knew the bitch still had the same number because when he was locked down, he used to call her from time to time to trade lies and find out what was going on 'Up the way.' He couldn't help but smile when Africa's phone started ringing. He knew the phony bitch was going to go crazy when she realized he was home. But, he would never let his guards down with her again.

The bitch was a cold-blooded snake. She'd shitted on him the entire time that he was locked down. Fucking both his so-called friends and sworn enemies and that was something that he could never pardon. But still, the thought of a little payback wasn't such a bad idea.

"Hello."

"What's up shorty, this Anthony." Billy Lo said, and Africa went off. The bitch wanted to know everything, from where he was to how long it would take him to get there. "Give me about twenty minutes."

"A'ight nigga, don't keep me waiting. I love you!" Africa replied and hung up.

Billy Lo looked at the phone, shaking his head. Had Africa just really said she loved him? The bitch couldn't be serious. The only thing she loved was money, sex, and weed and that was all he planned to feed her. When he finally pulled up in front of Africa's mother's house on Cordelia and saw her posted up on the front porch patiently waiting he had to take a moment to get his emotions in check because it was still hard to believe that Africa had crossed him like she did. Especially, after all the shit he'd done for her. But, after reminding himself how strong she'd made him. He remembered how grateful he was and hopped out of the car.

"Oh my God! My Motherfucking baby really home! Africa ran off the porch and jumped into Billy Lo's arms and started kissing all over him. "Boy! I thought you were playing."

Billy Lo backed up to get a good look at Africa. She was still the baddest black bitch in Park Heights, hands down. It was too bad she was only a pawn in the game Billy Lo was about to play.

"I've been thinking about you like crazy. I swear I was just telling my sister that I wished you were home so you could carry some of these bitch ass niggas out here. You know…"

Africa rumbled on and on about a bunch of shit that Billy Lo wasn't really trying to hear. "Look, man; we can talk about all that shit later. A nigga just touched down. I'm trying to get some of that pussy."

"Nigga, you ain't said nothing but a word," Africa said, grabbing Billy Lo by the hand, pulling him towards the house. "I'ma put this pussy on your ass like never before watch."

"Now you talking." Billy Lo followed behind Africa's 'pigeon-toed ass and couldn't do anything but watch her Apple Bottom. It was time to put all that nasty ass shit he'd seen and read about in all those 'Buttman' and freak novels in prison to use. "I see you still got that mean ass gap."

"And I hope you still know how to close it up," Africa replied giggling over her shoulder.

Billy Lo took Africa straight to her bedroom and started crushing her porn-style. He no longer had no respect for her whatsoever, so nothing was off limits. Tea-bagging, hair pulling, slapping her all in the face with the dick, making her gag, deepthroat, and some more nasty shit; was just a taste of what he had in store for her snake ass.

Africa cried and begged for mercy as Billy Lo tried to knock the bottom out of her ass, but he never let up. He treated her like the whore he knew she was and it felt so good. Almost as good as it felt when he finally pulled out, snatched her head back, made her open her mouth, and bust a nut all over her face. He couldn't believe that he'd ever fucked up his relationship with Lotti for this bitch.

"Did you call that nigga Card and tell him to come over like I said?" Billy Lo questioned still washing his nuts when Africa strolled into the bathroom butt naked.

"Yeah, but I don't understand why you just ain't go around there," Africa replied with a curious look on her face.

Billy Lo knew she was probably wondering if he knew she was fucking Card, which he did. A homeboy down 'The Cut' had already pulled his coat, but he played it cool. "I don't be liking dudes all up in my house because that's how shit gets started."

"Nah, I just wanted to surprise that nigga."

"Well, I told him, but he probably thought I was playing because I don't even be dealing with him like that. I mean, not since you been locked up." Africa added probably for her own benefit. "N-E-way. He said he ain't closing shop until around three."

"Then I'ma have to catch that nigga tomorrow because I got a job interview in the morning." Billy Lo disregarded Africa's little innocent act and pulled up his pants, after hanging somebody's washcloth back over the sink.

"So, what…you not staying?" Africa gave Billy Lo an evil look; he knew all too well.

"Nah, I told you I gotta take my aunt her car back." He lied. He knew that Africa just wanted to play house and get fucked again. But, he'd already blown her back out twice and he damn sure wasn't about to lay up with the bitch. "But, I'll see you once I'm finished though a'ight?"

"You better." Africa fired. "Don't make me come looking for your ass Anthony."

"I got you shorty." Billy Lo laughed and gave Africa a quick kiss on the cheek; before slapping her on the ass, telling her to clean that beat-up ass pussy, and heading for the door to further his plan and update his murder game. He drove past Card's strip twice. It had been about nine years since he'd actually laid eyes on him, when he had come through on a parole violation, but the ugly ass nigga looked exactly the same.

Billy Lo parked the car a few blocks over from Pamlico Road and made his way back towards Card's dope strip. Getting lost wasn't even a factor. Billy Lo knew Park Heights like the back of his hand. He looked around before approaching Card. He wasn't surprised that the nigga was still a creature of habit. He kept his money closer than his burner.

Card cracked a smile the moment he realized who Billy Lo was. "Oh shit! What's up slim? I heard you was home."

That bitch Africa thought Billy Lo but said. "Yeah, yeah. I heard you were jamming out here too. Got the Road on smash."

"You with me now slim." Card smiled. "If I don't know how to do nothing else I know how to get money."

"So, what's up?" Billy Lo asked.

"Same ole, same ole" Card replied. "Yo, come on walk up to this house with me. I got to put you down with a lot of shit. Niggas ain't the same slim. They be out here hating on a real nigga."

"What's up with Africa though?" Billy Lo questioned to see what Card would say.

"Oh, shorty good peoples slim. She was riding for you the whole time you was gone." Card shook his head before turning to tell his little pups to hold it down while he stepped off for a minute.

Billy Lo and Card walked up to the street to one of his spots talking. It was about five little niggas sitting on the front kicking it. "Come on in real quick. I got something for you." Card nodded towards the door, and Billy Lo followed him. "I'ma hit you with a couple stacks, then I want you to take a ride with me." Card said looking back as they stepped into the vestibule. "I got a lemon that owe me some paper and I need you to squeeze him for me."

"Say no more." Billy Lo followed Card inside the house.

After getting three stacks and a bunch of needed information on a few former friends. Billy Lo pulled out one of the glocks and laid it across his lap. Card got big eyed and started looking around for an exit route.

"What's up? You cool in here? You can put that up." Card tried to remain cool as he swallowed the fear in his throat.

"Where the rest of the bread at nigga?" Billy Lo asked calmly.

"Billy Lo, Slim, what is you..." Card started but was quickly cut off.

"Save all the slow singing Dog. And tell me where the bread at before I crush you."

Billy Lo picked the glock up and slid one into the chamber.

Shaking his head Card pointed at a bag of pampers hanging on the back of a stroller and Billy Lo got up and grabbed it before telling Card that he was gonna lock him in the basement.

"Don't come out for at least five minutes." Billy Lo said as he walked behind Card towards the steps.

"That's crazy slim, you on some wild shit." Card fired as he opened the basement door. "Niggas grew…"

Billy Lo silenced him with a shot to the back of the head and watched crumble and roll down the basement stairs. Then quickly headed for the door. What Card had forgotten about Billy Lo was that he did a grimy nigga worse, then he did a grimy bitch.

When he emerged from the house Card's lil' young boys were looking at him. Not really sure what was up, or if they had heard what one or two of them thought they heard. Billy Lo grabbed the closet one, pressed the hot glock to his skull and pulled the trigger before blocking the steps off as the rest of them started to scatter. He caught one and drug him back over to his homeboy's body. "If I find out 'ere one of you little niggas ran y'all mouth. I'ma come back and crush every last one of y'all." Billy Lo said through clenched teeth, shaking the little nigga by his collar. "You hear me nigga?"

The kid couldn't find his voice, so he just nodded. Billy Lo stepped over top of his homie and fired three more rounds into what was left of the back of his watermelon looking head to get his point across, before letting the kid go and breaking out. He cut through a few alleys, hopped a few gates, and made his way back to the car.

On his way home Billy Lo, tossed the gun into the Chesapeake Bay, ditched his gloves, and took one more look at his watch before heading home. He wanted to be back in bed before Lakeria got up for work.

******

"I think I better answer that." Detective Gibson exhaled deeply, running her hands through her sweaty hair, as she continued to ride her partner and sometime lover towards an orgasm. "Oh! I think I better answer that." She repeated but couldn't bring herself to stop riding some good dick just to pick up the phone.

"One-second baby." Detective Baker reached up and squeezed Gibson's breast. "One second, let me get this nut."

Gibson continued to let the phone ring, until both her and Baker reached their orgasms. Then she rolled off him onto her back and tried to catch her breath. "Gibson." She said picking up the cordless house phone still winded.

"Evening detective." The heavy familiar voice cracked.

"Captain." Gibson looked over at Baker sternly knowing that she should've taken the first two calls that came in on her department issued cell phone. "I was just about to call in."

"Listen, save the sweet talk for your partner. We got a problem." The Captain fired and went on to explain what was going on.

"You gotta be kidding me. Are you sure?" Gibson sat up. "Got damn it!" she pounded her fist into her pillow.

"I don't fucking believe this shit!"

"Just find your partner detective, if he's not already with you and have your asses in my office in an hour." The Captain hung up before Gibson could even think of a response.

Baker knew from the sudden look of disappointment on Gibson's face that something was wrong. "I take it, that wasn't good news."

"Worst. Somebody just killed our only witness on the Green and Chapple case." Gibson said staring at the wall.

"Fuck!" Baker barked jumping out of bed. "I bet you it was that fucking little bastard Pair!"

Gibson sat there trying to collect her thoughts. She could not believe that they had let some little wannabe gangsters get one over on them, she'd vowed to get them. And now it looked like they would slip through the cracks of justice again.

"Not this time." Baker was rumbling on as he got dressed. "Not this fucking time!"

"Bunchy, what are you doing?" Gibson spoke finally coming out of her daze. "We can't do nothing stupid to fuck this case up even further. The Captain's already pissed."

"We been going about this all wrong," Baker said pulling his jacket over his shoulders looking at Gibson. "We got to try the old approach. Because the new ones are not fucking working!"

"So, what now? We rush out in the streets in the middle of the night and try to find Pair? That's what you're thinking?" Gibson questioned looking at her partner like a fool. "You think we just going to go out in the streets and find something to hold up in court overnight?"

"Nope." Baker gave her a stupid ass smirk. "I was thinking more along the lines of driving over to White's house and making him give us something. I don't give a damn what it is."

"But, White was locked up when the murders happen." Gibson reminded Baker.

"So! You know them little punks told him something." Baker paused opening his hands as if giving her time to think. "You with me or not?"

"I don't know why, but you know I am," Gibson replied shaking her head, knowing that she'd live to regret it. "Hopefully we can at least get something that will stop the Captain from killing us in an hour."

******

"Get up Nigga!" Lil' Dray' yelled walking into Black's cell.

"Man… what the fuck is you all pumped up for?" Black asked laying the pictures of his daughter down and sitting up on the bunk agitated. Lil' Dray had fucked up his chain of thought.

"Yo, I just came back from seeing Wolf, and he said…"

"Wolf?" Black cut him off. "Who the hell is Wolf?"

"The Private Investigator dumb ass." Lil' Dray fired getting Black's full attention. "Anyway, he said that bitch ass nigga Card got spanked last night."

"Won't your dirty ass stop playing," Black said laying back down.

Everybody knew how much Lil' Dray liked to play. Even at the wrong times. It was one of the reasons why they stayed in so much shit on the section.

"Yo, that's my word! Needleman called Wolf late last night." Lil' Dray' retorted with a serious look on his face. "You know I ain't gonna play about our freedom," Wolf said somebody dogged that nigga up The Heights last night.

Black sat back up and looked at Lil' Dray. The nigga played so much that he couldn't tell if he was joking or not. "For real Dug? Put that on everything."

"Nigga, that's on everything! I ain't gonna tell your black ass again." Lil' Dray' replied. "Card a done deal. Go call your lawyer."

"If you playing Dug, I'ma fuck your dumb ass up watch," Black assured him, hopping off the bunk to go jump on the horn.

"Nigga, you remember them Harlem Park days." Lil' Dray said following Black out of the cell shadow-boxing. "You know I'm nice with my hands."

******

"Diamond!" Shabazz waved and gestured for Diamond to have a seat with him on the bleachers. Diamond saw Shabazz and made his way over. "Have a seat, Ock."

"What's happening old timer? I thought you were still on your visit?" Diamond said sitting down.

"I came out just before they called the code," Shabazz replied. "Did you get a look at the dude who they stabbed and beat over the head with the pool stick?"

"Nah, I heard dudes talking about it though. I was in the gym."

"I am telling you, Ock this guy must've really pissed them kids off."

"Damn. That's crazy." Diamond said knowing that it could be a million and one reasons why them kids went upside the guy's head. But, in the end, it all came down to one thing, and one thing only. *Respect!* That's what it was all about in prison. You either had it, or you submitted to and stayed out of the way of those who did. "Anyway, I talked to Billy Lo about that construction job last night. I told him that a friend of my wife's had mentioned it to her."

"Good. I'll see to it that he's hired if he decides to go in for an interview." Shabazz threw some more bread crumbs on the ground for the birds.

"Thanks." Diamond really appreciated the old wise mobster's help.

"Don't mention it." Shabazz knew that what Diamond thought was a simple gesture to help Billy Lo stay out of trouble was really no more than a strategic chess move to protect his interest and keep an eye on Diamond and his little friends. "Any friend of yours is a friend of mines." Shabazz smiled. In the game, no move was without reason, and no gift was without its price.

Chapter 5

"Damn baby! These joints a smash hit." Billy Lo said stuffing his mouth with another big ass bite of buttered-down French Toast Waffles off of Lakeria's plate. It had been years since Billy Lo had been able to relax and enjoy his food. In prison, he always ate in a hurry. Paying more attention to his surroundings than his meal. Making sure he wasn't the next one to get shanked in the back by some young crash dummy. "Baby make me a few more real quick."

"Boy, your butt is just greedy." Lakeria got up laughing. He'd already finished his own plate, before eating half of hers, but she loved every minute of it. The only thing she liked better than cooking was watching her man enjoy it. "You might as well, go ahead and finish the ones on my plate too."

"Oh, my bad baby." Billy Lo said laughing as he reached across the table and picked up Lakeria's last French Toast Waffle, before dipping it into the King's Syrup. "It's just that you put your foot in these joints. Mmh, mmh, mmh." Billy Lo closed his eyes and moaned like he was having sex after taking a bite. "Damn." He mumbled shaking his head. He still couldn't believe how good Lakeria's cooking was. "These joints banging baby." He added stuffing the last bite in his mouth. He knew that his baby loved to cook, but damn. Culinary Art School and her grandmother had taught her some stove top secrets that even a chef, who knew his way around the kitchen, couldn't fuck with.

"How many more you want babe?" Lakeria questioned grabbing the cinnamon off the table and opening the refrigerator to get the eggs and stuff.

Billy Lo thought for a second. "Bout seven or eight."

Lakeria just shook her head, smiled, and started cracking eggs.

Bodymore Murderland

After Lakeria made Billy Lo a few more French Toast Waffles, she washed the dishes and made the mistake of letting Billy Lo follow her to the shower, because he wouldn't let her out until he made her cum several times and busted his morning nut. So, by the time she got ready to leave for work. She was running almost two hours late.

"Baby don't forget to check out the house on Ward Street. I want to know if you like it. I think it's perfect for us, but it's going to need a little remodeling." Lakeria said slipping into the chocolate three-quarter Prada Boots that matched her briefcase and set off her crème business suit. "The lease is up on this place in March. And I can easily take out a loan now to start the remodeling process."

"I'll go check it out after I come from Motor Vehicles. I promise." Billy Lo replied. "But, I told you, baby. I don't care what it looks like, or where it's at. As long as I'm there with you, I'm good."

"Still go have a look okay?" Lakeria held his face and kissed him. "The wife only wants a fifteen percent rate increase on the sell. And that's because the house belonged to her grandmother. The only reason she is letting it go is because she and her husband have three children now and the house is too small."

"I got you." Billy Lo smiled and slapped her on the ass when she turned to leave. "Call me when you get to work too."

"Yes, daddy." Lakeria laughed, heading for the door. "I love you! I love you too!" Billy Lo, yelled back just before hearing her go out the door.

******

"Your Honor, there's no need for another postponement! The state has no case against my client. He has been sitting over at the Baltimore City Detention Center for the past nine and half months." Black's attorney fired, pleading his case in front of the Administrative Judge. "The state was requesting a continuance to come up with more evidence because their Star Witness had gotten killed. This is just another attempt by Ms. Royster to drag this case along. So again, I would like to move for a dismissal."

"Mr. Needleman, would you like to add to Misses Livingston's argument?" The Administrative Judge asked Lil' Dray attorney opening the floor.

"Well, umm, yes Your Honor." Needleman quickly got to his feet and cleared his throat. There wasn't too much to add. Mary had already covered just about everything. So, he would just support her motion because she too, had successfully defended some of the worst criminals to ever stand trial in the history of the State of Maryland. "First I would just like to second Misses Livingston's Motion to Dismiss. But, I would also add that Mr. Chapple has requested a Speedy Trial in this case. And furthermore, Your Honor, excuse my French, but this case died last week with the state's only eyewitness and I..."

"Your Honor, I assure you that the state already has a few more potential witnesses." The State's Attorney spoke up cutting Mr. Needleman off, as she quickly ruffled through her court files for something supporting her claim. She knew that if she could get Green and Chapple in front of a jury, the impression of guilt would work in her favor. It always did. She just needed the judge to buy what she was trying to sell. "The lead detective, in this case, is also currently, investigating a few major leads."

"Does these major leads involve eyewitnesses Ms. Royster?" The Administrative Judge questioned eyeing the state's attorney.

"Ummm... Well, we have surveillance footage from outside the Convenient Store where most of the murders took place that shows four occupants entering..."

"Four unidentified occupants!" Needleman interjected.

"Yeah, who just so happened to be in the same type of make and model Caravan where a body was found almost burnt beyond recognition."

"Circumstantial." Mr. Needleman assured her.

"*Circumstantial?*" The state's attorney repeated. "Well, let's add to that the fact that dental records show that the body found inside the Mini-Van was one of defendant's childhood friends, whose DNA and Willie Fryson just so happened to be at the Convenient Store with your client. A witness who no longer matters."

"Enough!" The Administrative Judge banged his gavel. This is not a trial counselors. "This is an evidentiary hearing."

"Your Honor, I am only requesting a small continuance so that the lab can try to enhance the surveillance footage."

"*Again, Your Honor,* this could take weeks." Ms. Livingston said knowing that advocacy was an art, not a science. "And at the most, would only end up being a silent witness. Because honestly, Your Honor and Ms. Royster knows this…I have personally, viewed this footage several times and even without the enhancement it is clear that the suspects faces are covered."

"Is that true counselor?" The Administrative Judge questioned looking at the state's attorney sternly over the rim of his glasses.

"Well, it does appear that the suspects are wearing some type of mask, but there are various distinguishing markings and things that the enhancement of this surveillance footage and 9-1-1- call could provide."

"*Again,* with the stall tactics." Ms. Livingston said shaking her head.

"Your Honor, what about my client's Six Amendment Rights? Doesn't that mean anything? The state has been diligently working on this case for the better part of year. There is no way they should need more time."

"I don't need you to do my job counselor." The Administrative Judge warned her with an evil eye, before turning his attention back to the state's attorney. "Without this video footage would the state be ready to proceed to trial today Ms. Royster?"

"Well, Your Honor, granted that I could have just a little time to go over what the lead detective has discovered. I think I could be ready to present my case no later than Thursday.

"That is not what I asked you, counselor."

"Your Honor, we are talking about five execution style murders. The possible ordered hit of a state witness and impersonating police officers. I…"

"It seems to me Ms. Royster, that what the state is asking this court to do is let them build a case, not postpone one." The Administrative Judge cut her off.

"That's not what I am asking at all Your Honor. I just…"

"I've heard enough from you for one day counselor." The Administrative Judge barked leaning forward to look down on everybody. "So, here's what's going to happen. The defendants are protected by the United States Constitution and so they have a right to a speedy trial…" The judge paused and directed his attention to the prosecutor. "Are you ready for trial Ms. Royster?"

"No, Your Honor." The state's attorney sounded defeated, and Black smiled at the ugly face bitch. "I am not."

"Then, unfortunately, in accordance with Maryland Law, I am bound to rule in favor of the defense." The judge set up straight. "With that being said. I am dismissing all charges against both Mr. Green and Mr. Chapple with prejudice. I am further ordering that all outstanding warrants on Michael Pair be hereby void. This court is adjourned." The judge banged his gavel.

******

"I don't fucking believe this shit!" Detective Gibson grumbled under her breath as the Administrative Judge called for the next case. "Did he really just release these fucking animals?"

Bodymore Murderland

Detective Baker sat there stuck on stupid. He didn't want to believe what he was hearing. The judge had to be a fucking retard or something not to find some grounds to hold Chapple and Green on. Surely, he could've violated a few rules. "This is exactly what I mean when I say most of those good for nothing ass laws only manage to get in the way of good police work."

"You know. Let's just get the hell out of here because these people are making me sick." Gibson spoke rising to her feet. She wished for a moment it was the judge instead of her and Baker, who had to step outside the courtroom and explain to five grieving families that some Constitutional bullshit had just allowed two guilty men to receive justice.

Detective Baker took a look over at Green's and Chapple's family, and supporters, and wondered how they could be smiling like they were attending a graduation instead of a pre-trial hearing for two sociopaths charged with multiple counts of murder. The worst part was that they were still on the Captain's shit-list for the little dry-room episode with White that hadn't gotten them anywhere.

******

"I love y'all baby!" Black yelled to Peanut and his baby girl after hugging his attorney.

"We love you too baby!" Peanut yelled back taking Leyonna's little hand, helping her wave at her father, as she smiled and giggled. Peanut was so happy that her baby was on his way home. She'd been missing him so much, and didn't care that her punk ass cousin had to get laid down for it to happen. If the wrong thing come out your mouth you deserve to die and besides, real niggas weren't supposed to make statements anyway. "When they gonna release you?"

Lil' Dray was in his own world, making faces with Tina. He couldn't get home to heat that pussy up quick enough. She'd been acting real crazy since he got jammed up. Fucking with other niggas and all that, but he knew that once he got home and threw her ass some dick, shit would be right back to normal. Lil' Dray looked around, it seemed the whole hood was present, but he knew only a few were there out of love. He cracked a huge smile when he spotted his mother and big brother in the back of the courtroom near the doors. They always had his back. No matter what.

"We still gotta get processed out, but it shouldn't take no more than a few hours."

Black was still running his mouth as the guards came over and started trying to escort him and Lil' Dray back to the holding cells to wait for transportation.

"Yo!" Lil' Dray barked snatching away from one of the guards. "Don't grab my fucking arm like that nigga! Fuck is wrong with you?"

"Just stay by the phone!" Black yelled as he and Lil' Dray were forced through the back courtroom doors. Shit was about to be on.

"So, you really going to stand by that black motherfucker, after I told you I think he had something to do with your cousin getting shot the other night?" Card's mother popped up out of nowhere.

Peanut didn't recall her aunt entering the courtroom with her and her brother. But they'd argued on the phone all night about Card's death and Black's possible involvement. "I'm not doing this right now." Peanut replied, stepping out into the aisle walking around her aunt. She refused to get into it with her while she had her daughter on her hip. Her aunt just wanted to make a big scene, but Peanut had already made her position clear when she said that she was standing by child's father at all cost and didn't plan to question him about anything he did or didn't do. "I'll call you later."

"Oh, no you won't neither." Her aunt spat. "Your trifling ass can just lose my number since you wanna go against your own family for that no good bastard!"

"Bitch!" Peanut's brother was about to go off, but Peanut stopped him and looked at her aunt. She fought real hard to hold her own tongue. She never made Black out to be an angel, but he would've never done what Card had done because he stood on his beliefs like a man, 'win, lose or draw,' and that was why she would always stand behind him.

Okay, if that's the way you want it, fine. Peanut replied, shook her head and walked off with a slight smirk on her face because she wasn't going to lose any sleep over Card's death or his mother's fit. Her baby was about to come home, and that was all that mattered.

******

For the past twenty four years, Diamond's mind had been like a sponge soaking up every aspect of the game. Keeping only what applied and squeezing off what didn't. Now, it was time to put everything he'd learned to work. The news that his little cousin was back on the streets was proof of what planning could do. However, now it was time to step shit all the way up.

After getting the news about Black and his man, Diamond instantly started making plans to get them and Billy Lo together. He knew that Billy Lo would buck at first because that wasn't initially a part of their plan. But, yet and still Diamond knew Billy Lo was loyal, and he felt he was sharp enough to keep Black and the rest of his little crazy homeboys free until he got home and they all got rich. With his mind, Black's crew, and Shabazz's plug wasn't no stopping them. To Diamond, the game hadn't really changed much. It was still the same old game, and all the old rules still applied. A nigga just had to work overtime to make sure that he wasn't the only one playing by them.

Diamond felt like a lot of niggas went wrong not being able to think. They didn't understand the importance of building a solid empire and letting their money work for them, but he did. Diamond looked at the game as a business. He'd been watching from the prison stands; as man, after man fell victim to the game in one fashion or another. It took him some time to realize that no matter how smart they thought they were. No matter how gangster they thought they were. They all made the mistake of trying to turn a 'Get In, Get Out,' game into a career. But, Diamond was out to be one of the greats and to be great, it took more than a strong team of wolves and a good plug. It took determination and commitment to your plan, but most importantly discipline.

Chapter 6

"Dug, you act like I'm saying something wrong." Mumbles said as Black pulled in front of Lil' Dray's house and hit the horn. "This nigga keep doing that sucker shit! I ain't say nothing at first, even though that shit the reason niggas got caught up for real, but come on Dug, again?"

"Yo, I'm not saying you not right Dug. That nigga definitely out of order for constantly putting his hands on that girl. You of all people know how I feel about that coward ass shit." Black looked over at Mumbles as if to remind him that they had murked his mother's boyfriend for the same violation. "All I'm saying is, let's take care of this business first. Then we can deal with D.W.'s dumb ass."

"Yeah, a'ight. You better hope she don't get his dumb ass locked up again." Mumbles said falling back in his seat, leaving it alone. If it was one thing that he hated. It was a nigga who couldn't keep his hands off women simply because he wasn't man enough to handle them. It was a cowardly act, and only bitch niggas would stoop so low because real men didn't hurt or destroy what they truly loved, respected, and desired.

"What's up niggas?" Lil' Dray fired, jumping in the back seat of the car, trying to twist both Black and Mumbles necks.

"Stop fucking playing nigga!" Mumbles barked looking at Lil' Dray with his face twisted up.

"Man, I ain't trying to hear that shit!" Lil' Dray replied thinking about the game they played. Mumbles had just caught him off guard the night before and popped his neck. "My neck still fucked up nigga!"

"Yo, fuck all that." Black looked at Lil' Dray and cut his eyes at Mumbles, signaling for him to leave him alone.

"What's up with this nigga you was talking about? How you stumble up on him?" Black asked pulling away from the curb. "It ain't the same Jerry we dogged over the jail, is it?"

"Nah, this a chump from down Baltimore and Gilmore that Tina started fucking with while we were over the jail." Lil' Dray replied.

"Come on with the crazy shit Dug." Black looked at Lil' Dray like he was crazy. "You wanna grab a nigga cause he was fucking with Tina, while we were over the jail? Is, you serious? Dug, you was *locked up*."

"Man, I wasn't even sweating that lame." Lil' Dray lied. He really did try to understand that Tina had needs and that he would've done the same shit if the shoe was on the other foot. But, still Tina was his baby, and the thought of her with another nigga drove him crazy, but he couldn't tell his niggas that. "But, I'm down 'Bills' earlier with Tina and Yo come up in the spot talking reckless and shit, with a couple of them B and G niggas…" Lil' Dray added remembering how the camera had been the only thing that had stopped him from pushing dudes shit back right there. "So, I told him he had it, and promised to see him again."

"Dug, do this nigga have some money for real? Or you just mad about Tina?" Mumbles questioned turning around to look at Lil' Dray. He wasn't going to keep getting caught because niggas couldn't control their women. "Didn't I just say I wasn't tripping over this punk till he tried me?" Lil' Dray balled his face up. "After that I made Tina tell me everything about him. He be pumping right off Gilmore, but he got a little spot over on Lombard near Steward Hill Elementary."

"So, you think he out there now?" Black asked looking in the rearview as they pulled up to a red light.

"He probably is. All you got to do is go through there and see.

"You toting?" Black looked over at Mumbles.

"Come on now, ain't I always?" Mumbles asked flashing his sawed-off.

"A'ight, fuck it. We gonna creep through." Black said as the light turned green and he started to pull off. "If yo out there we can grab him."

"I just know this nigga better have some money." Mumbles fired.

Black parked down the street from 'Bill's and waited until Lil' Dray' spotted the nigga they were looking for standing on the corner. Mumbles wanted to just snatch the nigga and get it over with, but nine months over the jail had given Black a lot of patience, so he convinced them to lay on the nigga until he was in a better position for them to grab him.

"He can't stand there all day," Black added.

The opportunity presented itself when the cops came through and made everybody take a walk. Black, stayed on the nigga and one of his homeboys for a good two blocks before they made their move.

Lil' Dray got out of the car with his heat ready and started walking as Black and Mumbles sped halfway up the block and pulled over so they could cut the niggas off. By the time, they realized what was about to happen it was too late.

"I told your bitch ass I'd be back." Lil' Dray, slapped the hustler upside the head with his heat when he saw Mumbles jump out of the car with a sawed-off shotgun and he tried to run. "So, you know what time it is nigga."

"Pop the trunk dug!" Mumbles yelled as they grabbed the hustler, and his homeboy, and started forcing them towards the back of the car. "Nigga, I ain't getting in no trunk!" The hustler's homeboy assured Mumbles struggling to break loose.

"A'ight." Mumbles nodded, as if he could careless, and shot the nigga in the head. "What about you Dug? You getting in or what?" He shrugged waving the gun.

Delmont M. Player

The hustler dived in the trunk, almost before Lil' Dray could get it open, and Mumbles quickly slammed it shut, before jumping back in the car with Black, and pulling off.

"Take this bitch somewhere quiet, so we can find out exactly where the money and house at." Lil' Dray ordered.

"I know just the spot too." Black responded.

It wasn't hard for Lil' Dray and them to find out everything they wanted to know. The nigga even told them some shit they hadn't even asked about, and before long they had the hustler gagged, and duct-taped to a chair in the basement of a row-home on Lombard Street; while they cleaned the house, and safe of all its valuables.

After clearing the spot out Black and Mumbles made their way out to the car and left Lil' Dray alone with the hustlers. Lil' Dray kicked the chair over, that the hustler was bound to, and stepped over top of him aiming at his head with the heat.

"Oh, ain't no sense in crying and shit now." Lil' Dray, smiled as the started swarming and trying to yell for help. "You should've thought about that before you decided to fuck my bitch and talk that slick shit." Lil' Dray shot the hustler in the head twice and made his way outside to the waiting car.

******

Diamond and Shabazz had been walking the penitentiary yard for the last twenty minutes, having a gentlemen conversation. Shabazz was as sharp as a tack and as focus as an Eagle. He was trying to explain to Diamond that in life, every gangster made mistakes that cost him more than he was hoping to lose.

"It is at that moment; a man learns that 'circumstances don't make men, they reveal them.'" Shabazz paused like he had forgotten something. "I've seen a lot of men come and go in this life, Ock. Some with honor, most by disgrace. But, what you gotta always remember is this. 'If it were easy, everybody would be doing it.'"

Diamond didn't reply. There was no need to. The old wise gangsta was giving him a lesson and he had come to learn. A couple young dudes walking the yard attempted to cut right between them before Shabazz could continue, but he wasn't having it.

"Ock, these lil' kids today don't have no fucking respect!" Shabazz closed his eyes for a moment and shook his head. "And they're so insecure that it's almost sad. Man, I don't even pay half them crash dummies no mind." Diamond said with a wave of the hand as if the lil' dudes ain't matter.

"But you should." Shabazz assured him knowing that when you didn't teach a person right, you automatically taught them wrong. "Because you can never trust an insecure man, Ock. A man that is not comfortable with himself is weak and will do anything, even if it means getting in over his head, to try to prove himself worthy. So, you should always pay him some mind."

Diamond heard one of the brothers calling The Adhan and knew it was time for the third Salah Prayer of the day. He looked over in the corner of the yard and saw the brothers lining up in the ranks, and knew he only had about two minutes.

"Listen Ock, when you get out there don't ever look back." Shabazz continued quickly, when he saw the Muslims getting ready to perform prayer.

"I like you, our thing is not about that. It never was. We are no different than a teacher and his student. You take what you learn, graduate, and run with it."

"I respect that, but I'ma still send word or something." Diamond assured although everything he'd said made perfect sense.

"Do you remember what I told you when we first met, Ock?"

"Yeah, iron sharpens iron, like a father sharpens the mind of his child before sending them out into the world." Diamond smiled. He had hung that statement on his wall, and read it every day until it made sense.

"And?"

"There is nothing to be learned where a man doesn't understand that he has one mouth and two ears to ahhh…" Diamond had to pause for a second to make sure that he had it right. "To do less talking and more listening."

"Exactly." Shabazz replied impressed. "Those are the two things I want you to focus on when you get out of this hell hole. Because those are the two things you'll need to succeed in a world that cares nothing about how you start and everything about how you finish."

"Oh, we got to finish this conversation after we make Salat." Diamond said excitedly. He loved when Shabazz spoke from experience. "You got to break that all the way down for me."

"A'ight." Shabazz nodded and followed Diamond over to the water cools to make Wu-Du before offering prayer.

******

"So, he does live." Detective Gibson, said to Baker when they pulled up in front of White's house and climbed out of the car to see Michael Pair.

"Well, well, well. I guess the whole gangs back together again." Detective Baker added walking over to the steps where everybody was sitting but nobody said a word.

"Long time no see Pair." Gibson smiled. She kind of admired the kid for being able to outsmart them this time. "I would take it that you heard the news about Fryson and the judge's ruling seeing as though you have decided to show your face again."

Again, nobody replied.

"You know, I kind of respect you guys for honoring the street code of silence." Gibson nodded and looked from on to the other and continued. "That's why I'ma really enjoy it when the tough guy acts start to disappear and the scared little boys come out."

"See you got us all fucked up." Lil' Dray' started, but Mumbles tipped his arm. What was understood didn't need to be explained so wasn't no need to reply.

"Oh, I have seen guys twice as smart and ten times tougher break when the temperature starts to raise. So, trust me when you break, and you will…" Gibson assured them. "I'll be the one there to throw you a life-line."

"So, Pair." Baker spoke up. "Where were you three weeks ago when Willie Fryson was shot to death?"

"I never answer questions I don't know the answers to detective. First I would have to know who Willie Fryson is."

"Man, why don't y'all just get the fuck away from my house, you bitches keep harassing niggas about nothing." D.W. barked unable to bite his tongue any longer. Taking niggas downtown and shit. We ain't no rats! We ain't telling y'all shit!"

"Chill Dug." Mumbles cut D.W. off. "Don't say nothing."

"Listen you little piece of shit." Baker fired through clenched teeth looking up at White, standing in the doorway, and pulling out his shield. "You see this badge mother fucker? It means that we can do what we want, when we want, how we want, to whomever we want. So, keep running your mouth, and I'll have your ass back in that dry-room so fast you won't even remember getting handcuffed."

D.W. just stared at Baker and shook his head.

"Now that we are all on the same page. I've got a little suggestion." Gibson said after a moment of silence. "Quit while you're ahead because, if you little motherfuckers don't. I promise you I'm going to bury every last one of y'all in prison."

******

After leaving the part-time job at the construction company Billy Lo swung pass Africa's spot to tighten her up and get some information. Billy Lo had been doing his homework, and now he was ready for some action. For, the last few weeks He'd been planning his attack and waiting for the right moment to have his first face to face with Diamond's people. Today everything was coming together.

After beating Africa's raggedy ass pussy out, the frame Billy Lo, headed for Lexington Terrace to hook up with Diamond's cousin and his men. Billy Lo, drove very slowly down Freemont Avenue, looking from a piece of paper to the faded out, chipped away house numbers, until he found the house that he was looking for. Then he pulled over and parked before getting out of the car more uneasy than nervous.

Billy Lo, knocked on the door, and waited. When the door opened he instantly recognized Diamond's little cousin Black from the Family Day.

"What's up homie? Black asked giving Billy Lo a hand shake before embracing him. "I thought you said nine o'clock?"

"Yeah, I just always like to show up a little early." Billy Lo smiled, as he followed Black inside to where three dudes, who he assumed were D.W., Mumbles and Lil' Dray' were chilling. Black introduced everybody in order, and Lil' Dray' and Mumbles tipped their hats off to Billy Lo, for Card 's murder although he continuously stressed that it wasn't his work.

Billy Lo, refused a drink from Black, and a blunt from D.W. more out of discipline than disrespect, because it was no longer his cup of tea. His whole existence and survival consist of being able to keep a clear head at all times. After some small talk, they got down to business and started laying their cards on the table.

"So, every move is like a check?" Black questioned focused like he didn't want to miss anything.

"Yeah, and all checks get cashed." Billy Lo responded, as he continued to size his new team up.

Black seemed to be the unwritten leader of the crew. D.W. was quiet, while Lil' Dray and Mumbles gave off 'a down for whatever 'vibe. "That way we don't ever have to worry about shit coming back to haunt us."

"I like that." Mumbles nodded approvingly.

Billy Lo gave them all burner cell phones from the bag he'd brought into the house. The numbers already programed in them joints. "They're strictly for business only. Don't be calling no Lil' Dummies from them joints. And definitely don't call none of your love ones."

Billy Lo looked around the room to make sure everybody understood what he was saying. Once he was certain that what he said had sunk-in, he went to cover the final and maybe most important part of his plan. "I got a few licks already lined up for us. So, y'all ain't got to sweat that. Plus, for now on, we only taking licks and dealing with niggas I approve of." Billy Lo said thinking they would go off, but they didn't.

In fact, everybody except Lil' Dray was cool with it. His only concern was their own little side 'stick-up' business. But, Billy Lo quickly informed him that all that side shit was a 'No Go', because they were a team.

"Hold up, so what about Herbert?" Lil' Dray' looked at Mumbles and them like they were crazy.

"Damn, niggas forgot about Herbert." Mumbles said.

"Who's Herbert?" Billy Lo questioned curiously.

"The Correctional Officer and Bounty Hunter chump we be getting police equipment and information up off of." Lil' Dray replied.

"How y'all hook up with him?"

"Through my faggy ass cousin, Wayne." Mumbles replied. "Yo, be giving us badges and shit. Keeping us ahead of investigations and shit when he can. That's how we got the jump on Card."

Billy Lo thought for a second. Police information and equipment could definitely come in handy one day. "Okay, Herbert good to go, but I want to meet this joker myself."

"No problem." Mumbles nodded.

"Oh, Herbert cool huh?" Lil' Dray asked sarcastically.

"Look homie, we're all in this shit together now, so you got to understand. If one of us fuck up, we all suffer. Trust me soldier, if we stick to my script you won't want for nothing. I'ma make sure everybody eats."

Billy Lo spoke with confidence knowing that when you tried to tell a young nigga, who got it how he live, how to eat, you had to be able to put food in his stomach. "All we got to do is move quick, strike hard, and make sure each man plays his part. We got to stay ten steps ahead of our prey. That means being patient, exploiting all known vices and capitalizing off any mistakes."

"So, when do we start?" Black asked hoping they were making the right decision.

"Next Week." Billy Lo smiled then went into their first lick. Tremaine and Cecil were a couple of childhood friends turned snakes. They had been some of the first niggas to act up and treat Billy Lo like he was expendable when he caught his time even though he had always been there for them. But, that ain't seem to count for shit when he fell. You would've thought Billy Lo was lying when he spoke about some of the things they did together. At least, by the way, they carried him. But, now that they were getting some change, Billy Lo felt like it was only fair that they be the first ones he burned and make pay for their sins against him.

"You sure these niggas gonna just up and let you right in the mix like that?" Black questioned jive leery.

"Trust me, soldier, it ain't gonna be hard to rock these niggas to sleep." Billy Lo replied. "They did a lot of fucked up shit while I was locked down, so they definitely gonna be trying to suck up to a nigga and feel him out. Especially Tremaine because that nigga knows I put that work in, and he still not sure what I do and don't know."

"What about the nigga Cecil?" Mumbles spoke up.

"Oh, niggas ain't even got to worry about him for real. First of all, he's a stone-cold bitch." Billy Lo replied remembering how Cecil had choked up back in the day, screaming about not wanting to die when a neighborhood beef got crazy and went haywire. "He told on my man Lil' Awnie about a body. Plus, he knows I think he had something to do with my baby Lotti getting shot."

"You don't think he's going to be paranoid."

"Nah, not really. He don't even know I'm hip to the shit with Lil' Awnie. And like I said. He's a homo-thug anyway, him and his best friend use to be fucking. We ain't got to worry about that punk." Billy Lo assured, before go on to lay out all the pros and cons of their first lick.

"I' m liking the sound of this shit already." Lil' Dray said rubbing his hands together as if he could already see the outcome.

"You ain't seen nothing yet. These niggas just target practice." Billy Lo said knowing that once he got up with his man Zimbabwe in a few days, and got the scoop on who was really doing what in the city it was on. "I'ma line a bunch of shit up for us. Just be cool."

Well, you line 'em 'up and watch how we lay 'em' down." Mumbles spit, and Billy Lo ain't need to hear no more. He knew that with most young niggas. If you weren't trying to help them come up, wasn't shit you could tell them.

Chapter 7

"Give us time to get inside then come right behind us. By then Mumbles, you should've drop on the two niggas out front. Me and Black gonna cover the house. If y'all don't see the lights flash in five minutes come in blazing. We can't afford to sleep on all these niggas." Billy Lo was going over the last few details of their first lick as they sat inside the used Ford Bronco he'd just gotten in the vacant Parking Lot of his mother's old church.

"Anybody got a problem with that?" Billy Lo waited for somebody to speak up. He knew that no plan was full proof, so he relied on his team to let him know if they had any better ideas. But, nobody said anything so he continued. "A'ight then. Let's go conduct this business."

Mumbles laid across the back floor of the Bronco as Lil' Dray and D.W. got out of the truck and climb back into the nearby stolen car as Billy Lo and them pulled off.

"A'ight, we coming up on the house now." Billy Lo, said over his shoulder slowing the Bronco down to pull into a parking space close to the house. "Remember Yo, wait for the lights to flash." Billy Lo added before grabbing the bag with the rope and duck-tape inside and exiting the truck with Black.

It was one of those cold, raining nights when Billy Lo, decided to make his move on Cecil and Tremaine. He'd hung out with them for two weeks and now had all the information needed to execute a successful string.

"What's up yo?" Billy Lo, asked Cecil's right-hand man walking up on the front.

"Ain't nothing to it."

"Where Cecil at?" Billy Lo, questioned looking around.

"Inside waiting for you." He replied, eyeing Black curiously.

"Oh yeah, this my man Black, I was telling y' all about." Billy Lo, said gesturing towards Black.

"Hell, yeah man." Cecil's man snapped his fingers excitedly. "I thought that was you. Damn, your lil' ass done got big as shit!"

It took Black a second to actually realize who the older dude was. "Oh, damn yo, what's up?" Black forced a phony smile and laugh.

"Ain't too much. What's up with you? How your father been doing?"

"Oh, everything good. Pops still standing and I'm out here trying to get this money." Black replied ready to cut the conversation short.

"I hear you. Your peoples still stay on Carrollton an…"

"Look yo, y'all can do all that later on. Let's us get in here and take of this business." Billy Lo, said interrupting the little reunion knowing that D.W. and Lil' Dray would be cutting the corner any minute now. "Plus, I'm trying to get out of this damn rain before my money get wet." He added holding up the bag real quick.

"Oh, my bad." Cecil's man banged on the door twice to give Cecil and whoever else may be inside the heads-up that they were coming in. "I'ma just catch you before you bounce Black."

"Bet." Black nodded and followed Billy Lo inside.

"Why you ain't tell me you knew that nigga?" Billy Lo, questioned as soon as he was sure that Cecil's man could no longer hear them.

"Yo, I ain't even realize who that nigga was until just now." Black assured him looking back towards the door. "I ain't seen yo, in years. He done lost weight and everything."

"You know we can't turn back right?" Billy Lo looked at Black seriously wondering how much he fucked with the nigga. "I mean, if you need me to…"

"I'm good Dug, trust me." Black cut him off. He wouldn't have no problem pulling the trigger on the shaky ass nigga. From what he remembered growing up the older G's had chased his faggy ass from the hood. "That nigga a nobody."

"Mumbles know him?" Billy Lo, paused before they stepped into the living room. He didn't want nobody having regrets in the morning.

"He might. I'm not sure. Yo, was all over Terry Springer for fucking with his faggy ass cousin Wayne or Tonya as he goes by. Plus, that Barbershop shooting was the talk of the Terrace. When we was coming up."

"Oh, you talking about that shit where the little boy got hit." Billy Lo, remembered the reckless ass hi-profile case like it was yesterday. He had been over the jail with the nigga who took the fall for it. The wrong nigga from what he understood. "Dude had something to do with that?"

"Yeah, he was the first one to start dropping names." Black laughed. "His bitch ass even fainted on the scene. I'm telling you Dug, this nigga a nobody."

"Ain't cool." Billy Lo, nodded and walked into the living room where Cecil was. It was nothing else to talk about. It was time to 'show and prove'.

"What's up nigga?" Cecil got up and gave Billy Lo some love before running his fingers across the bottom of his nose sniffing. "This your man?"

"Yeah, yeah." Billy Lo, replied eyeing the white shit around the rim of Cecil's nostrils. He knew the nigga was probably high. Every day that they'd hung out, the nigga treated his nose, but Billy Lo didn't care. The more Cecil sniffed. The more he talked and that was always a good thing in Billy Lo's line of work. It made his job a hell of a lot easier.

"I still say you should just hook-up with me and Maine." Cecil sniffed again and looked over at Black. "Let me tell you shorty. This nigga here. He ain't tell you how far we go back, did he? Man! I can tell you some stories."

Billy Lo just smiled. He'd been dealing with niggas like Cecil for the last fifteen years. The smile in your face, laugh, and talk behind your back type…so he knew that Cecil was nothing but another well-wishing, friendly-acting, envy-hiding snake who talked a good game.

"Yo, you got to fuck with me and Maine. We jamming up this bitch." Cecil said addressing Billy Lo again as he walked into the kitchen.

"Man, I ain't fucking with The Heights." Billy Lo assured him. First of all, he wasn't ever hustling again and secondly, he damn sure wasn't rolling with no fucking Rat. "Black got a nice lil' shop down the buildings."

"Suit yourself." Cecil opened one of the cabinets and started moving shit around. "So, what you say y' all was copping again?"

"Two onions." Billy Lo slowly sat the bag down and nodded for Black to make his move while Cecil's back was turned. "But I was thinking you could front us something too." Billy Lo added as Black eased up behind him with a big ass chrome Desert Eagle. It was time to go to work.

"I don't really be fucking with that fronting shit," Cecil said pulling the first container out and sitting it on the counter. "So, we gonna have…"

"In that case," Black mumbled pressing the cold steel against the back of Cecil's head. "We take whatever you got up in this motherfucker."

"Yo!" Cecil froze straight up and tried to look around to see Billy Lo. "What…what you doing man? Billy Lo?"

"Man, you ain't new to this." Billy Lo fired. "Who else in the house?"

Black cracked Cecil across the back of his head and knocked him off the counter onto the floor when he didn't reply quick enough. "Don't make him ask you again," Black ordered through clenched teeth sticking the D.E. right in Cecil's face.

"Nobody. I swear!" Cecil spat.

"Watch that bitch while I go make sure." Billy Lo said slowly moving for the stairs.

Mumbles eased up extra slow off the floor with the Army-green Mosberg Pump ready and saw two niggas sitting on the steps lolly-gagging. The one twisting the umbrella around in his hand was doing most of the talking. So, Mumbles rolled over and decided to make his move. Carefully crawling across the floor, Mumbles slowly pulled the door handle until the lock snapped and the door opened. Fortunately for him, the heavy rain and dark cloud worked in his favor. Mumbles said a silent prayer and carefully slid out of the truck on to the wet ground just as Lil' Dray and D.W. turned on to the block and cut their lights off.

"Yo, you see that?" Mumbles heard one of the niggas ask as he crept around the Bronco from what would soon be their blind side, if they kept watching the car slowly driving towards them. "They just cut their lights off."

Lil' Dray and D.W. drifted slowly down the street with their guns ready as Mumbles continued to creep around the truck.

"Yo, I think these niggas on one." The tall kid said sticking his hand into his dip as Lil' Dray and D.W. got closer. "What you want me to do yo? Bang on these niggas or what?" The tall kid was so busy worrying about what D.W. and Lil Dray may be up to, that he didn't even know what hit him when the lights went out.

"I want your bitch ass to reach nigga!" Mumbles barked stepping over the tall kid sticking the pump in the older nigga's face. "I'ma punish you out here!"

"Show time." Lil' Dray said hopping out of the car in the middle of the street rushing over to back Mumbles up as D.W. looked for somewhere to park. "Get up nigga!" Lil' Dray slapped the kid on the ground a few times until he was conscious enough to stand up on his own as he held the gun up under his chin and ran his pockets.

"Come on man, please. The niggas with the money inside."
The older dude said shaking as Mumbles pulled his 38 Revolver out
of his pants pocket and stuffed it in his dip. "I'll tell y'all whatever
y'all wanna know."

"Man shut your scared ass up and calm down." Mumbles
ordered as D.W. jogged over to join them. "And stop shaking
nigga!"

"Yo, they hitting the lights now." D.W. said looking up at the
windows.

"A'ight. Let's get these niggas inside." Mumbles order
snatching the older nigga by his collar, and moving towards the
door. All the flashy lights and shit were new to him. He was use to
pulling straight up C-Sections where when the nigga they wanted
did not come out they just went in and got him.

"Bitch!" Lil' Dray cracked the tall kid upside the head again
and forced him into the house behind Mumbles and the older
chump when he tried to buck.

D.W. took one more look up and down the block to make sure
the coast was clear before following them inside and locking the
door. Black and Billy Lo, already had Cecil laying across the floor
on his stomach with his hands tied behind his back.

"Lay them bitch ass niggas over there." Billy Lo ordered
pointing towards the couch, as him and Black continued to search
the living room.

"Lil' Leon', Come on man, tell 'em' I'm good peoples." The
older cat pleaded looking in Black's direction with tears in his eyes.

"Dug, after you tie that nigga up, gag his punk ass too."
Black fired, going in the bag tossing Mumbles some rope as they all
looked at each other trying to figure out how the hell the old bitch
ass nigga knew Black's real name. "I'll tell ya about it later. Tie them
niggas up."

For the next ten minutes D.W., Mumbles, and Lil' Dray tied
and gagged Cecil's homeboys while Billy Lo and Black beat him

with a frying-pan, until he told them everything they wanted to know, and agreed to call his brother. It was a known fact that fake thugs could only pretend for so long. The tall kid was the only one who had heart.

"A'ight look, put these niggas in the basement." Billy Lo ordered walking back into the room, carrying a pillow case after forcing Cecil to call Tremaine. "I'ma put this in the truck and me and Black gonna wait out front for Tremaine."

"Bet." Lil' Dray, replied reaching down and dragging the tall kid across the floor by his pants leg, until he was at the top of the basement stairs before kicking him down the stairs.

"Bring that old nigga over here too." Lil' Dray said once the tall kid finished rolling down the steps and he saw that he was still tied up nice and secure. Billy Lo, just smiled as D.W. pulled Cecil's man across the floor and kicked him down the steps too. He was starting to like these lil' niggas already.

"This should be him right here." Billy Lo tapped Black when he saw Tremaine's Lexus Coup coming down the street. "We gonna just rough whatever this nigga got. Slump these niggas and get out of dodge."

"It's whatever with me Dug," Black replied sincerely.

Tremaine pulled up and parked behind Billy Lo's Bronco and him and Black watched him, pull up his hood and hop out before setting the alarm.

"What's up nigga?" Tremaine asked kind of surprised to see Billy Lo sitting out on the front. "Fuck you sitting out in the rain for? My brother ain't open the door or something?'

"Nah, everything good." Billy Lo replied wiping a little bit of water off his face before giving Tremaine some love. "My truck was smoking. And you know how Cecil is? He ain't wanna have a bunch of niggas on the front."

"Where he at in the house?" Tremaine questioned looking pass Billy Lo.

"Yeah." Billy Lo nodded. "He was on the phone when I came out."

"Well, come on in and fuck with me for a minute." Tremaine waved his hand stepping in between Black and Billy Lo to make his way inside. "If your shit still acting crazy by the time I leave I'll run you home."

"My man." Billy Lo said getting up to follow Tremaine inside, "CECIL! CECIL! Fuck is that nigga at?" Tremaine looked back at Billy Lo for a second as they entered the house. "Ce...!" Tremaine was about to yell again but Billy Lo threw him in a wicked ass choke-hold.

"Don't fight it baby boy." Billy Lo whispered tightening his hold as Tremaine slung him around and scratched at his selves. "Just go to sleep."

"Fu...you...nigga!" Tremaine started swinging wildly.

"Wrong idea," Billy Lo said squeezing Tremaine's neck tighter.

Tremaine forced Billy Lo into the wall over and over again as he struggled like a motherfucker to break free. Black tried to keep him still, but Billy Lo wasn't worried. He was a beast, so he just held on and shook Tremaine until his watery eyes rolled into the back of his head and he passed out. Then he just let him fall to the floor.

"Yo, tie this nigga up." Billy Lo instructed looking at Black jive out of breath. "I'ma run upstairs and grab something I saw earlier."

"Man, I thought yo said this nigga was holding?" Black said rolling Tremaine over and checking his pocket. "This nigga ain't got shit!"

"Check him again. He said he was bringing it with him."

"Somebody lied."

"Well, now that we got everybody together we gonna find out who." Billy Lo smiled and took the steps two at a time as Black busied himself with the task of tying Tremaine up.

"Look." Billy Lo spoke calmly squatting down next to Tremaine with a pillow case in his hand. "I'm only going to ask you one more time before I start killing niggas up in here. Where the shit?"

"Come on Dug, we're like family. Why you doing…"

"Everybody keep saying that." Billy Lo smiled thinking about Card before calling out to black as he stuffed the gag back in Tremaine's mouth so he could watch in horror as Black carefully laid a pillow over his brother's head and pulled the trigger on the .38 Revolver Mumbles had handed him earlier.

Click. Click.

"What the fuck?" Black looked from the .38 to Mumbles before opening the barrow and realizing that the gun was never loaded. "Fuck you give me an empty gun for?" Black asked curiously and Mumbles started laughing.

"You bitch ass nigga." Mumbles fired kicking the older nigga in the face. "Hand that to me Dug." Mumbles ordered reaching out for the pillow, which he quickly laid across the older nigga's head before shooting him, with the pump.

"Oh, my god!" Cecil gave off a muffled cry when Mumbles removed the pillow or rather what was left of it, and he saw his man lying there with a softball size hole in his head and a permanent look of fear on his face.

"Now, you can either start talking…" Billy Lo tossed Black another pillow and removed Tremaine's gag again. "Or I'ma make sure Black use his own gun for your brother next time."

After Tremaine gave Billy Lo the information he wanted, the nigga started telling everybody else's business also who was getting money, who was fronting, who niggas got on, and all that good stuff. It was really too bad that he had to go because his ass had more street info than a 411 Operator.

In the end Billy Lo, and them came out with about sixteen-thousand dollars in cash and jewels, a couple ounces of raw dope and two nice .38 Revolvers. Mumbles and Lil' Dray shot Tremaine,

Cecil and the tall kid, execution style; while D.W. and them wiped the house down for prints, and all evidence tying them to the scene.

Outside Lil' Dray climbed into Tremaine's Lexus Coup with Billy Lo and followed the Bronco and stolen car off the block as the rain continued to fall.

"So, what now?" Lil' Dray questioned going through Tremaine's glove compartment.

"We go take care of these cars. "Billy Lo paused to observe the roads before turning. "Then shoot back over to the house to break down and go over our next lick.

"Sounds good to me." Lil' Dray nodded then continued to tear Tremaine's car apart.

Chapter 8

"Yo, you wasn't lying. These nigga's too sweet." Lil Dray said to Black and D.W. as they sat in Billy Lo's Bronco on Edmondson Avenue watching their next potential target conduct business.

"Now y'all see what I was saying." Black responded and continued checking out the layout. "These niggas out here getting it." Black added determined to keep his word from over the jail.

"Yeah, Billy Lo gonna like this shit." D.W. added watching the early morning drug traffic. "It ain't even nine o'clock and these lil' niggas out here jamming."

"Yo, all them niggas work for that tall dude leaning on the mailbox?" Lil' Dray questioned looking up and down the street. It had to be about fifteen of them lil' red bandanna wearing motherfuckers.

"Yeah." Black replied shaking his head. "But, I know all them niggas Piru. The tall one supposed to be something to that nigga from over the jail."

"Oh yeah!" Lil' Dray replied rubbing his hands together. As he remembered the nigga who stabbed Black. "Shid, we might just need to snatch that nigga."

"Nah, it's too many motherfuckers out here." D.W. assured him.

"Yeah, Dug right." Black seconded, although a quick ransom come-up sounded nice. "Those niggas mob deep, so you know it's a lot of heat out here."

"Or at least witnesses." D.W. laughed. "When they let you in the house to cop that weight. Was the tall nigga in there?"

"You thinking about grabbing the nigga from the house?" Lil' Dray asked with it still on his mind.

"Nah, I ain't see him." Black replied. "It was two other niggas, but I think somebody was upstairs too, because I kept hearing movement."

"So that's what we need to focus on." Lil' Dray said. "Them niggas pumping out the house, so they probably got all the heat out on the block."

"They so deep they don't even think a nigga gonna try 'em'." D.W. added.

"Y'all probably right." Black nodded in agreement. What Lil Dray and D.W. were saying made a lot of sense. Because when he'd entered the house to cop the quarter the two dudes in the living room barely looked up. "'Them niggas were definitely slipping when I was up in there."

"You say you heard something upstairs? Could you see where the steps were?" Lil' Dray asked wanting a mental picture. "Like were they off to the side, as soon as you came in or what?"

"They were like a lil' bit back, right across from the living room." Black thought hard for a moment. "Like when you come in the door. The steps like right here, and the living room off on this side. You got a straight shot back to the kitchen." Black demonstrated with his hands as he spoke. "The back door like beside the kitchen counter."

"A'ight, we still gotta do a lil' homework, but let's go run this shit past Billy Lo and see what he thinks." Lil' Dray said rolling up his window and leaning back as, Black pulled out into the light morning traffic. He knew it was personal for Black, but he still wanted to approach it like business.

******

"Michael, get off of him!" Cat demanded grabbing and pulling Mumbles by his shirt as he continued to kick, stump, and punch the nigga on the ground.

"I'll kill your chump ass nigga!" Mumbles hit him so hard it felt like his bone jumped out of place. "Clown ass nigga! Don't you ever..."

"Bitch don't touch him!" Cat barked looking at her neighbor's mother like she was crazy when she tried to pull Mumbles off her son. "Don't put your fucking hands on him!" Cat started tying her hair back into a ponytail in case she had to rumble.

"Michael baby, please stop!" Cat grilled her neighbor's mother before slowly pleading with Mumbles again. "The police coming and you gonna end up getting locked up."

"Nigga shouldn't jumped out there." Mumbles fired getting one more kick in before Cat could pull him through the crowd, "Get the fuck off me!" Mumbles barked snatching away from Cat walking up the street.

"What?" Cat stormed off behind him."

"You heard me!" Mumbles continued to walk. "Go help your Lil' boyfriend."

"Michael, don't play with me." Cat replied hot on his heels. "Michael stop, so I can talk to you."

"Man, just leave me the fuck alone."

"Leave you alone my ass. Nigga, you gonna talk to me. "Cat fired still following him up the street.

"I'm telling you Cat. Go ahead about your business. I'm done!"

"*You done?*" Cat repeated twisting her face up.

"Yeah, you heard me. I'm done." Mumbles looked at Cat and shook his head, "It's your fucking fault I'm around here scraping anyway. You ain't gonna be satisfied until I spank one of these Lil' dumb niggas, watch."

"You acting like I did something wrong."

"Man, don't play dumb with me. You know exactly what the fuck you did. You always be doing that shit! Running around here smiling all up in these niggas faces like they got a shot. Now, let that be me running around here leading these Lil' bitches on and you gonna have a fit, and you know it."

"No, I won't cause I know ain't none of them bitches got nothing an me."

Cat lied thinking about all the times he had to peel her up off same dizzy ass dumb bitch who had a thing for him or stop her from stomping a mud-hole in some Lil' chick around the way, who she thought overstepped her boundaries.

"Okay." Mumbles shook his head. "Remember that the next time you about to flip out and stab me with a broken bottle, or chase me up and down the street with a two-by-four and shit."

"Remember what?" Cat questioned giving Mumbles her signature look. "Don't get fucked up Michael, play if you want to. N-e-way, I told your ass to leave that shit alone." Cat tried to defend herself, but honestly, she knew she was dead wrong. She ain't have no business telling Mumbles what her neighbor had done because she of all people knew how stupid he could get, especially when it came to her. "He ain't mean no harm; he was drunk when that shit happens for real."

"I wouldn't give a fuck if that nigga was having an out of body experience." Mumbles fired looking at Cat like she was trying to make excuses for the clown. It wasn't any secret in the hood that he didn't play when it came to Cat. Anybody could get it, friend or foe. "His bitch ass shouldn't have did it! Period! He lucky I ain't put that 'tone on his bitch ass."

"Boy calm down, it's not even that serious."

"Oh yeah? A nigga kissing and grabbing all on you ain't serious huh?"

"You know what I meant." Cat rolled her eyes, as they turned onto Mumbles mother block.

"Yeah, whatever." Mumbles checked his pockets for his keys. "You might as well go back round your grandmother house because you're not coming in." Mumbles looked at Cat as they neared his mother's front door. "I' m not playing Cat. I' m done." Mumbles added when she ignored him.

"Boy please." Cat kept right on stepping. All the shit he had put her though. She wished he would try to act crazy for real; she followed him Right up to the door and stood there while he unlocked it. She knew exactly what she had to do to get his ass back in order.

"Seriously Cat, go back around the corner with your Lil' boyfriend." Mumbles stepped inside the house and tried to close the door, but Cat wasn't having it.

"Oh, for real?" Cat snapped pushing the door damn near making Mumbles fall. "I wish you would." Cat popped her neck and stood there with her hands on her hips, daring Mumbles to close the door in her face. "You know better...then again, you know what Michael? Go ahead and close the door. You ain't even got to worry about me no more. I'm not going to stand here and kiss your ass when you know I ain't do shit!

"Girl, get your Lil' ass in this house." Mumbles fired grabbing her when she turned like she was really going to leave. "You know you don't want me to let you leave for real."

"Nigga, try me." Cat turned around and sucked her teeth before pushing past Mumbles. "Move out my damn way! You playing, but I was about to be done for real cause you know I ain't the one."

Mumbles couldn't do anything but lock the door and smile as Cat continued to go off. She was so sexy when she got mad, and he loved when her gangster side came out. Mumbles double checked the door and followed Cat down stairs to his club size basement bedroom.

In his room, Mumbles grabbed Cat while she was still talking shit. Kissed her, undressed her, and laid her across the bed before slowly and gently kissing all over her soft body. When he got close to Cat's pussy, he threw one of her legs over his shoulder and went to work. He licked, kissed, teased and sucked all over her pussy, clit, ass, and thighs. One taste was never enough for him. Especially, once Cat started gripping his head, rolling her hips, and cumming all over his face, and in his mouth over and over again.

"Ssssss…baby!" Cat moaned trying to pry Mumbles' head from between her thighs. She couldn't take it anymore. Whenever Mumbles put that game on her she never could. Plus, she was ready to do her thing and show off. "Ohhh baby, let me get on it." Cat knew once she got him on his back where she wanted him. It was all she wrote.

Mumbles made Cat cum one more time before pulling down his sweatpants, and rolling over on his back to watch Cat ease down on his dick. He loved that shit; she felt so good, so wet, so tight. Mumbles knew he couldn't get what she was giving him nowhere else in the world.

"I swear to god you better not ever…" Mumbles bite his lip as his eyes rolled back up in his head and forced him to forget what he was about to say.

"You still want me to leave?" Cat exhaled rolling her hips in a very slow circular motion. "Huh?" She rose up until only the head of Mumbles' dick was inside of her. She knew it was her show now.

"You still done right?"

Mumbles tried to talk. He wanted to tell her how sorry he was for acting crazy. But, for some reason all he could do was squeeze Cat's hips, and threaten to kill her if she ever left him, or gave his pussy away. As she gripped his chest, came, and continued to ride him damn near until his toes broke.

"I love you so much, you know that?" Mumbles pulled Cat close and kissed her after busting his nut.

"I love you too Michael," Cat whispered softly, nibbling on his ear as she continued to grind on top of him slowly. She knew that he wasn't letting her go, nor was his ass going anywhere. Not in this lifetime. They were custom-made for each other. It didn't matter what they went through. They both knew there was honestly nobody else in the world who would accept them with all their strengths and weaknesses.

"And you gonna stop playing with these lil' dumb ass niggas too." Mumbles assured Cat trying to keep his eyes open. As always when he finished getting some of that amazing pussy he could barely move.

"Okay." Cat smiled before kissing him softly on the lips and chest.

"I'm not playing, I'm serious Cat." Mumbles said as Cat crawled up under his arm and laid her head across his chest.

"I am too." Cat replied sincerely, as she traced the tattooed portrait of her face over top of Mumbles' heart with the words '*2 die 4*' and '*My Queen*' written above and beneath it in bold cursive letters.

"Promise?"

"Promise." Cat kissed his chest again. She didn't want her baby to end up locked up over no bitch-made ass nigga that she would never be with anyway.

Satisfied. Mumbles kissed Cat on the top of her head, told her that he adored her, and dosed off knowing deep inside that she would always be his.

******

"Yo!" Diamond, yelled from behind the makeshift wall after someone called his name while he was getting ready for Ju'mah Service.

"Yo, let me holler at you for a minute."

"Pull the curtain." Diamond replied.

The blanket slid to the side, and the man behind the voice stepped inside the cramped cell. "What's up slim, you on?"

Diamond knew that there was no reason to lie. The penitentiary was too small, and word traveled extra fast. Diamond also understood that certain dude's palms had to be greased and the gangster standing in front of him was definitely one of them. The nigga's press game was so strong that he used to 'outline' his hand on blank pieces of paper and write get me' in the center to press niggas from behind the door on lock up, but penitentiary predators and gangsters could also work for you if you took care of them. So, Diamond always took care of them.

Diamond's game had been tight for years, but it wasn't always that way. It took him a minute to realize that he couldn't keep stabbing niggas, and trying to get home and get money at the same time. It didn't mix, so he started looking out for all the men and predators, who controlled the masses; that way he could fly under the radar because he knew like everybody else that only a certain caliber of men hustled and learned in 'The Pen' without paying taxes and constantly having problems.

"Yeah, I'm straight." The Imam's last warning echoed in Diamond's mind. He had just kicked another Muslim brother out of the community and banned him from the Masjid for violating Islamic Laws. The Imam went on about why good men wouldn't join the community. He felt a lot of brothers fit perfectly into the prison stereotype. To him, they were the reason most men who wanted to join the community felt like it was nothing more than a front to protect, harbor, and save known punks, drug dealers, and rats. But, he assured everybody that; that was about to stop. "When you plan on hollering at a nigga?"

"Come on slim, you know I got you." Diamond reached into his stash. He knew he could buck, but that would only bring trouble amongst the ranks, and Diamond knew that his higher-self 'Yusef' was out of order anyway. "I already had yours to the side."

"Good looking out soldier." The gangster hit him with a well-known 'I just pressed you, but your still cool' line, tucked his take off and walked out of the cell.

Diamond sat for a second collecting his thoughts. At one time, he would have flipped on a nigga for some shit like that. They knew not to try him with an aggressive lean, let alone a soft one. Diamond smiled and continued to get ready for service. He was really a different man and all he wanted to do was go home.

Yusef entered the Masjid, took his shoes off, and joined the ranks. The other Muslim Brothers were already on the prayer rug. Some are making Sunnah Prayer, others making Dhikr.

"As 'salaam alaikum." Yusef greeted another brother as he sat down next to him Indian style on the prayer rug just as the Khutba was about to begin.

******

"Look real close. Do you recognize any of these men?" Detective Gibson kept her fingers crossed as the witness looked closely at the six-man photo-array laid on the table in front of him.

"The mark right there look familiar." Don Poppa replied pointing at a photo of Andre Chapple when he still had corn-rows before looking up at the two detectives. "Number four."

"Take your time Shelton." Detective Baker tried to control his excitement. "Is he one of the men you saw sitting in the Caravan when you left out of the convenient store the day of the shooting?"

I...I...can't be sure." Don Poppa looked at the photo again. "I was moving so fast."

"Take one more look for me Shelton." Baker said to the high-level California Bounty Hunting Blood, who had allegedly migrated to Baltimore to rid the city of all fake Bloods and Sets. "Tell me you saw him in the Caravan." Baker really wanted to nail Chapple and them for the 'Red Maple' killings.

"You know I wanna help you Baker, them marks slaughtered one of my homies up in there, but I just can't be sure." Don Poppa repeated after studying Andre Chapple's photo again. "I didn't really see him head on."

"Okay Shelton." Gibson said laying another set of photographs in front of him. She wanted him to identify Chapple or one of them so badly that it made her pussy wet. But, she didn't want to push too hard since he'd been cooperating with them about Blood killings since his case made national headlines after he chopped one blood up with a Samurai. "Take a look at these and tell me if you recognize anybody."

"Oh hell yeah!" Don Poppa instantly fingered one of the photos excitedly. "I know this mark."

Baker and Gibson looked at each other and smiled. Shelton had just pointed out none other than Leon Green. This could be the break they needed. If they couldn't get them all, then they would pluck them off one by one.

"Where do you know him from?" Baker asked leaning forward.

"I saw him with Card a few times. I think that's his cousin's child father or something."

"Okay." Baker nodded his head. "Now tell me, did you see him in the caravan outside the 'Red Maple'?" Baker questioned knowing that it would really be nice to get Green back in custody since he and Chapple had walked on a legal technicality.

******

"Come on baby; we're going to be late," Lakeria said tapping on the bathroom door.

"Man, you got me looking like a cornball." Billy Lo said opening the bathroom door, stepping out in a navy-blue, two-button wool Brooks Brothers Suit with a crème colored cotton shirt, silk blue crème striped tie, and earth-tone Berluti leather shoes. All purchased by Lakeria, what a gangster wouldn't do for love and good pussy.

Billy Lo, hadn't worn a suit since he and Lotti's fifth grade graduation, but after walking in the bedroom a few night ago to find Lakeria up on the bed looking like a thicker version of Lil'

Kim off the cover of her *'Hardcore'* album he would've worn or done anything to impress her lil' work, buddies.

"Boy, you know you look good." Lakeria looked him up and down with a soft twinkle in her eyes. "I might have to get gangster tonight."

"A nigga do look good." Billy Lo laughed and struck a pose. "But damn baby, I must admit; you killing 'em'." Billy Lo added.

Lakeria was looking extra beautiful all dolled up. "You like?" Lakeria asked twirling around in a circle.

Everything on her from the body-hugging Gucci Dress, to the six-inch stilettos, which accentuated her legs and ass were perfect. Billy Lo couldn't help, but to lay a passionate kiss on her.

"What was that for?" Lakeria asked after Billy Lo finished.

"For being so damn fine." Billy Lo replied. "I'm glad your mines."

"I'm glad I' m yours too," Lakeria said.

She truly loved him to death, because she knew from experience that wounded people, especially men who'd been wronged by those they once loved and trusted only asked for one thing. A heart that loves and commits itself to them. Betrayal made them loyal only to those that were loyal to them.

"Now let's go before we are really late."

Lakeria and Billy Lo grabbed their coats and made their way out the door in route to the Prestigious Seminar. With any luck, they'd arrive just after 6 P.M. Which would be fine because the ceremony was scheduled to start at 6:20 and Lakeria wasn't big on small talk.

When Lakeria and Billy Lo, stepped inside the halls of Martin's West and made their way towards the secluded ballroom; they were truly impressed. The place was amazing, The lights were bright, the walls was lined with imported statues, and hand carved sculptures. The floors were marble and professionally waxed.

However, it was the beautiful Ballroom where the celebration was to take place that made the fabulous, well-polished, halls of

Bodymore Murderland

Martin's West seem insipid. The Ballroom could only be described in one word *Utopia*. The tables were perfectly placed and covered with rich silk linen, fine China, and sparkling mirror-like silverware. The room was covered with wall to wall plush white carpet. There were seating arrangements to make it easy for the guests to locate their tables, and pretty chandeliers hanging from the ceiling with scented candles. Lakeria had never seen a prettier sight.

"Name please?" An older gentleman in a black Tuxedo spoke as Lakeria and Billy Lo approached the guest of honor tables in the V.I.P. section. "Mr. and Mrs. Stanback." Lakeria smiled at Billy Lo.

"I like that." Billy Lo said kissing her on the cheek.

"Oh, here we are." The older gentlemen said after strolling down the guest's list. "Table four…that's just over by the front of the stage."

"Thank you," Lakeria said walking off with Billy Lo hand in hand.

Chapter 9

One of Baltimore's worst team of stick-up boys set two blocks away from there next lick in a stolen black MPV Mini-Van with shadow tints ready to go to work.

"Let's get in here, conduct this business and get out. No fuck ups! Everybody know what they gotta do." Billy Lo looked from one participant to the next as everyone nodded.

"What if these niggas buck?" D.W. questioned ready to waste a nigga. "I mean then what?"

Billy Lo chose his words carefully because he knew how trigger happy D.W. and them could be. He also understood that for this mission to come off good. Everybody had to be extra focused because not only was there a strong possibility that once they got inside, they'd be outnumbered. If the niggas controlling the block got wind of what was going down, they would be outgunned also.

"The plan is not to fire one shot. That's why we masked up, but our priority is to get this money and get out alive. So, if anybody gets in the way of that you know what's next."

"Say no more." D.W. nodded.

"A'ight. Let's go get these niggas." Mumbles said, cocking his baby, the untraceable army-green Mossberg Pump. Now this was his type of C-Section. He loved going in to get a nigga.

Lil' Dray was behind the wheel, as they pulled off exchanging hugs, and pounds with enough heavy-metal to start a rock band. D.W. had a lemon-squeeze 45; Billy Lo had twin nickel-platted .9's, Black had a fresh out of the box. 50 Caliber Desert Eagle and Lil' Dray had his Glock 40's.

Lil' Dray drove the two-block distance in no time. They had chosen a broad daylight lick for two reasons. One, most of the gang bangers would be too busy with the heavy morning drug traffic to be inside the house, and two the niggas inside wouldn't suspect motherfuckers to be that brave.

"Y'all niggas get ready." Lil' Dray commanded making a left into the Edmondson Avenue alley. Immediately everybody started double checking their guns, making sure their bullets were one step away from travel. "We're coming up on the house now."

It was all back-door action today. They knew the layout of the house, and everybody had strict directions. Two men would cover the first floor, Two men would take the second floor, and one would secure the basement. Billy Lo was hoping that the element of surprise would work in their favor. Lil' Dray pulled the MPV up just outside the gate as everybody slipped on baseball caps and tied blue bandannas over their faces. Another trick Billy Lo had come with to keep the niggas off their trail. Especially since Black and Lil' Dray had gotten into it with them over Steel-Side and had just come home for trashing a few of their homies up the Heights.

"A'ight, everybody stay focus." Billy Lo ordered pulling the sliding door open. "Let's move!"

They moved as a unit, Mumbles kicked the door open, and they rushed into the house. D.W. went straight for the basement, Black and Mumbles took the stairs two at a time, and Billy Lo and Lil' Dray covered the first floor.

In less than a minute they had the whole house under control. Six people in total, four four dudes, a baby girl that looked about two or three years old, and a bitch. Lil' Dray and Billy Lo caught three niggas in the living room playing a PS3 with guns and weed all over the table. Black and Mumbles caught the naked nigga and a bitch upstairs half asleep and snatched both of them out of bed before, waking the nigga all the way up with the butt of the Mossberg to the stomach and dragging him down the steps. The basement was empty, so D.W. ran upstairs and grabbed the little girl while Black handled the bitch.

"A'ight man, we ain't got all day. Y'all niggas know what this is." Billy Lo said as Lil' Dray started to beat one of the niggas, who kept trying to move senseless with the Glock. "So, where the shit at?"

"Right there under the couch homie." The dude, Lil' Dray had been beating, yelled out as blood poured from his head. The two niggas lying beside him looked scared to death, but the one-eyed monster was known to have that kind of effect on a nigga.

Lil' Dray and them watched as Billy Lo flipped the couch over and revealed a pile of clothes and an AK Assault Rifle with red bandannas tied around it, as the little girl continued to cry. "It-it's wrapped up in a white shirt." The bloody nigga added.

Billy Lo kicked the clothes around until what looked like about six pounds of weed and two thousand E-pills fell out. "Oh, you think we playing huh? Kill that nigga shorty."

"Hold up homie. Hold up!" The nigga pleaded trying to cover his head when Lil' Dray aimed the Glock. 40 at him.

"Then tell us where the money at bitch!" Lil' Dray barked through clenched teeth, cracking the nigga with the Glock again.

"Ahhhh!" He spat out blood and broken teeth. "I only control the drugs homie, I swear."

"Well, you better tell whoever control the money to give it up." Mumbles fired grabbing the weed and shit off the table stuffing his pockets. "Because we're gonna smash you first."

The nigga shook his head like he was disappointed and got silent for a second; before looking over at the naked dude and telling him to tell Billy Lo and them where the money was. "Go ahead homie. Tell them where that shit at.

"It ain't nothing." Another one of the scared niggas spoke up.

"Yeah homie, you heard your man." Billy Lo walked over to the naked nigga.

"Tell us where the money at."

"Y'all niggas pussies!" The naked nigga fired looking at his homies. "Fuck these crabs!"

Billy Lo stuck one of the nickel-platted .9's in his dip before kneeling down and mashing the nigga's head into the floor and pressing the other one to his temple. "Oh, you gonna tell us where that money at bitch. Trust me."

"Fuck you crabs! Y' all ain't getting shit up off me." The naked nigga assured Billy Lo and tried to hawk-spit on him.

"Last chance." Billy Lo said calmly cocking the hammer on the .9 back. He jive admired the nigga, but not enough to walk up outta there empty handed. So, he was about to lay down the law. "Hand me one of them cushions off the floor."

"Nah, Nah, hold up, chill Dug!" .D.W. stopped Mumbles from passing Billy Lo, the cushion once he realized that the nigga was willing to die than submit to what he thought was an archenemy. "This nigga ain't gonna bend I got another idea."

"I don't feed crabs nigga! I eat 'em!" The nigga was still talking shit as Billy Lo mashed his face into the floor.

"Let's see how gangster you really is nigga." D.W. ripped the little girl from her mother 's arms, and slung her across the coffee table on her stomach, before snatching her little colorful training-draws down and placing the nose of his .45 at the entrance of her little coochie before anybody could realize what was happening.

"You ready to talk now gangster?" D.W. questioned acting like he was about to force the gun into the little girl as she cried and screamed for her mother.

"Please don't hurt my daughter." The bitch begged as one of the scared niggas tried to jump up and stop D.W., but ended up getting stretched out by Lil' Dray with the quickness.

"What's it gonna be homie?" D.W. asked again, but the nigga never flinched. All he did was stare at D.W. with bloodshot red eyes so, D.W. pushed a few inches of the .45 into the little girl and made her scream louder.

"Man, just pop that Lil' bitch!" Lil' Dray fired. He was tired of watching the sick scene play itself out "Fuck all that crazy shit!"

"*No!*" The female shrieked looking at the stubborn ass naked nigga. My brother gonna kill your punk ass watch!" She added before addressing D.W. "The money upstairs inside my daughter's doll house."

Billy Lo signaled for Lil' Dray and them to hold it down and took off up the steps as somebody started knocking on the front door in code.

"What the fuck that mean nigga?" Mumbles jammed the pump into one of the scared niggas backs. "Huh?"

"Little homie's need another pack." The nigga replied.

"Man! One of y'all stupid ass niggas in there open the fucking door and stop playing!" The dude yelled from outside banging on the door.

"Shit!" Lil' Dray mumbled looking towards the steps. "Where this nigga at."

"Homie, them crabs in here trying to…" Lil' Dray's killer instincts kicked in, he shot the naked nigga two times in the head with the Glock, before he could continue, and ordered everybody to get down. As the nigga on the other side of the door started shooting through the windows and door.

Billy Lo came flying down the steps shooting at the door, yelling for everybody to get to the MPV. D.W. shot one of the scared niggas in the back, and ran for the back door with everybody else, as the bitch rolled over and pulled a .22 out of nowhere and started dumping.

Billy Lo heard what sounded like the front door smashing open, as he cut out the back door, and ran for the MPV with everybody else.

"They going out the back door!"

"Go! Go! Go!" Black yelled hitting the back of Lil' Dray's seat repeatedly before Billy Lo was all the way inside.

Lil' Dray mashed the gas and burnt rubber down the alley as bullets tore into the frame of the MPV. Mumbles knocked the back window of the MPV out and started letting the chopper (Ak-47 Assault Rifle) go, as Lil' Dray came bouncing out of the alley doing about 80 miles per hour before side-swiping a car and losing a hubcap.

Lil' Dray put the MPV in reverse and backed up off the car as Billy Lo fought hard to close the sliding door and keep from falling out. Niggas were shooting from everywhere, so Lil' Dray just threw that motherfucker back in drive, and got the hell out of there as Mumbles continued to let the chopper off out the back window wildly like he was in a Hollywood movie.

******

"Damn, you a nasty Lil' bitch." Billy Lo moaned biting his bottom lip as Africa's sixteen-year-old little sister slobbered all over his dick, while he stood in the middle of the locked bathroom with Africa waiting for him downstairs.

"Mmmmh…hmmmm," India mumbled, slurped, and sucked as Billy Lo pushed her long hair out of his view and clutched the back of her head. She'd been sucking his dick for weeks now whenever her sister wasn't home or not paying attention.

94

"You gonna get a nigga caught up watch." Billy Lo shook his head but couldn't bring himself to stop her. "Come on, take some more for me, baby."

"You know I can't, I'ma choke, it's too big." India stopped sucking for a moment to caught her breath and stroke Billy Lo's saliva covered dick.

"Try to spit on it again. Get it real wet." Billy Lo said rubbing the head back and forth across her lips. "You can do it." India tried. She spit, gagged, and damn near choked to death, but she was still only able to get about half of it down her throat. Even with all the extra encouragement from Billy Lo.

"See." India came up coughing and tried to catch her breath as she wiped her watery eyes.

"A'ight. Just open your mouth real wide for me." Billy Lo breathed jerking his dick, as India tilted her head slightly back, held her mouth wide open, and look right into his eyes. "That's it; here it comes...stick that tongue out. Ahhh...good girl...good girl. Eat that shit up." Billy Lo shook and watched as his nut rolled off India's tongue down into her little throat. "Shit! Your Lil' ass too young to be a monster like that."

India stood up and smiled before wiping her face. "If you stop being scared and fuck me. I can really show you something. You know milk ain't the only thing that does a body good."

"Your lil ass off the chain." Billy Lo laughed fixing his jeans. It still amazed him how the once little bad baby girl, who use to run around the house in pissy pampers before he fell, had turned out to be a bad Lil' chocolate thing who could put most grown women to shame. "I keep telling your Lil' ass you ain't ready."

"Boy please, I done fucked dudes with dicks twice your size," India assured and started to come up out of her clothes. So, you can hit this pussy right now."

"Yo, India, stop playing." Billy Lo said anxiously listening for Africa's footsteps, knowing that she was bound to come looking for him soon. "You know your sister right downstairs waiting for me." "So!" India rolled her Lil' eyes. "I'm trying to fuck! I ain't just going to keep sucking your dick."

"I got you shorty, that's my word. Next time we gonna hit the motel." Billy Lo replied seriously.

He wanted to get up in her little guts anyway for real. Her Lil' body was tight. She ain't have no stretch marks or nothing. And her Lil' baby phat was in all the right places. But it was no way that he could really beat that Lil' pussy up the way he wanted to with Africa in the house.

"Now go ahead and get up outta here, before Africa bring her nosey ass up here looking for me."

"I ain't worried about that bitch!" India sucked her teeth and wiggled back into her tight little jeans. "She fucked two of my boyfriend's anyway."

"Well, I'm glad because I'm trying to get up in that wet Lil' pussy." Billy Lo said walking up behind India and using both hands to shake her ass cheeks as she unlocked the bathroom door.

"Yeah, whatever." India popped her neck and shit. "You just make sure you ready to throw me some of that dick next time nigga."

"I got you shorty." Billy Lo smiled and shook his head as India eased the bathroom door open and crept back across the hall to her room with her Lil' Phat ass jiggling. Billy Lo couldn't wait to hit.

******

"What's up fam?" Diamond said giving his cousin some love, embracing him in a hug across the visiting room counter.

"Cooling, you know me; taking it one day at a time," Black replied taking his seat. "What's good with you?"

"Waiting to get the fuck up outta here, so I can show niggas how it supposed to be done." Diamond looked around the visiting room full of women and children and wondered where all the so-called 'Real Niggas' were at.

Black smiled. "It shouldn't be long now right?"

"Nah, not really, especially since the dude Walter Lomax got me some good days back." Diamond replied.

"Cuz, I can't wait till you come home." Black declared. His cousin had shown him that the true definition of a gangster, wasn't how much work he put in, but rather how firm he stood in a game where mostly everybody was making up their own rules as they went along. "My niggas dying to meet you, cause they done heard so many stories from other G's around the way that it ain't even funny."

"All y'all Lil' niggas wild as shit man." Diamond started laughing. His Lil' cousin's crew name was ringing bells all the way from West Baltimore to the penitentiary, and that could be both good and bad.

"Nah Cuz, we just holding it down. Watch when you get home." Black assured Diamond. He had always looked up to his big cousin.

"So, what's up? How is shit looking out there?"

"Ahhhh man, sweet," Black replied. "You already know how we living, but your man. Billy Lo... oh, he a fool with it. I fuck with that nigga."

Diamond smiled. "What about Mumbles and them?"

"Oh, they fucks with dug too.'" Diamond paused as something else popped in his mind. "Oh yeah, fam, whatever happen about that other thing?"

"What other thing?" Black asked confused.

"'With the lil folks." Diamond replied referring to the Lil' C.O. bitch he had bringing work in for him.

"Oh." Black paused remembering what happened when he and Lil' Dray tried to drop an ounce of blow off for Diamond. "Man, shorty crazy as a motherfucker. First she act like she trying to throw a young nigga some pussy. And when that ain't work she started talking about more money and all this other shit. So, I pulled right off on her dumb ass."

"Oh yeah?" Diamond smiled. "That bitch came in here telling me a bunch of other shit. Like y'all was trying to fuck her and holler at her."

"What?" Black bust out laughing. "That was funny. Don't nobody want that big head, flat butt bitch! Niggas got dimes out here. She stuntin' Cuz. She might be something in here to these niggas, but uptown she ain't shit! She probably just ain't want to bust that move."

"Yeah. That's exactly what I thought. "Diamond agreed. They had never had any problem before. "Because I tried to get her to holler at somebody else and she played games again."

"Why she just ain't say she ain't want to do it?" Black couldn't understand some people. They would rather play games instead of just saying no. "Fuck she geeking for all of a sudden?"

"Man, you wouldn't believe me if I told you."

"What?" Black was really curious to know. "I know you ain't fucking with that bitch on no personal level?"

"Hell no!" Diamond fired.

"Oh, I was about to say you been locked up too long. These jailhouse bitches ain't nothing."

"Nah, ever since her home girl got knocked off horsing for some clown ass nigga that told on her, she's been on some real bullshit."

"Hold up Cuz. You telling me that a nigga in here, a prisoner, told on a female that was helping him out?" Black wondered what the game was coming to.

"Not only did he tell, but he set the bitch up."

"That's crazy." Black shook his head. He'd never heard no shit like that in his life. It was bad enough that niggas were snitching on niggas, but now they were even telling on the police. "No wonder that bitch was playing games. Niggas in here bitches."

"That's why a nigga got to get in, get out, and legitimize his shit." Diamond said, and all Black could do was shake his head in agreement.

Chapter 10

"Yeah, we're still on for tonight." Billy Lo, spoke on his cell phone as he made his way into the downtown Real Estate Firm. "I'ma meet y'all niggas at Africa's around six. A'ight bet."

Billy Lo, ended the call as he approached the receptionist desk. He and the crew had a nice sting set up for later that night. A couple of New York boys down in South Baltimore that his man Zimbabwe had turned on to. For the last month Billy Lo, and them had only been on two licks. The first one hadn't gone so well, but the second one was a little more rewarding. They had hit a hot ass nigga name Elway, whose time should've been up, over in East Baltimore for $17,000 in cash, some jewels, and a bunch of pills before tossing his body in a dumpster. But niggas stomachs were still growling.

"Good afternoon Sir, how may I help you?" The pretty little female behind the desk with the Headset and tiny felt-tipped wire curved around her face to the marble-size mic asked smiling.

"Yeah, umm... I'm here to see Ms. Stanback." Billy Lo thought for a second. "Should have an appointment."

"One moment please." The receptionist picked up the phone and tapped a few numbers before looking back up. "Name Sir."

"Oh, Anthony Izzard." Billy Lo, replied as the receptionist asked for Lakeria's extension and started typing on her computer again.

"Hello! Ahh yes, good morning Ms. Stanback, this is Latabitha at the front desk. There's a gentleman, named Mr. Izzard out here, who says he has an appointment, but I can't seem to find his name in the system."

Billy Lo's plan was to smash Lakeria then shoot on down south to make sure everything was still everything with Zimbabwe.

"Yes Ma' am. I'll send him right in." The receptionist gently placed the phone back in its hook. "Umm…you can go on back Mr. Izzard. It's the last door on the left.

"Thank you." Billy Lo nodded.

"You're welcome." She smiled and turned back to her computer as Billy Lo walked off, when Billy Lo entered Lakeria's office, she was sitting at her desk flipping through papers and talking to one of her clients on the phone, so she held up one of her fingers and signaled for him to hold on.

"I understand that, but there is no way that I can secure that property without the acquisition cost. This is why…" Lakeria, continued her conversation while Billy Lo walked around her office checking out awards and picking up books.

"Hey, baby." Lakeria hung up the phone and turned her attention to him.

"You look so sexy when you're working." Billy Lo said making her blush as he came around the desk.

"Yeah well, girlfriend got me working overtime to get control of this, 43,000 acres of land down there in Fells Point," Lakeria said closing a folder.

"How's your day going?"

"Fine now." Billy Lo replied kissing her.

"Anthony." Lakeria inhaled as Billy Lo slowly spread her legs. She was both afraid and excited. "I am at work."

"I'ma be quick baby, I swear." Billy Lo whispered carefully putting her legs up over the arms of her chair before going to his knees. "I only wanna taste it."

Lakeria felt his tongue make contact with her clit and it was over. She grabbed the back of his head, told him to hurry up, closed her eyes, bit her lip, and instantly started cumming all in his mouth.

******

Zimbabwe was another wild ass stick up boy from up the Heights that Billy Lo had met and celled with over the jail while they were both fighting their cases. They had been known to each other due to the 'Up Top, Down Bottom' Park Heights rivalry. But, it was an Edmondson Avenue robbery and 'Cross the Tracks' shooting that brought them together in the square (a makeshift top tier gladiator ring where men went to earn their bones and put in work) and forged their bond.

"What's good my nigga?" Zimbabwe asked giving Billy Lo a pound and hug after he got out of the car.

"You." Billy Lo replied. "So how we looking for tonight?"

"Everything straight. Y'all niggas just camp up the block and wait for my signal. Once them niggas wet, I'ma dip out and leave the door unlock."

"Yo, you got to make sure all them niggas downstairs in the basement." Billy Lo reminded him. He wasn't trying to fuck around and get to shooting all crazy in South Baltimore like they had to do up North and Longwood because them crackers were definitely going to call the police.

"I got my end," Zimbabwe assured him.

"What about your girl's cousin Dug? You sure you don't want to wait till shorty not gonna be there? I mean, I don't need you feeling sorry about that shit later because you know what time it is after we conduct that business.

"Man, fuck that bitch! If you can spare her, spare her." Zimbabwe looked Billy Lo right in the eyes and shook his head. "If not, do what you do, because that bitch is definitely going to say something."

"A'ight then nigga, that's what it is." Billy Lo gave Zimbabwe some more love and climbed back into the car. "I'll stop pass your spot in a day or two." Billy Lo added before hitting the horn twice and pulling off in route to Africa's house.

******

"There it is." Billy Lo said tapping Black on his leg as he watched Zimbabwe stand on the steps of the house they'd been watching for the last three hours giving them the green light. "Make sure them niggas ready to rock and roll."

Black picked up his cell phone and called Lil' Dray, who was sitting down the street in another car waiting for the word with Mumbles and D.W.

When Lil' Dray answered the phone, Black simply said two words "Work Call." and hung up.

"Make sure you stay beside me." Billy Lo said after him, and Black climbed out of the truck and started walking down the block adjusting their police caps and badges.

"I'm right up on you Dug." Black saw Lil' Dray and them coming towards them as they neared the house and it was on.

"Everybody head straight for the basement." Billy Lo, spoke simultaneously pulling his gun, as they all met up in front of the house. After everybody had nodded Billy Lo, walked up the steps and marched right through the front door with Black and them behind him.

"Ummm, excuse me." A little- white bitch came strolling out of the kitchen in some cut-off jean shorts and a pink body-hugging hoodie about to start talking shit. "Don't just be walking into my house."

"We're with the Police Department Ma'am." Billy Lo whispered flashing her his badge.

"I don't care. You still don't…"

Billy Lo made her swallow the rest of her statement with a heavy backhand.

"Somebody handle this dumb bitch!" Billy Lo barked and continued for the basement. "And check upstairs. Make sure the rest of the house clear." He wasn't leaving anything to chance.

Billy Lo put his ear to the basement door and listened for a second. He could hear one of the New York niggas freestyling over a Jadakiss instrumental as his homeboys egged him on. Billy Lo put his finger up to his lips and slowly opened the basement door before easing down the steps and waving for everybody to follow.

"Son, I'ma wig splitter/outta town money getter. This the Negro League/ put them G's on your head nigga! Been hitting shit since eighty-eight/ fuck the Jake."

"Oh, my gosh! Please don't hurt me!" The little white bitch's face was as red as a cherry. "I didn't do anything officer. I was only saying…"

"Just shut the fuck up bitch, damn!" D.W. barked as the white woman's plea for mercy fell on deaf ears. "Now tell me who else upstairs."

"Nobody, I swear." The white bitch submitted.

"Bitch! If I find out your lying I'ma kill your dumb ass." D.W. fired pushing her over to the couch as he checked out her long legs and tight little ass. "Now turn around bitch! What you got on you?"

"I don't have nothing." She replied as D.W. started to check her for nothing in particular. "Is this necessary?"

"Didn't I say shut up?" D.W. was rubbing all over her, groping her ass and little titties. "You got something bitch!" He stuck his hands down inside her shorts and slipped a finger into her Lil' phat pussy after realizing that she didn't have on any panties. "It's probably stashed up in this pussy."

D.W. smiled when the bitch moaned and tried to wiggle away. He had been hearing stories about how nasty white girls were since he first started going to Charles Hickey Training School for boys.

"That's my word son! Ain't nothing here." The New York boy Zimbabwe had identified as Preacher was balled up on the basement floor crying.

"Then you better start telling me where it's at nigga because we're not leaving here without something. Your money or your life. Now, what's it going to be?" Billy Lo questioned as if the nigga really had an option. Because truth be told, it didn't matter if he gave the money up or not; shit was going to end badly.

"Come on son! I'm telling you the truth. My man just left with the doe." Preach replied. "That's on my old earth."

"Man, this nigga bluffing." Black stepped forward and aimed his gun.

"Hold up; I got this bitch." Billy Lo smiled before walking over and snatching the phone cord out the wall. "Tie them, niggas, up. I'll be right back." He added headed towards the steps.

Billy Lo ran back up the stairs to the kitchen and started going through the draws until he found exactly what he was looking for. "Okay. This what I'm talking about." Billy Lo said to himself analyzing his weapon of choice before peeping into the living room and asking D.W. if he cleared the house.

"Yeah Dug, we good." He lied. "Ain't nobody up there."

'A'ight, then bring that lil' bitch downstairs with everybody else."

Lil' Dray watched as Billy Lo came down the steps followed by D.W. pulling the white bitch by her hair as he finished tying the last of the three New York boys up with the phone cord Billy Lo had ripped from the wall.

"Gag them, niggas, too." Billy Lo ordered kicking some dirty ass socks across the floor from over near the washer and dryer.

"What about the bitch?" D.W. questioned slinging her to the floor.

"What about her?" Billy Lo repeated. "Tie her ass up too." After everybody was secure, Billy Lo, called a little huddle over by the foot of the stairs and laid out his blueprint.

"And y'all niggas thought I was crazy." Lil' Dray said as the huddle broke and Billy Lo walked over to the closest New York nigga and cut his throat wide open with a Butcher's Knife to set the tone. "It's your turn son!" Billy Lo mocked slamming the knife into the next New York boy's side just under the ribcage forcing him to scream into the gag and damn near pop the phone cord. Billy Lo slowly pulled the knife out and slammed it into his thigh this time with a smile before looking over at Preacher. "You ready to talk son? Or do I got to kill the God? Now, remember, once he's dead. You're up next."

Billy Lo saw the fear in Preacher's eyes as he stood there with the ten-inch blood-soaked Butcher's Knife waiting for an answer and watching Preacher and the white bitch cry and pray that they would wake up from what they thought was a nightmare.

"I'm not going to ask your punk ass again."

Preacher nodded, and Lil' Dray quickly removed his gag so he could talk.

"Come on, talk nigga!" Lil' Dray slapped him with the gun.

"I...I got a Lil' spot. It...it's ahh." Preacher was having trouble catching his breath as he tried to talk, cough, and breathe all at the same time. "It's a townhouse out in Woodlawn."

"Is the money out there?" Billy Lo questioned.

"Yeah, son." Preacher confessed. "Take you straight to it. Just don't let my man die kid."

Billy Lo looked over at the New York nigga slowly bleeding to death and the swarming lil' white bitch before he spoke. "A'ight listen. After we get the money. I'ma let your man and the bitch go. That's my word, but if you play any fucking games, everybody dies."

"I swear son. The money at the house." Preacher assured him.

"On your feet nigga." Billy Lo fired snatching Preacher up off the floor before looking at D.W. "You hold this shit down and wait for my call. If I don't call in half an hour, kill both of 'em'."

"I got you." D.W. smiled and nodded. "You crazy as shit Dug. From now on I'ma start calling you the robbery negotiator."

"Yeah, I heard that." Billy Lo replied, and everybody couldn't help but, laugh because Billy Lo had put on one hell of a show.

Black, Mumbles, Lil' Dray, Billy Lo, and Preacher arrived at the Spring Hill Circle Townhouses without incident and just like Preacher had said nobody appeared to be home.

"You sure ain't nobody inside?" Billy Lo questioned Preacher a third time.

"Yeah, I'm the only one with a key."

"A'ight." Billy Lo gestured to Black and Lil' Dray. "Y'all niggas go check that shit out. If there's anybody inside kill em and get out of there, if not, y'all know what to do."

Billy Lo continued to question Preacher as Lil' Dray and Black headed for the townhouse. He wanted to get as much information as possible out of him.

It took Black and Lil' Dray five minutes to call with the all clear. Billy Lo immediately started asking Preacher more questions about the money, floor safe and combination, as he checked in with D.W.

"Tell them to look in the last bedroom. It's right in there. They're gonna have to move the dresser, pull the carpet back and lift up the floor broads." Preacher continued to explain as Billy Lo repeated everything to Black over the phone. "The combination is two-one-eighty-four."

Black nodded and relayed the information to Lil' Dray as they moved towards the bedroom. If what Preacher said was true, then they were about to be straight, Black told Billy Lo to hold so he could help Lil' Dray move the dresser. Then he stood back and left Lil Dray crack the safe.

"Jack Pot!" Lil' Dray looked up at Black smiling when he opened the safe and saw all the money.

Billy Lo kept asking if everything was straight, so Black told him the good news. Homeboy wasn't lying Dug."

"Yeah...a'ight, bet." Black shook his head and ended the call. "Bag that shit up so we can get up outta here."

"Dug, this nigga was loaded." Lil' Dray said opening the back door of the truck tossing the heavy bag full of money across the back seat next to Preacher. "No wonder you New York niggas be running down here."

"Come on, so we can get this shit over with." Billy Lo said pushing Preacher out of the truck. "I' ma tie you up in the house and we gone."

"You still gonna make the call about my man son?" Preacher, questioned as he struggled to keep his balance because his hands were still tied behind his back, "You gave me your word kid."

"Just keep moving nigga. You did your part, now I' ma do mines."

"Come on son, let me go right here, kid. I swear I won't tell on y'all son. I ain't no rat nah-mean." Preacher kept looking around. It was like he felt something. Like maybe history was finally catching up to him for all the foul shit he'd done over the years. "This not about the money is it son? Ahh, son! Come on Dog, I ain't..."

"Shut the fuck up!" Mumbles barked about to slap him with the gun. "Fuck you trying to do, make a scene?"

"Nah son, my bad. I just thought…" Preacher pushed Billy Lo, into Mumbles and took off in a dead run. "Help! Somebody Help!"

Billy Lo and Mumbles instantly opened fire and took off behind him.

Preacher was fast, but not that fast. Hot rocks from both Billy Lo's and Mumbles tones quickly chased him down before he could benefit from Billy Lo's slight mistake.

"Oh, you Lil' bitch." Billy Lo ran up on Preacher after he fell to the ground and shot him in the head a few times to make sure the deed was done. Their freedom depended on it.

"Come on nigga! Let go!" Lil' Dray yelled from the truck, and Billy Lo and Mumbles ran back over to the truck, so they could get the fuck out of there before motherfuckers started peeking out windows, taking notes and shit.

******

"Yo!" D.W. answered the phone out of breath. "What's up?

"Fuck took you so long?" Billy Lo snapped.

"I thought I heard something upstairs." D.W. replied.

"A'ight. Cash them checks and meet us back at the spot." Billy Lo hung up.

D.W. tossed his phone back on the pile of clothes and smiled. He had been fucking the dog shit out of the Lil' white bitch for close to the last hour. He had gotten head and everything else. Those niggas out training school hadn't lied. Them white bitches were down for anything.

"Was that your friends?" The naked white girl asked looking up at D.W. from her knees. "Did everything go okay?"

"Yeah, shorty, everything good. They're on their way back."
D.W. lied waving his dangling dick in front of her face as he spoke.
"Get it hard again."

The white girl got back to work. Eating the dick up like her life
depended on it. In a funny way, it did. Still, even under the
circumstances, she seemed to be enjoying herself. In her mind it
wasn't rape, it was her game of escape.

"Damn! That's what I'm talking about." D.W. ran his hand
over her head as she continued to polish his dick like a porn star.
Swallowing that motherfucker like she had a snake in her throat.

"You like that?" The white bitch asked coming up for air
before licking his nuts while she jerked his saliva covered dick as
spit dripped from her mouth and chin all over her wrist and chest.

"I love that nasty shit bitch!" D.W. replied going up on his
tippy-toes when the nasty bitch's tongue touched his ass. D.W.
knew that he didn't have much time, so he decided to hurry up and
get that last nut. "Come on stand up bitch! I'm trying to hit that shit
from the back again. This time I want you to bend all the way over
the table. I want you to grab the edge too."

The Lil' nasty bitch hopped right up and quickly laid across the
table grabbing the other side before looking back over her shoulder
wiggling her little tight ass.

"Like this daddy?" She smiled.

"Yeah, just like that." D.W. got behind her and spread her little
ass cheeks some more before sliding in. Her pussy was still nice and
loose. And her asshole showed evidence of the earlier pounding it
had taken. D.W. slide in and out of her pussy a few times to get his
dick nice and wet before pulling out to hit her in the ass again.

"Ahhhh!" The white bitch moaned as D.W. stretched her little
pink asshole opened again. "Ahhhh!"

"What? You want me to stop?" D.W. slowed down.

"No!" She pushed her ass back to him. "Please don't stop."

"You gonna relax and open that ass up for me again?"

"Yes, God yes."

"Good girl." D.W. slapped her across the ass and then started pounding away until he nutted all up in her.

Once he was done, he zipped up his pants, and shot the white bitch in the face two times and laughed at the silly look on her face. She really thought she'd survive; the ass was good, but not that good. The New York boy had bled to death not long after Black and them had left, but D.W. popped him in the head twice just to be sure. And left him looking like 'DMX' on the front of the 'Flesh of my flesh, Blood of my Blood' CD cover. Too many niggas were still in the penitentiary for that mistake. So it was better to be safe than sorry.

Chapter 11

The New Year had come and gone like all the rest in the history of Baltimore City. All night parties, midnight gunshots, and early morning homicide discoveries. It was only ten days into 2014, and the murder rate was already pushing twenty. Billy Lo and them had been laying low since their last sting. The news wasn't saying too much about the home invasion, but the word was that the Feds were somehow involved.

Billy Lo had blessed Zimbabwe with fifteen grand and a brand spanking new two tone, blue-steel P90 for his assistance. He also got Black to get with Herbert about what the police were saying and was jive surprised when he came back talking about the Lil' white bitch being raped. Billy Lo immediately stepped to D.W., but he assured him that he had stuck to the script and could never do no sick ass shit like that. So, he left it at that.

"What time are you going to work?" Lakeria asked walking into the bedroom dressed for work.

"Around ten, ten thirty. Why?" Billy Lo rolled over to peep at the clock; He'd just gotten the part-time construction job Diamond turned him on to.

"Because I need you to change the bulbs in the kitchen and bathroom like I asked you to do yesterday please."

"Damn, I forgot." Billy Lo grumbled. "I'll do it as soon as I get up."

"Thank, you baby." Lakeria walked over to the bed and kissed him. "Ewwww boy! Your breath stink."

"It must be all that fish I ate last night." Billy Lo laughed when Lakeria finally caught on to the joke and hit him with a pillow.

"Then why were you acting like you were at all you can eat?" Lakeria rolled her eyes and popped her neck before placing her hands on her hip.

"I'm from Park Heights baby; you ain't never heard of the Lake Trout?" Billy Lo replied pulling her into his arms. "Nah baby, I'm only playing. You know your stuff taste like heaven guurrrllll. A nigga can't get enough."

Don't touch me!" Lakeria shouted and acted like she was really trying to get away when Billy Lo started kissing all over her face. "Anthony stop! You're going to make me late."

"I know." Billy Lo said pulling her skirt up as he rolled over on top of her. "But I can't help myself."

******

"YUSEF BRINKLEY! REPORT TO CENTER HALL!"
Diamond heard his name being called over the loud yard speaker and looked up as if he wasn't expecting it. He and Shabazz had been walking the track bundled up in big (Ben's) prison-issued coats since the first call for recreation in silence. They both wanted to enjoy their last bit of time together.

"I guess this is it, Ock." Shabazz stopped and stuck his hand out. "You take care out there. It's a cold world."

"Ain't no colder than this." Diamond said shaking Shabazz's hand firmly. He surely would miss the old, wise man, who had helped make his boots much tighter and his skin a lot thicker. "So, I'ma really be good out there."

"Prison is nothing compared to all the responsibilities you will face out there. All you have to be in here to survive is a solid man but in the real world... Out there." Shabazz waved towards the other side of the gun tower. "You got to be more than just a solid man. You got to be great, Ock. You got to be patient, flexible. You got to be a husband, father, and gangster all rolled into one. And that's just the beginning. We got it easy in here, Ock."

"I guess you're right." Diamond thought for a second and nodded his head. "You gotta walk slow and think fast out there, Ock. That's the only way you get what your hand calls for." Shabazz paused to look at Diamond.

"But always remember what I said because nobody likes to be disappointed. Especially not a man in prison."

Shabazz's words flashed in Diamond's mind. "I will." Diamond assured him because he had no plans of letting the gangsta down.

"Good." Shabazz patted Diamond on the shoulder. "Now go ahead and get outta here before they find another reason to keep you."

Diamond stood there for a moment and watched Shabazz walk off. No good- byes, warnings, or words of encouragement were needed. Diamond knew how lucky he was. Most men that came into the penitentiary on murder wraps never got the chance to see daylight again.

Diamond thought about all the good, stand up men that had taught him one thing or another on his journey and smiled. He wished he didn't have to leave them behind, but he was 'no good' to anybody caged up, so he looked at Shabazz one more time and then headed for center hall.

As he passed under the lock-up windows, he heard some young clowns yelling and frowned. He surely would not miss the weak, watered-down suckers with no morals and principles. He damn sure wasn't gonna miss the sex-jokes and new 'Color Craze' gang shit that allowed a lot of cowards to abuse the power of unity and slip through untested.

"You act like you don't want to leave Mr. Brinkley." The little skinny, brown-skin sergeant with the overbite said when Diamond got to center hall. "Got that beautiful family out there waiting for you and you want to be walking the yard."

"Nah." Diamond laughed. He had always been fond of the attractive little sister. "I was just getting my last lap. I ain't think I was leaving before lunch."

"Oh! what you wanna eat first?" She questioned raising an eyebrow.

"No Ma'am." Diamond shook his head.

"Okay then, let's go." She said moving towards the steps that lead to the front doors. Diamond had signed all the necessary release papers a few days ago, so all she had to do was open the doors as Diamond followed her towards freedom. He started to get a little nervous. It had been a long time since he'd been on the streets and he'd gotten jive institutionalize. So much had changed, there was so much to do, so much to see, and so much that he wanted to accomplish.

"Here we are Mr. Brinkley." The Sergeant said as they came up on a door that read 'Parking Lot Exit' in bright orange letters. "Let me give you a bit of advice Mr. Brinkley. Don't go out there trying to save the world or make up for lost time. You can't, just take your time and work on getting to know your family again and doing something they can be proud of. I done seen a lot of guys walk out these doors to nothing, so it's obvious that your family believes in you if they stuck around all this time.

"I appreciate that." Diamond said sincerely. It was no wonder why her cocked-eye ass husband loved her so much.

"Then make sure you take heed and don't come back." She unlocked the door. "This ain't no place for a good man."

"This part of my life over. I can promise you that. I'm looking ahead." Diamond thought about all the mother fuckers that had written him off and counted him out when he first fell. All the lames with so much to say, who knew that face to face he clowned niggas and smiled. "I'ma different man now."

"A'ight then." She said and pushed the heavy steel door open and just like that Diamond was one step away from freedom. "See you around."

Diamond stepped out and took his first real breath of fresh air in almost twenty-five years. For some reason, the sun seemed to be shining extra bright. The sergeant stood there in the doorway watching. She always enjoyed this part the most. When black men reunited with their true loved ones if they were lucky enough to make it out in time. Some tried to play it cool, but most cried while others just went stare crazy not knowing what to do.

Diamond looked at his family, mother, wife, son and granddaughter. The only people besides Allah that had never truly given up on him. The only people he felt he owed anything to. Sure, it wasn't always easy, especially in the beginning, but unconditional love and Allah had pulled them through.

His wife Khadijah was dressed in full Garb, and like the rest of the family, she was only able to stare. Nobody moved. With his heart in full submission Diamond silently said a prayer because he knew that it was the will of Allah that had brought him up out of the pits of hell a better man.

Diamond knew that society would be hard on him. Being both a Muslim and convicted felon made you like a terrorist in America, but he knew that the true terrorist were the tyrants who had robbed, raped, kidnapped, and killed his people without mercy and now forced them to live in poverty. It was just too bad that people were afraid to see it.

Diamond's granddaughter was the first one to break the silence she ran over to hug him.

"I missed you!"

"I missed you too beautiful." Diamond snatched her up in the air as the rest of the family came forward. "I missed you too."

"Aham-du-di-lar!" Diamond repeated as he hugged and kissed his family. "Aham-du-di-lar."

Like all those before him, Diamond took one last look at the place that had taken so, much from him on one hand and taught him so much on the other. The joint was a fucking 'menticide' madhouse, and Diamond hoped that somebody would burn that bitch down one day. I prayed to Allah to keep you safe Abu." His granddaughter said hugging him tightly as he held her in his arms.

"And it worked." Diamond came out of his trance and kissed her on the forehead. "Now let's go home."

******

Mumbles parked in front of D.W.'s house and jumped out of the car bloodthirsty. He had just gotten into it with a few Westport niggas while dropping Cat off at the best friend's house. He had already known it was coming because he had been catching ill looks out there ever since the little football game drama jumped off between their neighborhoods. So, today after Cat got out the car niggas started acting crazy. Throwing bottle and screaming threats.

So, Mumbles threw the car in park and hopped out to see what was up and 'shit instantly erupted into a huge tussling match with Cat right up in the middle grabbing niggas with him. Ebony and her father had to come out and break shit up. After Ebony's father had assured Mumbles that Cat was safe, he jumped back in the car and headed for D.W.'s with it on his mind. Because, there was no way that he was going to swallow his pride, and let that shit slide.

Mumbles banged on D.W.'s door like he was crazy until he heard Tiara asking who was at the door. It's Mumbles! Open the door." Mumbles ordered, he was ready to get back out Westport and drop his nuts.

"Donald and them, aren't here," Tiara said. "They left about an hour ago."

"Man, Tiara stop playing with me and open the door." Mumbles yelled. He didn't need D.W. and them to grab what he was trying to get his hands on. He knew exactly where the AK-47 was at. "I gotta get something girl."

Mumbles heard Tiara huffing and puffing, sucking her teeth and shit as she fumbled with the lock.

"Yo! What 's wrong with you?" Mumbles questioned her attitude when she finally got the door open and stepped behind it to let him inside the dark house. "You in this motherfucker all in the dark and shit."

"Nothing," Tiara replied closing the door. "Can you just hurry up please?"

"Aye Yo!" Mumbles fired when the light from outside flashed across Tiara's face. "Man...I know you ain't let that nigga put his fucking hands on you again? Hold up!" Mumbles walked over and flicked the light now. Nah Nah, fuck no! That nigga did that?"

"Michael, please just leave it alone," Tiara said trying to cover her battered face. "Get what you got to get and leave."

"Nah man, fuck that!" Mumbles pulled her hands down so that he could survey all the damage. "Yo, I swear to God. I told this nigga to keep his fucking hands off you. You know what? You don't know where they went at?"

"No."

"They probably walked 'round Lil' Dray's house." Mumbles said quickly moving to the door. "Watch me go around there and whip that nigga's ass."

"Michael please," Tiara jumped in front of the door.

"Move yo, I'ma give his punk ass a dose of his own medicine." Mumbles spit trying to pull Tiara from in front the door, "I'm serious Tiara, watch out. I wanna see how much he like having his shit all lumped up."

"It wasn't even his fault."

"Stop trying to protect that nigga" Mumbles barked at her angrily, "It's his job to protect you and ain't no fucking reason in the world why he should be putting his damn hands on you."

"I love him, Michael." Tiara just broke down crying.

"I know." Mumbles pulled her into his arms and tried to comfort her; it was crazy how D.W. could wrong something so precious. Mumbles never claimed to be perfect, but all he wanted to do was love, protect, and take care of Cat.

"But you can't keep letting him beat on you and treat you like shit. Love is not like that yo. Love is beautiful."

"I just don't know what to do." She admitted almost ashamed. "I never thought that I would be the woman that stayed after a nigga put his hands on me. Especially after watching my mother go through the same shit. But look at me. I'm so scared to be alone that I allow this nigga to keep disrespecting me and then keep telling myself he'll get better."

"I'll help you figure something out okay?" Mumbles held her tight as she continued crying. Maybe he could get Cat to talk to her or something. He just couldn't figure out why women choose to stay with niggas that beat on them. Especially, the ones with kids. It just sent the wrong message. They had to know that they could do better.

"I do know one thing though…If you continue to accept that shit, it's only going to get worst. That's how them bitch ass niggas do. They beat on their women to make themselves feel more like a man because they know deep down inside they lack what it really takes to be one."

******

"Shit about to be on nigga, my cousin home now." Black said hitting the blunt.

"Man, nigga, pass that piff." D.W. reached for the Backwoods when Black went into a coughing fit. "Before you hurt yourself." Black took another hit and passed the blunt to D.W. The weed was good and strong. "Nigga, I got Indian in my family. I can smoke like a chimney."

"A'ight Chief," D.W. replied laughing before hitting the blunt until his lungs felt like they were about to collapse.

"So, that old cousin of yours is finally home huh?" Lil' Dray asked. He was tired of hearing about the 'Life and Times of *Yusef Diamond Brinkley*, the Lexington Terrace Legend, who had played the game by all the rules that mattered. "I'm ready to meet this nigga."

"Yeah, me too Dug." D.W. seconded taking a swallow of Jack Daniels. "I hope this nigga about that paper like you said."

"Aye yo, what if he on that "I' ma Muslim now, no more dope slinging' shit?" Lil' Dray questioned laughing. "You know how them dudes in the joint be."

"Hell yeah!" D.W. burst out laughing. "All them niggas be coming home on that 'I don't eat no pork, Bean pie! Bullshit."

"Aaah nigga, you ain't got to worry about that. My cousin a fucking gangster!" Black corrected. The thought of Diamond being on some brainwash jail shit wasn't even a question. "I just can't wait to show that nigga how much I done came up out here. How I been keeping the legacy alive."

"You mean we nigga!" D.W. fired. "You ain't the only one out here putting in work; fuck is you hollering about?"

"Man shut the fuck up and pass the blunt." Lil' Dray barked at D.W. "You're scared ass ain't going to bust a grape in a fruit fight."

"You ain't lying about that!" Black added laughing. "Yo, remember the time when he froze up down the shopping center? Bluffing motherfucker! He was…"

Chapter 12

"So now we on some hustling shit?" Lil' Dray questioned as Black's cousin Diamond paced the floor of D.W.'s living room laying out his plans.

"Yeah." Diamond replied. He'd been home all of three weeks, and it was time to put shit together.

"Man, I ain't feeling this shit!" Mumbles said. He'd been listening to Diamond for the past thirty minutes, and he still wasn't convinced. "We got a good thing going with this robbery stuff. The money sweet and the team is strong."

"Yeah, but the risk is high." Diamond fired. He knew it would be hard to turn a bunch of young hoodlums into hustlers. As hard as it was to turn a hoe into a housewife, but he was up for the challenge. "What happens when shit goes bad huh? Or niggas run out of good strings?"

"You act like ain't no risk in fucking with them Muslim motherfuckers!" Mumbles barked. The whole idea was crazy to him. "What happens if they start playing games?"

"Hold up yo." Black saw where things were going and decided to intervene.

"Listen. It's always a risk, but I'm like Mumbles. I don't trust them weird ass motherfuckers. For real we can get them for all I care. But, on the flip side if what you're saying is true. Then I say fuck it! Let's get rich."

"How much money we talking about?" D.W.'s greed started to kick in.

"Enough to retire with." Diamond knew that no smart nigga, gangster or otherwise, wanted to have to rob, kill, and deal their entire lives. "I already got a meeting set up with my man's nephew in a few days. Once that's done all we got to do is go hard for about six months and then we can call it quits."

"What if the shit some garbage?" Black asked.

"Yeah, a nigga can't do nothing with no huff," D.W. added.

"Oh! We ain't got to worry about that; trust me." Diamond smiled. He'd already been assured that the product would be even better than the prices. "This shit gonna be A-one."

"Billy Lo." Mumbles looked across the room seeking a man's judgment he had come to respect and trust. All the shit Diamond was talking sounded good, but to him, Diamond was just another one of them slick talking old heads, that came home thinking that they deserved a reward or something for standing up. "What do you think about all this?"

Billy Lo had been leaning against the wall listening to Diamond the entire time; never voicing his opinion. He wasn't feeling how Diamond just came out of left field with all the put down the guns, pick up the pack' bullshit. That wasn't what they had discussed, nor planned.

"I don't like it." Billy Lo replied honestly. He wanted to stick to the script that kept him from being directly involved. The script that had Diamond coming home to get money; while he faded to black and only came out to eliminate the competition. "But, if it makes money, it makes sense, so I'm in, but I want you to understand this yo. If them bean pie eating motherfuckers play any games. We crushing 'em'."

"You think I don't know that?" Diamond eyed Billy Lo as Shabazz's advice came to mind. "I know that, but they not gonna try to fuck us slim, believe that. All we got to do is get this money and get the fuck out of the game."

Mumbles remained silent and smiled on the inside. He admired Billy Lo for always being straight up and calling shit like it was.

"Where the hell we gonna set up shop?" Black asked nobody, in particular, looking around the room. "We going to have drugs with no corner.

"Shid, what about the Pole-Homes?" Lil' Dray paused to let everybody consider that.

"Nah, we're gonna need a good dopestrip," Black replied.

"Yeah, we'll probably have to give out testers and shit to build something up." Diamond thought for a second. "What about that little cut right there by the store on Saratoga? I saw a few kids jamming out there."

"You been gone too long Dug." Mumbles shook his head and started laughing. "Niggas not just going to let you take over their block."

"Them Lil' ass kids" Diamond retorted. "Shorty, I probably raised them Lil' niggas fathers."

"That don't mean shit. Niggas respect work. All that living off your name shit died in the eighties."

"Mumbles right Cuz," Black said knowing it was a new day. "Niggas not going to just sit back and let us get rich. We gonna have to crack some heads."

"Money and blood don't mix." Diamond spoke from experience. "One always consumes the other."

"They used to say the same thing about street niggas and courtrooms. Now, look how good they get along." Mumbles said. "Personally, I don't think you can get money without blood. And I know you can't keep it without drama."

"Well, let's just focus on getting the work first." Diamond said a little disappointed. He'd thought that Mumbles and them would fall to his feet when he came home. That was how it use to be when a reputable gangster hit the bricks back in the day, but he guessed shit had truly changed.

"Bet." Mumbles replied. "All you got to do is tell us when you're ready."

Diamond looked around as everybody nodded in agreement and wondered for a moment if Black had really told Mumbles and them about all the work he used to put in back in the day.

******

The call came around six o'clock in the evening. The caller simply said... "There's a car waiting for you out front. You got two minutes to get in it..." and hung up.

Diamond quickly left the house that he shared with his wife and children and climb into the back seat of a late model, tinted window Lincoln Continental with two other big beard muslims , who never uttered a word.

It felt like some shit straight out of a movie. First, he was driven to a dock near the Inner Harbor's Water and searched. Then he was escorted to another car that would eventually pull up behind a nice Halaal restaurant in a part of the city known as baby Mecca due to its high number of Muslims.

"As-salaam alaikum." Samad got to his feet and greeted Diamond with a handshake, when he entered the small private room that was used to conduct the sought of business that had brought them together.

"Wa-alaikum as-salaam." Diamond replied.

"Have a seat, Ock." Samad gestured towards the table.

"Thanks." Diamond sized Samad's bodyguard up and sat down.

"Let's eat. Then we can talk business." It was more of a statement than question. Samad Knight was an American Born Muslim with a bull's neck. He was known in the community for his quick temper and ability to drop a fly from a thousand meters. An old sniper trick he'd picked up in the military before Allah changed his heart and brought him home to serve as the head of security for the Al-Haqq Masjid and Imam Paul 'Walaa' Rhodes, who instantly took to him, and not only because he was Shabazz's nephew.

Walaa and Samad's uncle Shabazz had come through the trenches together, and at first a lot of the Saudi Aradia brothers felt like he was just a slick talking American punk, who hadn't truly earned his position, but they quickly learned that Samad was just as dangerous as he was sharp, when he stopped a non-believer from killing Imam with a Pianoforte Wire. So, from then on they learned to accept his position and gangster status.

"Tariq!" Samad yelled and looked towards the closed door where the two men, who'd driver Diamond to the restaurant, stood outside on guard.

The door cracked and the slim, older, baldheaded brother with the salt and pepper beard poked his in. "What's up, Ock?"

"Have one of the sisters come back here for me."

Tariq nodded and closed the door.

Samad and Diamond talked about Shabazz while they waited for one of the sisters to show up. Samad was halfway through the Cuban Cigar when Tariq opened the door again and let a fine little sister in full garb enter. Samad spoke in Arabic as she scribbled on a small white writing-pad before nodding and exiting the room just as quickly as she'd come.

I still can't get that Arabit down pat." Diamond said.

"You just got to keep studying." Samad said. "But basically. I just ordered us some cheese and mushroom covered spaghetti, with a side of freshly toasted garlic bread and red wine."

"That's my shot." Diamond said more out of respect than anyting.

"Well enough about my uncle. Let me introduce you to the other brothers while we wait." Samad sucked on his cigar again and continued. "This here is Jabbar." He pointed to the bodyguard, who had come in while they were talking about Shabazz.

Jabbar Branch was a young Muslim from West Baltimore's Sandtown with extra-long thumbs and a tender trigger finger. "And this brother here is Mosi." Samad gestured towards the first bodyguard. Another West Baltimore born and bred member of the Al-Haqq Masjid. "And finally the two brothers that picked you up were Tariq and Adnan."

Samad said referring to Tariq Grandison, the one time prize-fighter with the meaty hands that now claimed fame as one of the best gung-ho gun-slingers in the baby Mecca community, and Adnan Shyydie, a light skinned, baldhead Pakistani known for always getting the right guy with the first shot.

Neither brother had said a word to Diamond, nor greeted him in the car. Both for different reasons. Tariq was a man of few words, and Adnan, well he just didn't trust Jews and Kuffer lovers. A decade old throat scar from the Pirani and four .357 Magnum slugs to the chest during an old fashioned religious war gave him good reason.

After the sister had cleared the table, Samad and Diamond got down to business. They went over prices, delivery, and quota. Samad asked Diamond not to accept more than he would be able to move because that would surely cause problems. Samad agreed to four- kilos a month for the time being and promised that if demand went up, the load would increase and the numbers would come down. There was only one problem. Diamond needed a productive piece of drug Real Estate.

"Pick any two streets that cross on the East Coast and in twenty-four hours they're yours," Samad said.

"Just like that huh?" Diamond smiled thinking about Shabazz.

"Just like that," Samad assured him. All he had to do was hold up his end of the deal.

"Well, in that case. I got the perfect place." Diamond shook his head and went on to tell Samad exactly where he wanted to set up shop.

"I assure you that won't be a problem," Samad replied; when Diamond finished laying out his request and just like that, Diamond's little problem was solved.

"Then let's get some money." Diamond stood and shook Samad's hand to seal the deal. It was a simple gesture that represented so much more in the underworld. Agreement, consent, whatever the case Diamond knew there was no turning back. In the morning, he would have the corners of his choice and four bricks of pure, uncut grade one heroin

"I like the sound of that." Samad patted Diamond's shoulder. "Adnan and Tariq will see to it that you get home safely. Please don't take my antics personal. I mean you no disrespect, but I am sure that you can understand that with so many suckers infiltrating our world that we must protect ourselves?"

"'It's all good." The only thing on Diamond's mind was telling his team that he was about to make them rich. "You gotta do what you gotta do."

******

"So, what ya think about this dude Mosi'?" Samad asked once Diamond was gone.

"I don't like him, Ock, it seems like something's off with slim, but you know how some dudes can be when they first come, thinking they know everything."

"Inshallah, you're wrong, Ock." Samad shook his head. He trusted his uncle's judgment. "You got to learn to see with your brain sometimes. Don't always use your eyes."

"You asked me what I think about this dude, and I told you the truth, so don't go off on me Ock."

"You think too much, Ock." Samad laughed.

******

"Money, money, money, money, MONEY!" D.W. sung hanging the phone up.

"Nigga! What the fuck he say?" Lil' Dray barked with his half hidden in a thick cloud of weed smoke.

"Nigga we got some mob ties now!" D.W. grabbed Lil' Dray by his face and leaned towards him.

"Yo!" Lil' Dray snatched free with the quickness and drew his gun. "If you put your fucking crusty ass lips on me I' ma spank your dumb ass down here. I don't play that touchy, feely gay shit nigga."

"Nigga, we on some Scarface, Good Fellas shit now. Niggas gonna start calling me Gotti or something."

"Man shut the fuck up and hand me that Hen-rock." Lil' Dray fired. "You sound scared. Them niggas ain't no different than us. They put their pants on one leg at a time too."

"I'm just saying, we fucking with some terrorist, Al Qaeda type niggas." D.W. gave him the bottle. "So, we about to have motherfuckers shook."

"Fuck is you talking about nigga? I been had niggas shook."
Lil' Dray grizzled the Hennessy. "You better ask somebody."

"You a bluffing ass nigga, with your dirty ass." D.W. laughed
and tried to pop Lil' Dray's neck. "Well, now you about to be scary
and rich."

"Now you're speaking my language."

"Yeah, I bet I'm, and for the record nigga I don't fear nothing
but, God himself, believe that."

"Oh, shit yo!" Lil' Dray snapped remembering the lick
Mumbles and Black had set-up for that night. "Call that nigga back.
You forgot about the shit; we gotta take care of our Westport
later."

"Damn! You right." D.W. was about to pick up the phone but
stopped. "Hold up, we still gonna do that shit? We on now, I mean,
I know yo getting some money. He just busted with that new
Navigator, but like I said we on, and that's Dug's cousin baby
father."

"Man, fuck that flashy ass nigga. He shouldn't have got with
that bullshit out there." Lil' Dray barked.

"Oh, it ain't him I'm worried about. It's Ebony Lil' crazy ass."

"Ebony cool yo, Mumbles gave her and Cat his word that he
wasn't gonna sweat that shit."

"Yeah, but they ain't dumb, and that's her baby father, Dug."

"You act like we gonna body the nigga or go running to Ebony
like 'Yo, we just got your baby father." Lil' Dray shook his head.
"Come on now, think about all the niggas we done got that fuck
with people we know."

"You right," D.W. admitted remembering how they used to
put each other on dudes they knew in the hood. Most who still ain't
know they got em'.

"At the end of the day if that shit come out Black got to deal with Ebony, not us. Him and Mumbles, they going to be the ones that get the blame for yo getting ganked."

"Hell yeah." D.W. laughed and picked up the phone. Wasn't no sense in letting a good string slip through their fingers. Especially, after they had already done their homework. "I'ma call that nigga back right now."

Chapter 13

Money was rolling, and Diamond, Billy Lo, Black, Mumbles, D.W. and Lil' Dray were enjoying the ride. Some a little too much, everybody had whips, but only Diamond and Billy Lo were preparing for a rainy day. Black did bless Peanut with some change to attend business school. Mumbles copped a Range Rover and got a nice spot for him and Cat not too far from her grandmother's. D.W. was spending his money like it was going out of style and all Lil' Dray did was buy guns, trick on bitches, and shit on haters. Billy Lo tried to talk some sense into them, but they were wild, young, money, getting niggas, full of cum, a lethal combination.

The Muslims had shown their hand. Diamond had requested a strip, and they laid out the red carpet. Literally, and before the blood dried up Diamond and them were out on the block in full force; jamming with 50's of raw dope and weight. D.W. and them were definitely respecting a G. When it came to getting money, and organizing shit Diamond knew what the fuck he was doing. The heroin they were getting was so pure you couldn't even touch the wrapper without catching a contact, but Diamond showed them how to step, walk, and even dance on that shit before it hit the street.

Money was coming in so fast that Samad had to up delivery and Diamond was forced to reach out to his Muslim Brother Joe Louis. An old-school gangster from Edmondson and Brice, who had earned his name by shooting his way up out of the City Jail in the late 80's with another gangsta, before leaving a trail of bodies from Baltimore to Washington D.C. to protect himself from going back.

Mumbles pulled up in his pearl white Range Rover and called one of their runners's over to the truck after electronically lowering the window. "What's up unc? You straight?"

"Yeah, I'm good nephew." He replied walking up on the truck pulling his hood down before blowing hot air into his closed fist to catch some heat.

"How it's looking out here?" Mumbles asked, scanning the block.

"Ain't nothing unusual; jump-out boys came through earlier, but that s about it. They ain't slow nothing up though. Traffic still moving." He replied. "We gonna need another loaf in about an hour too. You know today check-day and these motherfuckers hungry."

"A'ight just hit me when y'all ready. I'ma be around on Division anyway."

"That'll work." He pulled his hood up and back up off the Range stuffing his hands into his pockets as Mumbles slowly pulled off rolling his window up.

"Check this nigga out," D.W. said when he spotted Mumbles' Range coming off Gold Street. "He just thinks he's the slickest thing moving."

"That joint is tough though." Lil' Dray said giving Mumbles his props as he pulled up and parked behind his BMW.

"You ain't lying about that, but watch how I bust out on niggas next month.

"What's up with y'all niggas?" Mumbles walked up giving D.W. and Lil' Dray some love.

"Shit," D.W. replied as Lil' Dray shook his head. "Chilling."

"Fuck everybody at?" Mumbles questioned looking around,

"Billy Lo up in the nest, Joe in the hole." Lil' Dray gestured towards the alley with his head. "And Diamond and Black went around Peaches house with them Baker Street niggas to shoot some dice."

Mumbles looked up and saw Billy Lo. That was the best thing Diamond could've done for that nigga; because he hated to show his face, but he damn sure loved to protect his interest.

Mumbles stood around kicking it with D.W. and Lil' Dray for a minute. Talking about the latest hood drama and shit before he decided to slide around Peaches' spot to see if he could come up real quick.

******

"Come on bitch!" Mumbles threw the red and white dice across the cold concrete up against the wall. "Six/Four."

"I gotta yard say this nigga go out." Another neighborhood hustler in a butter-soft leather said tossing a $100-dollar bill on the ground.

"Bet!" Black fired ready to ride with his man. Everybody knew that Mumbles was like the Golden Child when he got them bones in his hand.

The back yard was packed with enough dope boys to supply half of the city. The money on the ground alone was enough to take ten bad bitches on a Saks Fifth Avenue shopping spree. Black smiled to himself. Niggas were lucky him and his Dug's weren't on their dumb shit right now because they would lay everybody out that bitch down.

"That's right Dug!" Mumbles said shaking the dice hyped up as Black pulled a yard from the pile of money in front of him threw it in with the hustlers. "Fuck with your man, I'ma help you get that Valentine's Day paper."

Mumbles sounded off throwing the bones. "Here it comes nigga, here it comes. Nine hoes and a pimp...*Sweet!*"

"Bet back nigga, bet back." The hustler said as Black and Mumbles picked up their winnings. "Matter fact bet two."

"You ain't said nothing nigga. Bet!" Black smiled throwing another $100-dollar bill on the ground. "I ain't got.no problem taking you nigga's money."

******

"Please baby, let me peek." Lakeria was blindfolded as Billy Lo guided her through the crowded Downtown Gallery.

"Nope." Billy Lo smiled as he continued to guide her steps. It was Valentine's Day, and he wanted everything to be special. He had already woken her up to breakfast in bed singing an old, early 1990's cut called '*Fire*' by a group name '*Subway.*' "You gotta wait."

Billy Lo knew that one of Lakeria's favorite R&B Groups were doing a special Valentine 's Day performance at the Harbor View Fug Factory'. So, he slowly guided her over and removed her blindfold.

"Oh, my god Anthony!" Lakeria instantly covered her mouth with both hands and started jumping up and down once she realized what was about to. happen. "Oh, my God! I love you so much!" She put so much tongue in his mouth that it was crazy. "Wait until we get home, boy! Mmmmh."

"I love you too baby." Billy Lo smiled. Making her happy was all that mattered. But getting that '*You did good'* pussy was always a blessing.

Billy Lo and Lakeria stayed through the entire show. Dru Hill hit every classic from '*We're Not Making Love No More'* to '*Never*

Bodymore Murderland

Make a Promise' to *'Incomplete.'* Billy Lo even got them niggas to take a few photos and personally autograph them for his baby. But, he was just getting started. The Inner Harbor had a lot of romantic stuff to offer. The World Trade Center, The Baltimore Aquarium, couples' boat rides, and exclusive restaurants like Quzo Bay and Oregon Grille and Billy Lo planned to take his baby to them all.

******

Diamond couldn't believe he'd allowed Khadijah to talk him into going to some little book singing out in Owings Mills, but it was Valentine's Day, and she was crazy about them urban books. Especially, anything *NeNe Capri* wrote or put out.

"You better be lucky I love you." Diamond said as he held the door of the Books and Cafe spot open so his wife could walk in. This was as close to celebrating a holiday they were going to get.

"No! You better be lucky you love me." Khadijah's eyes lit up behind her Garb. "You know I'm crazy," Khadijah added laughing.

As soon as they got inside Khadijah took off and jumped in line to get her books signed. Diamond's plan was just to stroll around and chill while his wife got her books signed, but all that changed the moment he laid eyes on a former enemy.

Diamond couldn't believe it. The last he'd heard was that somebody had caught the nigga slipping on a mountain-bike and left him with wheels for legs. But, it was obvious from looking at the nigga that what he heard was untrue...

Diamond thought back to how Fly Feet and another nigga had brought him a move down the old penitentiary, back in the day and vowed to settle the score. Diamond looked to make sure his wife was still busy, then dipped outside to call his man Joe Louis as the situation started to play itself out in his head like it was yesterday...

"I'm dirty yo." Some nigga, who had just come off lock-up said pulling his property into the cell.

"I got you." Diamond quickly got on point and stepped outside the cell to keep an eye out for the guard while he got straight.

Once the nigga was unpacked, and they were locked in. He started pulling out a bunch of weird shit. *"What's that slim?"* Diamond questioned when the nigga attempted to stuff some milk cartons behind the bunk.

"Nah, yo." He smiled. *"I said I was dirty; this so nothing won't fall down on you."*

"What?" Diamond was confused, he knew there were some fucked up dudes in the joint, but this nigga couldn't be telling him that he was dirty like 'filthy. He ain't play that. He could deal with a lot of shit in the cell. But, a dirty or smelly nigga wasn't one of them.

"You mean like breaking law dirty right?"

"Nah, like dirt and stuff falling down on you from my bunk." He replied.

"Oh, hell no!" Diamond balled his face. *"You ain't staying in here slim. You gotta go."*

That was how it all started, two days later, after Diamond had checked the nigga in. Fly Feet and his man ran down on him on his way to eat. It turns out that the dirty nigga was supposed to be Fly Feet's stepson…

When Diamond got back inside Khadijah had all her books signed and was ready to go. Which was cool with him because he needed an excuse to take her home anyway, so he could scoop Joe Louis and get back out there before Fly Feet decided to bounce.

******

"Head's up Ock." Diamond tapped Joe Louis's leg when he saw Fly Feet coming out of the Books and Cafe spot with a small crowd. "Here he comes now."

"A'ight slim, handle your business." Joe Louie came up outta a slight nod as Diamond rolled the ski mask down over his face.

"Oh! I got him slim." Diamond assured Joe Louis picking the gun up out of his lap, reaching for the door handle.

"I'ma start this bitch up as soon as you start busting." Joe Louis said and watched Diamond nod, ease out the car, and jog across the street so he could approach Fly Feet from the blind.

"Fuck is you doing?" Joe Louis mumbled to himself watching Diamond suddenly change directions when he could've walked Fly Feet right down. "The nigga gonna see you, man!" Joe Louis was just about to say fuck it and run Fly Feet's ass down with the car when he looked up and saw the danger approaching.

"Shit!" Joe Louis fired jumping out of the car as Fly Feet pulled out a small caliber pistol and started walking towards Diamond shooting without a moment's hesitation as everybody else ran for cover.

Diamond squeezed off a few shots and went down behind a car, and Joe Louis wasn't sure if he was hit or not.

Fly Feet walked around the car like a professional to finish Diamond and was instantly knocked off his feet with two rounds from Joe Louis's big ass .357 Magnum before he quickly advanced to point blank range. Joe Louis wasn't taking no prisoners. He was a professional too, and although he didn't personally know Fly Feet, from the looks of what he'd just tried to put down, he knew he wasn't the type of nigga you crossed and allowed to continue breathing.

Joe Louis stood over Fly Feet and issued two more shots to the dome before turning around to help Diamond to his feet and push him towards the car.

"My shit jammed on me." Diamond felt the need to defend himself as they jumped back in the whip. "That's why I ain't get him at first."

"You ain't hit, are you?" Joe Louis questioned making a U-turn heading for the city as Diamond snatched his mask off. They could talk about all that other shit later.

"Nah, I don't think so." Diamond replied double-checking himself.

"You a lucky motherfucker Ock." Joe Louis took his eyes off the road for a second to check the rearview. "Slim wasn't playing."

"You know what they say. The prey gets preyed on. Killers get prayed for."

"And that's for sure." Joe Louis said smiling. Somebody had definitely been praying to Allah for Diamond today.

Chapter 14

"You no pay! You no leave!" Mumbles heard someone shout and turned around to see the old, ugly, cat-faced lady who owned the Chinese Store grabbing hold of Peaches' son.

"Me call cops now!" The funny looking bitch started mumbling in Chinese acting all crazy, trying to pull him to the back of the store.

"Bitch!" He snatched away turning towards her. "Touch me again. I dare you." He stood there with his little fist balled up.

"Nah shorty, chill I got it." Mumbles ain't want to see him get locked up. Plus, he wasn't for no nigga putting his hands on no female, so he pulled out a fat ass knot of bills. "How much that shit cost?"

"Five ninety-nine." The old Chinese lady barked.

"Everything always ninety-nine." Mumbles couldn't tell if the old wrinkled cat-faced bitch was smiling or frowning when he gave her a $10 spot and told her to keep the change before walking out of the store with Peaches' son.

"Man, you ain't have to give that bitch shit!" Peaches' son fired once they were outside. "I was about to pluck her dumb ass."

"Nah man, you don't put your hands on no female."

"Man, fuck that ugly ass bitch!"

"Your Lil' ass crazy shorty. How you gonna try to steal from the Chinese Store? You know them sneaky motherfuckers be watching a nigga like a hawk."

"They ain't even got no cameras in that bitch."

Mumbles looked at him and shook his head. The little nigga couldn't be no more than 60lbs pounds tops, but he always stayed in some shit. "Fuck is you stealing for anyway?"

"What's up with all the questions homeboy?" He looked up at Mumbles. "You five-0 or something?"

"Nah shorty, I ain't no police." Mumbles laughed. "I just wanted to know."

"Well, I gotta feed my Lil' Sister."

Mumbles didn't know how to respond to that. He knew that his mother got high and tricked. Shid, he was probably one of the only dudes around the strip besides Billy Lo who hadn't crept her off, but he had no idea it was that bad.

"You know what? What's your Lil' bad ass name again?"

"Charm." He replied.

"Well, I got a job for you Charm."

"A job?" Charm stopped walking to look him up and down.

"Yeah, a job. A J-0-B." Mumbles smiled. He liked shorty's spirit. He reminded him of Black when they were little. "What time do you get out of school?"

"I ain't got time for school. I'm too busy taking care of my Lil' Sister."

"Yeah well, your Lil' bad ass ain't working for me during no school hours. You still want the job?" Mumbles watched Charm as he considered the offer.

"What I gotta do?" Charm asked curiously.

"Nothing really. Just keep an eye on a few guys for me." Mumbles replied.

"*Keep an eye on a few guys*!?Charm repeated balling his face up.

"Yeah Lil' nigga, keep an eye on a few dudes for me and I'ma pay you twenty dollars a night. You got a problem with that."

"I ain't snitching on nobody." Charm assured him.

"Who said anything about snitching shorty? I know you a soldier."

"A'ight then, give me twenty-five, and I'll start tomorrow."

"Twenty-five huh?" Mumbles smiled. He liked Charm's style. "You know what?"

"You got that." He said as Charm's Lil' bad ass homeboys pulled up in a stolen money-green Chevy Tahoe hitting the horn. "Come see me tomorrow after school."

"A'ight bet." Charm nodded jumping into the truck before it pulled off.

******

"Damn Miss. Peaches, you gonna make a nigga fall in love." D.W. shook his head and looked down as Peaches continued slowly swallowing his dick down to the nuts before slowly coughing, gagging, and spitting him back up again.

Slurp, "Umm...umm...!" Peaches cupped his balls and deep-throated him again before getting real sloppy with it. "Mmmmmh...hmm!"

D.W. tilted Peaches' head back until he got the angle he wanted. Then started fucking her throat like he was in some pussy. "I'ma bout to bust!"

Peaches had offered D.W. some slow neck for a blast when he came out of her bathroom one day and he had already heard what the head was hitting for and wasn't about to pass up a chance to get a firsthand experience. Especially, not with her standing there naked with her phat Lil' pussy, nice tittie's, and a wiggly little butt on display. The fact that Baltimore City had the second highest ranked H.I.V./AIDS diagnoses in the nation meant nothing to neither one of them.

"Here it comes!" D.W. took one more look at all the saliva in and around Peaches' mouth, threw his head back, and nutted all her down her throat.

D.W. handed Peaches a $50 of dope and tried to catch his breath as she got up off her knees, and made her way over to the bathroom sink to spit out a glob of cum and gargle with some water.

"Yeah." D.W. licked his lips and eyed Peaches' lil' fair Caramel complexion body, before fixing his pants, and slapping her on the ass. "Next time I'm trying to get some of that pussy and ass." Damn, he wished Black wasn't waiting for him.

"Yeah well, you better bring more than a fifty." Peaches said firmly.

******

"Damn nigga! It took you long enough." Black fired shaking his head.

"I told you my stomach was on the half," D.W. said rubbing his stomach.

"Man, just come on," Black ordered ready to go pick Peanut up from class.

******

"You know you're the only one he'll listen to." Lil' Dray was up in the nest trying to convince Billy Lo to holler at Diamond for him because he was tired of keeping niggas on hold because of the bullshit ass 'Stop Snitching' DVD indictment. The game didn't stop because a few niggas got knocked off.

"I told you I got you. Just sit tight for a minute," Billy Lo spoke but never took his eyes off the strip. He knew that Lil' Dray wasn't hurting for money. The area they were in was a fucking goldmine. DNA of the most heroin plagued spots in the United States. "Let shit settle down first.

"Okay." Lil' Dray looked at Billy Lo strangely and walked out. It was like he was the only one willing to speak out against some of the bullshit Diamond was pulling. It wasn't supposed to be no big I's and little U's, but Diamond was really starting to act like he was the fucking boss because he had the plug.

"What 's up slim?" Joe Louis asked when Lil' Dray took a seat on the steps with him.

"Ain't shit Dug." Lil' Dray looked back towards the nest. "Diamond holding me up on the weight tip and that shit starting to get on my nerves."

"He ain't bless you yet?" Joe Louis was kind of surprised. Especially, since Diamond had hit him off last night with an ounce for himself.

"Nah, he still yapping about that 'Stop Snitching' shit." Lil' Dray replied zipping his leather up. "That fat, freckled-face State's Attorney bitch got that nigga shook."

"Man, that old bitch better worry about that faggot ass Police Commissioner stealing the City's Tax Payers money." Joe Louis fired thinking about how the bitch had made her career off convicting a few good men he knew. "She always trying to take a nigga down. The bitch went off about that 'Legends of the Unwired, Baltimore Street Chronicles' joint that dudes were pushing, and that was on some positive shit."

"Legends of the Unwired?" Lil' Dray thought for a second and snapped his fingers when it came to him. "Oh yeah, the demos the dude Bodie Barksdale be putting out about all the old school gangsters, right?" Lil' Dray remembered watching the one about the dudes Marlow, and Timirror over Black's house one night.

"Yeah." Joe Louis nodded in agreement. "The only one I ain't seen yet is the joint with my man Francis Byrd."

"I like how yo put them demos together. Because them crackers were getting all that money off The Wire." Lil' Dray said wondering how motherfuckers could profile real gangster's name and stories without paying up.

"Yeah, all they did was mix the stories up and left a lot of shit out." Joe Louis said knowing that he could tell Lil' Dray some shit. "But, you see that bitch ain't have no problem with that, did she?"

"Hell no."

"Yeah, that's because all them bitches were eating off that shit one way or another. Acting and all that shit! See it's only a problem when they can't exploit us and make money. That old bitch don't give a fuck about no snitch. She throws them to the wolves after they tell every time. She just don't want people to find out how they be giving them coward ass niggas that get out of jail free cards to lie and all that other shit."

"How about that." Lil' Dray shook his head. He knew a few rats that the Feds paid, supplied with drugs, and guns, and let run wild just as long as they said what they needed them to say when they needed them in court.

"Don't look now, but here comes your man."

"Who?" Lil' Dray looked down the street and started laughing when he saw Keystone, the $10-dollar man coming up the block pushing a shopping -cart full of junk a brown Quarter-Roy Pants jumpsuit.

"Dray, my main man. What's up home slice?" Keystone brought the cart to a stop. "I got something nice for you today baby."

"Man, Keystone I ain't fucking with your crazy ass today. You already got me cursed out by my girl for taking them damn used panties home."

"She played you man, all eleven of them were still in the pack." Keystone said moving around the cart. "But, you make it up with this nice T.V. set."

"Oh shit!" Joe Louis burst out laughing when Keystone pulled the dirty blanket back to reveal two old ass looking T.V.'s sitting in the cart. "Yo got the black and white hook-up."

"Keystone, man." Lil' Dray shook his head and laughed. One of the T.V.'s had a big ass hole in the tube. "What the hell am I supposed to do with that? I'ma flat screen nigga."

"Come on home slice. This stuff A-B-C. You put this one on the bottom." Keystone replied pointing to the T.V. with the hole in the tube. "It still has the sound, and this one got the nice color picture." He added pointing to the other T.V. "All I want is twenty dollars for the whole set. You can't beat that baby. That's a sweet deal."

Lil' Dray stood there tripping off Keystone. He couldn't believe he was really trying to convince him to buy some broke ass T.V.s. But he shouldn't have been too surprised. Keystone's crazy ass was always up to something.

"Man, Keystone, kick rocks nigga." Lil' Dray spit as Joe Louis continued to laugh until tears came to his eyes. Everybody knew that Keystone was a stone-cold con-artist. "I don't want that shit!"

"A'ight well, loan me a few dollars. My old lady got them hemorrhoids, and we can't even have sex until I can get her some of them little bullet things to stick up in a--"

"Whoa man! Don't nobody wanna hear that shit!" Lil' Dray barked going into his pocket to pull out a $20. "Here man, just go ahead about your business."

"Thanks, home slice, you always look out." Keystone said and took off before Lil' Dray could come up with a reply.

"Man, that nigga is crazy." Joe Louis said watching Keystone fly up the street with his cart.

"You ain't got to tell me." Lil' Dray said still laughing. "I already know. Somehow this motherfucker put some dirty, dyed drawers in a factory pack and sold them to me. I wanted to beat his old ass, but I couldn't do nothing but laugh."

Chapter 15

"Oooh...Bruce!" Detective Gibson's back arched up off the bed as Detective Baker, gently spread her pussy lips, and softly blew on her clit. "Why you like doing that so much?" She trembled.

Baker didn't answer, he just pushed her legs back some more and continued going to work. Gibson kept her pubic hair neatly trimmed so that her phat clit was always on display. She knew her pussy was good, because she'd tested it so many times herself.

"You gonna make me cum!" Gibson grabbed a mean hold of Baker's head as her flawless, toasted brown body started twisting, turning, and bending like she was having a seizure. "You... oh my, you...!"

"Don't run." Baker gripped her soft thighs and tried to pin her down to the bed in her small one bedroom apartment out in Brooklyn. He took the tip of his tongue, and repeatedly licked her from her ass to her clit slowly, driving her crazy because he knew that behind the tough girl demeanor was nothing more than a woman who loved to be made love to. "That's it; that's my girl. Give me that honey Pooh bear."

Gibson came all over Baker's face as he continued to play all the perfect notes on her harmonica with his mouth and fingers until her favorite song ended.

******

"Turn that up for me Bunchy!" Gibson yelled from the steam filled bathroom reaching for a thick towel as she stepped out of the shower.

Bodymore Murderland

"Owings Mills, Maryland, detectives are still investigating the bizarre Valentine's Day shoot-out and murder of an aspiring author and his longtime friend outside of a 'Books and Cafe Shop' that took place just last week."

"Detectives have little leads but believe that at least one of the victims were the intended target. Witnesses tell us the two unidentified men came out of nowhere and opened fire as the two victims were exiting the Books and Cafe Shop, where renowned author NeNe Capri, was promoting her latest series The Pussy Trap. Authorities won't say if they believe NeNe Capri or another of her peoples were involved, but they are asking for any leads."

Gibson walked out of the bathroom, wrapped in her towel, and took a seat on the side of the bed next to the nightstand so she could lotion up.

"In other news, several juveniles were arrested in the thirteen hundred block of Arlington for the stabbing death of Shawn Stanfield. A twenty-one-year-old male, whose court records show had just been released on bond for several child-molestation charges. Sources close to the investigation tell us that Stanfield was also sexually assaulted while being detained at the Central Bookings Intake Center and that they're looking into the possibility that the juvenile suspects may be related to at least one of Stanfield's' victims..."

"Sick motherfucker!" Gibson looked up at the photo of a relatively handsome dark skin kid with a couple of golds in his mouth before picking up the remote control and clicking the T.V. off. "That's what he gets." Gibson ain't have no sympathy for motherfuckers who preyed on children. "They shouldn't have let him out. Nothing says poetic justice like a rapist or child molester, who cute enough to get a woman his own age if he tried, going to jail to become somebody's little bitch."

"They always let them bastards out." Baker shook his head. Rapist and child molesters were the two type of sick motherfuckers he believed should face a firing squad. "And they're probably going to charge those kids as adults."

148

"What is world coming to when we can't even protect our babies anymore?"

Gibson tossed the remote back on the bed and continued to lotion up.

******

"Damn baby, that feels good." Billy Lo mumbled as Lakeria massaged his shoulders, while he sat in the bathtub full of hot water with his arms up on the edges and his head tilted forward.

Lakeria just smiled, she knew he'd had a hard day and she knew exactly what he needed. A hot bath, some good food, and some nasty sex; she planned to give it to him in perfect order.

Billy Lo truly appreciated Lakeria; she was the best thing that had happened to him in a long time. To top it off, she was strong, black, beautiful, and independent. Just like a queen was supposed to be.

Lakeria massaged Billy Lo's shoulders until she knew he was nice and relaxed. Then she kissed him on his back and told him to take his time while she went to the kitchen to finish washing off the Pork-Chops and Broccoli that she'd set out earlier. Everything else was already done. The phone rung while Lakeria was prepping, seasoning and frying the Pork Chops, but she answered without missing a beat. Her head and shoulder held the cordless phone, her mouth and ear focused on the conversation, and her hands continued to poke, flip, and shake the Pork-Chops around in the pan.

"See Ma, I know, I'll tell him soon." Lakeria rolled her eyes. "Look Ma, let me call you back, I'm still cooking." Lakeria burst out laughing. "No, I am not fattening up the frog for the snake oh, uh unh see ya bye." Lakeria laughed harder. "I am not messing with your crazy tail today...yes...okay. I promise...I love you too!"

Bodymore Murderland

By the time, Billy Lo walked into the kitchen Lakeria had once again outdone herself. Gravy covered Rice, Pork-Chops, Broccoli, cold Ice-Tea, and Mac and Cheese. Billy Lo kissed her and sat down to eat. It was definitely time to pop the question.

******

"I don't think it's a good idea period." Diamond said to Black as soon as he got back into the car. "I thought about it. Nah, I ain't with that."

"Why not?" Black tossed the Crazy John's Pizza bag into Diamond's lap and opened his own. "We got the clout, and you know that dope sells coke. That's easy money."

"Yeah, but all money ain't good money shorty." Diamond checked his side mirror, before pulling out into traffic. "Plus, ain't no sense in fucking with the coke anyway. I'm shutting down just before Baltimore City Day."

The Downtown streets were jammed packed. It didn't matter if you were walking or in a car. You weren't going anywhere fast. There was some kind of 'Purple Party' being sponsored by Baltimore City's own Jada Pinkett and Carmelo Anthony down the Baltimore Arena.

"That's the reason why we should do this. I know everybody can use a lil' extra money." Black added trying to get his cousin to feel their master plan.

Diamond took the first left after the light-rail passed by. He knew Lil' Dray, and them had put his cousin up to this bullshit. "Listen fam; I can't help it if niggas been fucking their money off. That's on them."

"What happened to being a team? You were the main one talking about making sure everybody was good before niggas called it quits."

"Fuck all that team shit!" Diamond looked over at Black. "We not no team! Let's get that straight. You my family and Billy Lo my man, but that's where its stops. It's strictly business for me; Mumbles and them your people."

"Damn Dug, you on some wild shit!" Black stared back at him not feeling the little selfish shit. "It's like you saying fuck niggas."

"Nah, it's not that. I just understand business." Diamond said steering the Benz through the streets.

"We do too," Black assured him as they fell back into heavy traffic.

"I can't tell." Diamond fired getting a little agitated.

Black took a deep breath before he spoke. He respected his cousin like a man, but he was on some sucker shit. "Look Cuz; I know you already had a plan. I understand, but we just wanna get right before you walk away." Black said hoping that Diamond could feel where he was coming from and get on the same page. "You know niggas like us only get this type of opportunity once in a lifetime."

Black saw Diamond about to come with some off the wall shit and continued before he could get it out. "Me and these niggas will kill for each other, steal for each other, all that shit. We done went to jail and did bids for each other. Them my brothers and I want all of us to shine."

"And I respect that." Diamond said taking his eyes off the road again. "I mean especially nowadays with all the telling going on, but like I said before. Ain't no sense getting no coke because we about the close shop."

"I heard that." Black nodded and decided to fall back until Diamond dropped him off.

"So, we good?" Diamond tried to read Black.

"Yeah, we good," Black replied and left it at that. Diamond was so lucky that they were family.

******

"Cream out! Cream out!" Charm yelled as Mumbles and D.W. watched him. Lil' Dray was in the nest holding them down. "Hitting in the hole! No ones! No fives!"

"Man, that lil' nigga gangster." D.W. pointed at Charm.

"Yeah, I know." Mumbles said with a wide grin. He had promoted Charm from lookout to runner after he got snatched up with his cousin for questioning in a murder and kept his mouth shut. "That's my Lil' Brother, I'ma lace that nigga boots up too."

"Backup Bitch!" Charm barked on a fiend twice his size. "Do I look like I'm serving? The line over there."

D.W. and Mumbles fell out laughing. The streets had a way of making a young nigga cold hearted. They watched as Charm directed and controlled the dope line before walking back over to the steps looking like a mini Mumbles in his little Seven jeans and dope Penny Hardaways.

"Where your lil' ass get all that heart shorty?" D.W. asked as Charm jumped back up on the steps.

"I don't know." Charm hunched his shoulders. "That's just me."

"You hear this lil' nigga?" D.W. tapped Mumbles and smiled. Charm was ahead of his time. "He says that's just him."

"That's right. Some niggas born gangsters, some niggas become gangsters." Mumbles said rubbing Charm's head.

"You keep teaching this Lil' nigga all that gangster shit, and his Lil' ass gonna fuck around and take over."

"Charm City nigga," Mumbles said giving Charm a pound.

"You better know it." Charm added laughing.

"Oh yeah? So, who--" D.W. paused when an unmarked car pulled up and the last two motherfuckers in the world they wanted to see hopped out.

"Well, well, well. If it isn't two of our old buddies." Detective Baker said walking up on D.W. "I guess it is true what they say. Some gangsters have more balls than brains."

"Get up against the damn wall!" Gibson demanded. She knew at least one of them had to be carrying. "You didn't think I'd let y'all little wannabe gangsters get away that easy now, did you? Come on, y'all know me better than that. I' ma nail your asses!"

"Where's the rest of the gang?" Baker questioned looking around for Chapple and Green. "I don't want you little punks going too far off before we can reopen that Park Heights case."

Charm knew he had to do something. Both D.W. and Mumbles had a lot of cash on them. "Ummm, excuse me, officer." Charm said in his boyish voice as Gibson pushed Mumbles up against the wall.

"Hey, little man." Gibson kicked Mumbles legs apart and looked at Charm.

"Why are you messing with my brother? My teacher said all police were like Officer Friendly." Charm said with a smile. "He didn't do nothing. He just came to pick me up and take me to Chucky Cheese's for my birthday."

Gibson didn't know what to say. She didn't want to rough Pair and White in front of some innocent little kid and traumatize him for life. So, she looked at him and winked. She knew that there was always tomorrow.

"Today's your lucky day Pair," Gibson said backing up off him. "What's your name kid."

"Calvin." Charm replied.

"Well, Calvin." She said softly not wanting another neighborhood kid to grow up hating the police. "You enjoy your birthday okay, and don't forget to make a wish."

"Yes Ma'am." Charm shook his head up and down.

Mumbles and D.W. couldn't fucking believe it. Hard ass Gibson and her good for nothing ass partner had went for the okey-doke. They stood there and watched until the detective's car disappeared.

"Yo, wait till I tell Black about this shit!" Mumbles grabbed Charm in a head-lock. "He's not going to believe it."

"Here shorty." D.W. went into his pocket and pulled out a fifty- dollar bill.

"You earned that."

"Hell yeah." Mumbles said following suit. "Now I see why they call your lil' ass Charm. You can get out of anything boy."

"I told you." Charm said stuffing the bills in his pocket. "I told you."

Chapter 16

Black and Peanut were on the front row laughing hard as shit as they watched one of the Queens of Comedy live on stage inside the Lyric Opera House. It was a Saturday night in late March, and the spot was sold out. Peanut and Black had blown some piff with her crazy ass mother Creola before showing up, so everything was extra funny. Mumbles and them had wanted Black to hang out tonight. Underground Night Club Owner Ricky Duvall was throwing a party for Baltimore City's own 'American Gangster' Little Melvin Williams and every 'G' from across the state was scheduled to pay their respects. But nobody in the world mattered to Black more than Peanut.

"Listen up big girls... stay on your job. Don't trust these skinny ass bitches around your man." Big Monique had the crowd crying-laughing. "See they ain't used to think we were a threat. So, they wasn't checking for our niggas, but see now you got to watch them boney, good for nothing, sneaky bitches..."

******

Lil' Dray, D.W., Billy Lo, Mumbles, Diamond, and Joe Louis were all inside the famous Underground Night Club on Edmondson Avenue having a ball. All the Baltimore hood celebrities had come out to have a good time and pay homage to Little Melvin. Sam Cassel, Skip Wise, Reggie Gross, Heavyweight Boxing Champ Hasim Rahman, and so forth. Joe Louis kept trying to lay his mack down on the fine little XXL Eye Candy and King Magazine Beauty of the Year bitch Robin V., but the pretty dike broad *Snoop* from 'The Wire' was all in his way.

"A yo, come mere real quick Dug." Lil' Dray popped out of the crowd getting Billy Lo's attention. "Hurry up!"

Billy Lo got up from one of the two tables they had in a dark corner and followed Lil' Dray to the other side of the club.

"What's up?" Billy Lo asked curiously once they reached the bar.

Lil' Dray leaned over and whispered so the approaching Bar Tender couldn't hear what he was about to say. "Don't look now, but check out your ten o'clock. Ain't that them A-T-L niggas that be stuntin' all the time?"

Billy Lo waited until the Bar Tender was taking the orders from Lil' Dray to look over and clock the V.I.P. Section. He knew Lil' Dray was talking about the two brothers sitting under the club's speakers surrounded by a gang of well-known Baltimore City freaks in big jewels.

"Yea, that's them. Why? What's up?" Billy Lo asked not really understanding Lil' Dray's point.

"I'm trying to snatch them, niggas." Lil' Dray replied eyeing the biggest brother like a hawk as he adjusted his Atlanta Falcon's fitted cap.

"Pump your breaks man, you drunk. You know I ain't with that spirit of the moment shit." Billy Lo said grabbing one of the two drinks from the Bar Tender. "Let them niggas slide through shorty, everybody chilling. This a gangster party."

"Yeah, you right Dug. Fuck that shit! Let's finish partying." Lil' Dray said to put Billy Lo at ease because he still had it on his mind, and wasn't feeling none of that soft shit he was kicking. "The night still young."

"And you know it." Billy Lo raise his glass in the air. "To us."

"To us." Lil' Dray toasted before following Billy Lo back over to the tables like everything was cool. He knew who he had to holler at if he wanted to show niggas that they still had to 'B-more Careful' when they came to the Charm City.

Lil' Dray waited until Billy Lo, forgot about the Atlanta niggas and hit the dance floor, before he pitched his idea to Joe Louis, Mumbles and D.W. Niggas who knew blood money was still money, and you could never have enough of it. D.W. and Joe Louis ain't need much convincing. They were with it, but Mumbles said he was carrying his drunk ass home. So, when the club started breaking up, and everybody started departing, Lil' Dray and them gave Billy Lo and Diamond some love and went duck hunting,

******

Mumbles was standing up in the middle of the floor sweating like crazy as Cat rode him damn near to death. "I love you so much, baby." He clutched his jaws, squeezed her ass cheeks, and continued to help bounce her up, and down on his dick like he too was crazy.

"I want you to hit it from the back." Cat held Mumbles' neck and leaned all the way back to look him in the eyes, while carefully rolling her hips in a circular motion. She didn't want him to nut yet.

"Nah." Mumbles managed between breaths. "Unh uh. "

"No." Cat moaned forcing herself to stop riding him because she knew that if she continued he was cumming. He couldn't handle her rodeo game. "Cause I don't want your drunk ass to cum yet."

"Oh, you wanna play?" Mumbles nodded. He was ready to get gangster up in that motherfucker now. Straight Bedroom Bully shit. "Get on the bed."

Cat crawled up on the bed on her hands and knees as ordered and waited for Mumbles to make his next move. Mumbles stood there for a second taking Cat all in as she looked back at him over her shoulder. Even in the doggy-style position, she was a fucking dime.

"Come on and get this pussy Daddy." Cat bit her sexy Lil' bottom lip.

"Hold up." Mumbles said crawling on the back behind her with other plans.

Her lil' black pussy was so pretty sitting there in front of him like that. The way the lips came out like a heel and curled up just before they got to the clit. Mumbles kissed her pussy softly and slowly ran his tongue up to her clit, tasting her before straightening up.

"I love the way you taste." Mumbles rubbed his dick between Cat's pussy lips a few times then it was ready to go to work.

"And I love how you feel." Cat inhaled as he slid in and it was on. For the next five minutes, all that could be heard inside the bedroom was the sound of sweaty skin slapping.

"Throw it back!" Mumbles barked slapping Cat across the ass and pushing her face down into the mattress. "Good girl."

Mumbles grabbed Cat's waist and watched her phat ole' ass shake all over the place. He talked a lot of shit to his niggas, flirted with a lot of bitches, and even threaten to leave a few times, but the truth be told, he knew he wasn't ever going nowhere. Cat was his life, and she had the best pussy on the face of the Earth.

"Get it, Daddy! Get that pussy "Cat gripped the sheets, bit down on a pillow and started throwing her ass back like she had something to prove. Mumbles moaned and slapped her across the ass again. He loved when she got all nasty and aggressive on him because it let him know that she was about to get hers and he knew that he wouldn't be able to stand up in that pussy too long after she started cumming.

******

"Don't get too close," D.W. said from the passenger's seat as they continued to follow the ATL niggas through the city streets.

"I got these niggas Dug." Lil' Dray assured him keeping his eyes on the Charcoal-grey Lincoln Navigator. "Fall back."

"Man, just stay with 'em' slim." Joe Louis fired from the backseat. He didn't give a fuck if Lil' Dray drove beside the niggas as long as they got the chance to move on them.

Lil' Dray and them followed the brothers from one Strip Club to the next until they ended up at El' Dorado's. Baltimore's No.1 Candy Shop.

******

"Damn that bitch bad." D.W. spit as they watched a fine Cocoa Brown dancer by the named Dream do a full split, lay her upper body flat across the stage and make her ass move like wild-waves. It was a trick called 'The Dream Catcher,' and D.W. understood why. It was hard to believe that an ass could move like that. "I'd suck a bone out that pussy."

"Shid. You and me both." Lil' Dray was so amazed that he almost came in his pants when Dream did her signature tongue and nipple trick. It was no wonder why everybody said that El' Dorado's only hired the baddest strippers in the city.

After Dream picked up all of her earnings and left the stage. Another bad, peanut butter flavored bitch named China Doll took the stage in her red leather 'Come-Fuck-Me' boots and started her routine. She wasn't sacked like Dream, but the bitch could definitely hold her own.

By the time, China Doll got into her pole routine the ATL niggas were moving like they were about to bounce so Lil' Dray, D.W. and Joe Louis quickly exited the club to get in position. The plan was to take the brothers in the parking lot.

"Here they come now," D.W. whispered to Lil' Dray. "Let's make it happen."

"Let Joe get up on them first." Lil' Dray grabbed D.W.'s. arm. "Once he got their attention then we can drop 'em'."

Lil' Dray and D.W. watched as Joe Louis approached the ATL dudes and flashed one of the Police Badges Lil' Dray kept for situations like this on them. Once the brothers were distracted Lil' Dray, and D.W. started moving.

Like a lot of out of towners, the brothers never knew what hit them. By the time, they thought to question Joe Louis, it was too late because he was stretching one of them with a mean overhand as D.W. brought his Glock across the back of his brother's head and Lil' Dray kept an eye out for any witnesses.

Once they knew the coast was clear, D.W. kept lookout while Joe Louis and Lil' Dray dragged the brothers up in between the cars and ran their pants. The one Joe Louis knocked out had the keys to the truck, so he popped all the locks and checked it out real quick to see if anything worth taking was inside. "Go get the car Dug." Lil' Dray said tossing D.W. his keys.

D.W. pulled the car up right behind the truck and popped the trunk so Joe Louis and Lil' Dray could stuff the brothers inside. "Hold up. What we leaving the Nav?" D.W. questioned after Joe Louis and Lil' Dray finished struggling to get the two big ass ATL niggas in Lil' Dray's small as trunk and got in the car.

"Yeah, let the police find it." Joe Louis replied. "Ain't nothing up in that bitch. It's a rental rock."

Lil' Dray and them drove over to the side of town that was once known for giving birth to more head-hitters than anything and stripped the brothers of all their valuables. Big faced, iced-out, Presidential Watches, heavy crushed-ice platinum chains, and nice sized pinky rings, huge Diamond studded earrings and mad cash before issuing a few head-shots, dumping the bodies in McElderry Park and calling it a night.

Chapter 17

Mumbles stood over top of Ms. Candy's naked ass while she bagged up his blow waiting for Charm to come back from taking his little sister to school so he could put his foot in Peaches' ass for stealing Charm's money and chasing him from the house in tears. Peaches had his blood boiling because Mumbles knew that all Charm wanted to do was take care of his little sister. It was bad enough that he was already being forced to act like a grown man because Peaches was getting high. But, now she wanted to steal from him too. Nah, fuck that! Mumbles wasn't having it, not this time.

When Charm came back, Mumbles handed him the duck-taped handled .32 revolver and told him to keep an eye on Ms. Candy while he went around his house to step to Peaches.

"Don't let her ass leave the table for nothing." Mumbles ordered Charm looking at Ms. Candy's slick ass. "And don't play my lil' brother Ms. Candy."

"Nigga go ahead and take care of what you're going to take care of. He okay, I got his lil' ass." Ms. Candy smiled.

"I' m good Dug." Charm assured him looking at the older, fine, dark skin chick with short hair and gangster rep. "Go ahead."

"A' ight." Mumbles nodded and made his way out the door.

******

"Damn, my bad." Mumbles came through Peaches back door and ran right into the neighborhood hustle man. "Where Peaches at?"

"Mumbles, my main man." Keystone smiled and pointed at him. "You just the man I need to see. Dig it; I had this dream last night--"

"Man, where the fuck Peaches at?" Mumbles fired cutting him off. I ain't got time for that shit today."

"Nah, listen man. I got a good lottery number, all I need is ten slugs to--"

"Here man! Damn!" Mumbles barked stuffing a $20 in Keystone's hand after going in his pocket. "Where's Peaches!"

"Right upstairs in her bedroom." Keystone replied and hauled ass-out the back door as Mumbles marched up the steps and banged on her bedroom door.

"I said hold up!" Peaches yelled trying to hide her stash as the bedroom door burst open. "Nigga what's wrong with you? Don't be just opening my damn door like you pay bills or live up in this motherfucker! What the fuck you--"

Mumbles cleared the floor and grabbed Peaches by her throat so fast that she choked on the rest of her words.

"Listen to me and listen good bitch!" Mumbles spoke as Peaches started gasping for air. Her hands shot up and tried to break his hold as tears welled up in her eyes. "That money you stole from Charm was mine, but I'ma let your junky ass slide because I know you got that monkey on your back. But, the next time you take anything from shorty I'ma come around here and kill your dumb ass myself. You got that?"

All Peaches could do was manage to shake her head up and down quickly. Mumbles let go of her throat, and she fell to the floor half dizzy, choking, and holding her chest like she was having an asthma attack. Mumbles kicked over the nightstand where she had tried to hide the mirror with her little dope lines on it and walked out. He was pretty sure that he'd made himself very clear.

******

"What's up?" Mumbles asked locking the door after Charm let him in. "You been watching her?"

"Yeah." Charm nodded. "She just finished too."

"You watched her the whole time? Because she'll pull a fast on a nigga in a heartbeat." Mumbles walked over to the table and started flipping through the tan bags of raw heroin trying to take a visual count.

"I was on her the whole time yo." Charm replied winking at Ms. Candy behind Mumble's back. "I didn't let her go nowhere or nothing."

"A'ight. I got it from here." Mumbles said pushing the bags of dope into one pile. He would physically count them after he searched Ms. Candy's ass. "Come on so I can search your ass." Mumbles stepped back and gestured for her to get up from the table. "What you bring back anyway?"

"I got a little over a thousand fifty's." Ms. Candy put her hands on the table and poked her ass out as Mumbles ran his hands all over her naked body. "But that's because I kept the bags healthy."

Mumbles now knew from experience how a fiend could hide an ounce of dope in plain sight if they wanted it bad enough. And Ms. Candy was as slick as they came, so he checked her hair, ears, mouth, pussy, ass and feet.

"A'ight. Tap your nails on the table."

"Come on now Mumbles." Ms. Candy looked at him like he was crazy. "How many times we gonna go through this? He told you I ain't move shit."

"Man, Miss Candy, just tap your nails on the table so I can pay you and get outta here." Mumbles trusted Charm, but he also knew that the hands were much quicker than the eyes. Plus, Diamond had just pulled all their coats to the new little trick fiends were working while they bagged up. Stuffing their nails with blow. "I ain't got all day."

Ms. Candy tried to tap her nails lightly, but a little bit of dope still came out. Mumbles smiled. He wasn't mad. A fiend was going to be a fiend. He respected her hustle.

"You see that Charm? Let it be a lesson to you." Mumbles said never taking his eyes off Ms. Candy. "What do I always tell you?"

"Trust nothing, expect anything." Charm replied eyeing Ms. Candy stupidly.

"Now you see why; you can never trust your eyes. All real gangsters rule with their minds. Just because you didn't see it doesn't mean it ain't happen."

Charm was hurt. Ms. Candy had played him. Mumbles had told him over and over again 'that any pure woman of the street could never be trusted because all of her life she'd been taught to get over, and it was the only way she knew how to survive.'

"Sorry sugar." Ms. Candy smiled at Charm. "Don't take it personally. I had to try you, but didn't I take care you?"

"Yeah, don't trip lil' homie. You live, and you learn." Mumbles said as he picked up an Ace of Spade's playing card and started cleaning Ms. Candy's nails.

Charm ain't hear nothing Mumbles said as he reached for the .32 revolver he had given him, pulled it out and fired wildly.

"Ahhhhhh!" Ms. Candy's leg gave out, and she tried to grab the table before she hit the floor. "You little motherfucker I'ma kick your ass!"

"YO!" Mumbles jumped out of the way not wanting to get shot and looked at Charm. "Is you crazy nigga? Man, give me that got damn gun!"

Charm kept the 32 pointed at Ms. Candy until Mumbles came over and snatched it out of his hand and stuffed it back into his dip.

"Ahhhhh!" Ms. Candy cried out again getting back to her feet and sat down in the chair, taking a look at her thigh. "That little bastard shot me."

"Man, Miss Candy stop faking, that shit don't hurt that bad." Mumbles fired knowing the flesh wound wasn't as bad as it looked.

"Nigga, you see my damn thigh?" Ms. Candy started acting all dramatic, putting on a good. "I think I'ma bout to pass out."

"Cut the bullshit." Mumbles spat trying to clean up and tell Ms. Candy what to say when the police arrived at the same time. "Just tell them that a trick shot you. A white dude or something." Mumbles said handing her about ten fifties. "I'll look out for you again when their gone."

Ms. Candy nodded and watched Mumbles and Charm head for the door. "I'ma still kick his little ass!"

******

"Stop and get some fruit. I got a taste for some grapes." Detective Gibson said when she saw the fruit man pulling his horse and carriage down North Avenue.

"*WATERMELONS! CANTALOUPES! BANANAS!*" The old man yelled as Baker slowly pulled up alongside him. "*APPLES! ORANGES! GRAPES!*" The fruit man barked at the horse and

166

pulled the leather straps to bring him to a stop once the detectives got his attention from the unmarked car.

"How much for a bushel of grapes?" Gibson questioned reaching for her purse. It had been a long night. She and Baker had picked up two well-known Cherry Hill shooters in connection with a couple of West Baltimore robbery/murders and spent the night trying to get one to believe that he was the lesser of two evils.

The game was to get them to turn against each other or give up some silly alibi or explanation. 'I only did this; I only did that. Unaware that Maryland Law allowed them to be charged as if they had pulled the trigger themselves. Gibson and Baker especially loved those so-called gangsters, who couldn't keep their mouths shut. The too slick ones, who disregarded anything you say or do, can and will be used against you', and talked their way into trouble trying to prove to themselves that they were as real as they had managed to convince everyone else they were.

However, the shooters they had picked up last night were professionals who didn't succumb to the games and fake belief, that by snitching they would get a better shake. These guys knew the drill. Some big shot lawyer worth his or her fees had probably taught them all about the landmark Escondido and Miranda Decision. So, after listening to their rights, they both requested lawyers.

No alibis, no explanations, no expressions of polite dismay or blanket denials. Nothing. They never even considered risking, hurting themselves, let alone each other. They both understood that they could always make a statement, but that once a statement was made, they could never take it back.

"Thank you," Gibson said handing the fruit man a few dollars.

"So, what now?" Baker asked pulling off. "Wanna head back over to the station and work on that Gold Street shooting?"

"Honestly." Gibson paused to dangle the grapes out the window and pour water over them. "I was thinking about maybe going over to the city lock-up to take another crack at Ebb and Edison."

"After last night, you gotta be kidding?" Baker watched Gibson eat a few grapes. "Did I miss something? Because I'm pretty sure that those two assholes proved to us they would rather be tried by twelve then labeled a snitch."

"Yeah, you're right." Gibson tossed a few more juicy grapes in her mouth. "Damn, these grapes are good. But, yeah, I want these guys. Look at how often their name have been connected to city murders. Remember their names even came up during the Fryson murder."

"Yeah, but these guys are old school," Baker said knowing that they couldn't take Ebb's and Edison's refusal to cooperate personally. They had a good run last month. Seven for Seven, but they couldn't expect everybody to snitch. "They still live and die by the code of the streets. They're not like these young kids who want to be known."

"Well, I guess we got our work cut out for us then."

"Yes indeed." Baker smiled. Wasn't nothing like good old fashion, hard police work. He enjoyed the challenge. "No snitches and no cooperation always make it feel so much better when you take them down."

Chapter 18

Diamond got out of bed and went to the bathroom to wet his hands, mouth, face, head, ears, forearms and feet before offering his morning, Salah. Nothing in the world was more important than Allah. The most gracious, the most beneficent, and the most merciful.

After prayer Diamond started getting himself ready to hit the streets. First, he stopped to lift the cloth that covered the photos of the few good men he had left behind. It was a daily reminder of where he came from and refused to go back to. The photos assured him that failure was not an option.

Diamond took care of his hygiene, got dressed, and headed on downstairs to eat the breakfast his wife left in the oven before locking up the house and bouncing. Billy Lo had summoned everybody to Africa's crib for an afternoon sit-down.

******

"I'm serious Cat!" Mumbles fired trying to block the doorway so she couldn't throw his boots out in the street.

"*I'm serious Cat.*" She teased dancing around in a circle.

"Okay…you playing now watch when I get your dusty ass back. Don't start crying." Mumbles acted like he ain't care then rushed her and tried to snatch the boots. "Stop playing."

Cat laughed and slung one of the boots pass him as they tussled for the other.

"Oh, it's on now." Mumbles grabbed Cat and tickled her so bad that she dropped the boot and farted. "Lil' dirty ass."

"Nah, don't run now!" Cat said jumping on Mumbles back.

Bodymore Murderland

"Get off me yo! You stink!" Mumbles fell to the floor laughing. He couldn't believe his baby's fart stink so bad. "It went in my mouth too."

"Oh! I know you ain't talking. Your boots smell like doo-doo." Cat laughed rolling around on the floor with him. Mumbles rolled on top of Cat, quickly picked up the boot and put it in her face. "What now!"

"Ewwww boy! I'ma fuck you up." Cat covered her nose and mouth and tried to get away.

"Nah, Nah, I got your bad ass now." Mumbles retorted chasing her through the house with the boot. It was no question how much he loved Cat. They had been through the storm together. Their love was tried, tested, and proven. Sometimes Mumbles could not believe how lucky he got, but when love was as powerful and authentic as theirs, there could be no other outcome.

Cat was one of those women who would never cross a friend and who would go off the edge of the earth for her man and Mumbles was both.

"A'ight, you win! You win!" Cat submitted when Mumbles caught up to her.

"I win?" Mumbles questioned holding the shoe up.

"Yeah." Cat smiled.

"You gonna stop playing so much?"

"Yes." Cat replied grabbing Mumbles arm when he acted like he was gonna bring it to her face again.

"Who got the juice?"

"You do," Cat said defeated.

"Who?" Mumbles shook the boot.

"I said you boy, damn."

"Now give me a kiss." Mumbles demanded, grabbing Cat up in a bear-hug, poking his lips out.

170

"Kiss this punk!" Cat snatched the boot and pushed it into his face forcing Mumbles to let go as she laughed and took off running again.

"Oh yeah?" Mumbles said repeatedly spitting the taste of boot out of his mouth before picking the boot back up and chasing after her laughing. He knew they weren't perfect, but they loved each other more than anything in the world. "I got your ass now!"

******

"You gonna be okay until I get back?" Billy Lo asked Lakeria as she sat at her computer creating contracts so voluminous and incoherent that even he couldn't understand it. Ever since she had told him that she was pregnant, he'd been waiting on her hands and feet.

"Yes, Anthony." Lakeria shook her head and blushed.

"A'ight. Hit me if you need anything." Billy Lo said rubbing her stomach. "You or the baby."

"Yes, Daddy." Lakeria giggled when Billy Lo kissed her belly.

"I love you." Billy Lo kissed her forehead. He felt blessed. There was nothing in the world greater than a strong Black woman. He admired Lakeria's beauty for a second then eased out the door.

******

Billy Lo walked into the smoke clouded basement and looked at Africa with a touch of contempt. Here it was her little bad ass brother was upstairs opening doors in nothing but a ski-mask and socks while her dumb ass downstairs worrying about being in a weed cypher.

"What's up nigga?" Lil' Dray got up and gave Billy Lo some love.

"Ain't shit." Billy Lo replied wishing he had stayed his ass home with Lakeria. However, he knew that some serious business needed to be discussed.

"Where's Diamond at?" Billy Lo looked around the room. He knew from the cars outside that everybody was present.

"In the bathroom," D.W. answered.

"A'ight, look umm…" Billy Lo looked from India to Africa. "I'ma need y'all to bounce for a few minutes."

"We were only chilling," Africa said getting up not smart enough to recognized on Billy Lo's face that he really didn't a fuck.

"A'ight, well chill somewhere else." Billy Lo watched as India and another lil' bitch followed Africa out of the basement. But India made it a point to roll her eyes and let him know that she wasn't feeling him. But, Billy Lo wasn't paying her young ass no mind. She had been tripping ever since he had left her out the Motel 6 on Route 40 when Lakeria needed him to come home.

******

"Now the reason I called this meeting is because I feel like niggas need to get some shit off their chest." Billy Lo had waited until Diamond came back to address everybody. It was a lot of issues that needed to be cleared up. Billy Lo didn't want them to get caught up in no female back-biting shit. "We're all men, so now is the time to speak up or forever hold your peace."

Billy Lo paused then decided to lead by example. "I'll go first. My issue is with niggas making moves without niggas being on point. I mean, it's got to be honor amongst men. Lil' Dray last week--"

"Don't even say his name." Lil' Dray fired knowing where Billy Lo was about to go. "I tried to put you niggas on point, but you was acting all crazy--"

"Just listen man." Billy Lo put his hand up. "My point is that you hit them, niggas, anyway. I read the shit in the newspaper. I mean, all is well that ends well, but I'm just saying y'all niggas could've handled that a lot better."

"I respect that." Lil' Dray nodded.

"Without honor, discipline, and communication we ain't got shit! We got to keep it clean with each other." Billy Lo added.

They went around the room and talked about everything from giving Charm his own coke shop to shutting down as planned. Everything was going good until Black and Diamond got into it.

"I'm just trying to figure out this plan you keep talking about." Black stared at his cousin. "Who all in on this plan? Cause I don't know shit."

"Me neither." Lil' Dray seconded.

"I'm talking about the 'Get in, get out' plan we all agreed on." Diamond chose his words carefully. "That's why I been telling you, little niggas, to stack your doe."

"Everybody not you Dug!" Black fired back. "Everybody don't know how to save money when it's always coming. So, you got to stop putting everybody in your shoes."

"I'm not saying that everybody is me." Diamond assured him. He was one of a kind. Niggas couldn't even hold a torch to his flame. "But I told niggas from the jump. Stack your chips because we can't make no career out this shit."

"You know what trips me out about you Dug?" Lil' Dray spoke up again." You came home talking all that old-school gangster shit, but you ain't sat a nigga down and laced his boots up yet."

Diamond didn't know how to respond to that.

Bodymore Murderland

"Niggas fucked up, we been blowing everything. Now we're trying to get right before the summer hits. We wanna retire too." Lil' Dray said.

"Okay. I'ma grab something extra." Diamond said getting to his feet ready to go. "But I'm still sticking to the plan. After B-Day shop closes."

Black smiled and let out a sarcastic grunt as he got to his feet.

"Hold up! I got an issue too." Mumbles spoke up for the first time, causing everybody to stop and look at him.

"What's on your mind slim?" Diamond questioned ready to go.

"I said shit good, I'ma get the coke for y'all."

"Man, I ain't even talking about that." Mumbles replied and continued. "My problem is with D.W."

"What?" D.W. fired. "Fuck you talking about nigga? You ain't got no problem with me."

"'I got a problem with you constantly putting your hands-on Tiara and jeopardizing niggas hustle--"

"Hold up Dug. I'ma grown ass man." D.W. barked. "I don't need you telling me how to handle my bitch nigga."

"I can't tell nigga" Mumbles spit. "It's obvious somebody need to tell you something."

"You ain't going to tell me shit Dug." D.W. walked towards Mumbles aggressively.

"Nigga, I'll tell you what the fuck I want to when it comes to fucking up my money." Mumbles never backed down from a challenge. "You out there beating on shorty all in the streets. That's bitch shit."

"Come on Dug, kill that." Lil' Dray stepped between them.

"Nah Dug, let that nigga keep running his mouth. I'ma show him who the real bitch is."

174

"Fuck you nigga!" Mumbles tried to move Lil', Dray. "I'm not Tiara nigga. I'll crush your bitch ass."

"Dug, you ain't like that for real."

"What's up then nigga?" Mumbles threw his hands up. "You know you don't want that. You couldn't even do nothing with Lil' Melvin down Ramsey Street. "

"You just talking nigga. You ain't 'bout that." D.W. waved him off like he was nothing headed for the steps. "Like I said, I'ma grown ass man and ain't no nobody gonna tell me how to handle my bitch."

"You hear this nigga?" Mumbles said to nobody in particular laughing. "Yo think he a man cause he put his hands on a female half his size, who he knows can't really hurt him. Nigga, you's a coward."

"What if I put my hands on you too" D.W. stopped in his tracks and turned around. "Then what?"

"Then I'ma trash your whore ass up in here."

"Chill man." Lil' Dray said trying to defuse the situation again.

"Nah Lil' Dray, let them niggas get that shit off their chest," Black said.

Billy Lo knew he had to step in and do something before shit really got out of hand. Niggas had come too far to throw it all away over an ego trip. Billy Lo had seen it coming all along, and now it was time to bring it to a close.

"Look, man; it's only one way to settle this shit." Billy Lo knew what had to be done for niggas to be able to put this behind them and move on. "Black run upstairs and wet about five or six towels real quick. We're gonna take this shit to the old school. Wrap these niggas hands up and let 'em' work."

"I like that." Lil' Dray said nodding. "I might be trying to see something too."

"Okay, while we wait both of y'all lil' niggas take off y'all shirts and give Diamond y'allburners." Billy Lo didn't trust them under the circumstances. "Move them tables Lil' Dray, let niggas get some leg room."

Mumbles pulled out a big ass 'cock end pop' .357 Bulldog and handed it to Diamond, D.W. followed suit with his Four-five.

"I'm ready to do this." Mumbles said cracking his knuckles.

"Yeah nigga, me too." D.W. started shadow-boxing.

"Hold up, wait for the towels first."

When Black returned with the wet towels it was on. Billy Lo wrapped Mumbles and D.W.'s hands and stepped back still holding his arms up between them. "I'ma let y'all little niggas go until one of y'all get knocked out, or tap out." Billy Lo said dropping his arms and stepping out of the way.

Mumbles and D.W. closed in at the same time and started exchanging blows. D.W. caught Mumbles with a quick two-piece and tried to slam him, but Mumbles wasn't having it. He kneed D.W. in the stomach and hit him with a hard right on the temple.

"Okay bitch, let's work." D.W. said rushing Mumbles up against the wall.

"Stop trying to wrestle and throw hands nigga!" Mumbles said as he and D.W. knocked into the table.

"Hold up ma." Billy Lo separated them again. "Y'all niggas gonna go or what? Fuck all the wrestling shit."

"That's what I am saying." Mumbles squared up and threw his hands back up. "Let's go."

When Mumbles and D.W. got to working again it looked like a modern day 'Thrills in Manilla.' They were going back and forth, tagging the shit out of each other. Mumble's shit got split first, but he opened half of D.W.'s face up. About three minutes into the fight everybody could tell that Mumbles was gonna win, but D.W. refused to tap out.

"You done dug?" Mumbles asked bobbing and weaving around D.W.

"You gonna have to kill me dug." D.W. said spitting blood on the floor.

Mumbles faked a jab and caught D.W. slipping with a wicked ass body-shot followed by a straight right. The body-shot landed so hard that Billy Lo and them could see the water jump off the now blood covered wet towel. D.W. folded over and went to one knee as Mumbles closed in for the kill.

D.W. was punch drunk so Mumbles danced around and waited for him to try and come back up so that he could hit him with the signature combination that his older brothers had shown him years ago.

"I told you that you gonna have to..." D.W. was pushing himself up off his knee saying when Mumbles laid him out could with two clean uppercuts to the chin, and a sharp right hook, and it was game over.

"Somebody get that bitch up, so I can see if he wants some more." Mumbles back up still throwing his hands. "Cause I still got something to teach him about putting his hands on women."

"Dug that nigga done." Lil' Dray laughed and Billy Lo and Diamond tried to bring him back to reality with ice and shit. "I like that nigga, you might gotta see me next."

"I am down for whatever." Mumbles said and everybody started laughing. "You see how I just whipped that nigga ass, so you know my shit up to date."

Chapter 19

The first day of summer was around the corner and with almost a month left to stack everybody was looking to be straight. Diamond could tell that it was going to be hard for Black and them to call it quits, but that was going to be their problems. He had done his part. To him, the game was a stepping stone, and he planned to get out before it was too late. Samad had already assured him that he wouldn't do business with nobody but him, so that was a dead issue anyway. Besides, Diamond had made a promise to his wife a long time ago that he would never jeopardize the things that mattered the most for things that didn't matter at all.

******

"Charm!" Billy Lo, yelled from across the street jogging over.

"What's up?" Charm stopped and questioned.

"Hi, Mr. Billy." Charm's little sister Tiffany waved her small hand. "I got a hundred on my spelling test."

"That's good baby girl. I'ma take you to the Penny Candy Store when you get out of school okay?" Billy Lo saw her missing tooth smile and continued. "Yo, I need you to watch the block real quick while I run around to the barber shop to get D.W. or Mumbles."

"Yo, I got to get Tiffany to school." Charm said looking at his watch. "I'ma only be a minute." Billy Lo assured him. "My girl just called me, and I need to get to the hospital asap"

"Man." Charm breathed and shook his head. He hated having his little sister anywhere near drugs. "I don't want her to be late."

"I just need to run around there and tell one of them, niggas, to come on."

"Man, hurry up yo, if you take too long I'm gone."

"Good looking out." Billy Lo replied already moving, "Black down the street and Lil' Dray up in the nest." Billy Lo added before he took off in a slow jog towards the barber shop.

******

"I'm from Linda's Lane, right off Timothy's Turn Pike." Mumbles fired reclining in the barber shop chair as D.W. continued to get his normal line-up and flip through a street magazine. "There's only two other niggas cut from that cloth. That's my brothers Jarod and Lil' Timmy."

"Y'all hear this shit, right?" D.W. questioned looking around the shop. He and Mumbles had come to respect each other a lot more since going a few rounds in Africa's basement even though Mumbles had got out on him each time. "Wait till I tell Black about this one. As much as you being set tripping too."

Mumbles burst out laughing. He knew D.W. was right. He stayed on his L.T. shit, but after reading the latest Don Diva article about how one in every four niggas were telling; he wasn't claiming anything but his roots. The Lion and the Pitbull.

******

"He gonna say the same thing, watch."

"What's up Lil' Gangster!" Black walked up on Charm. "Where Billy Lo at?"

"He ran around to New Identity's real quick." Charm replied and looked at his watch again. "You good? Because I got to get my little sister to this school."

"Yeah, go ahead. I got this. And make--" Black's voice was suddenly drowned out by the explosive sound of rapid gunfire. "*Move! Move! Move!*"

Black dove for cover behind a parked car as pieces of broken glass and concrete flew everywhere. Black spotted a jet-black Beamer flying towards him with niggas hanging all out the passenger side window and sunroof and pulled his .45 and started dumping just as the chopper AK-47 went off.

******

Lil' Dray had peeped the black, tinted window BMW the first two times it had come through, but thought nothing of it. The motherfucker could be lost. However, he clocked it every time so when the Mac- tooting nigga popped up out of the sun-roof on the third trip Lil' Dray instantly knew it was a hit and brought the AK up to cut him down from the window.

Lil' Dray saw Soft Ball sized holes popping up all over the BMW as one-foot sparks jumped out of the burrow and sides of the AK. Lil' Dray saw the nigga hanging out the sunroof bend forward and slam into the roof of the car before losing his Mac as chopper rounds slammed into his back. He'd been waiting to give a nigga that AK business, and watch him ball up since they first got that motherfucker.

Lil' Dray emptied the clip. Hitting wheels, windows and rims. He even knocked the trunk off that bitch before watching it crash into the side of a house near the corner.

Black heard the crash and looked up to see a wild dread pulling one of his partners through one of the broken windows and started running at him dumping again.

The nigga left his homeboy half hanging out the car and took off with Black on his ass. Black saw the nigga drop and thought he had him, but the nigga hopped right back up and continued to run towards North Avenue, but Black was committed so either he was going to catch this nigga or run out of shells.

When Mumbles heard the shots, he knew in his gut that his men were in the middle of it and wasted no time running up outta New Identity's Barber Shop with D.W. hot on his heels.

"Yo!" Mumbles and D.W. ran right into Billy Lo. "What's up?"

"I don't know." Billy Lo replied jive out of breath. "Niggas around Division shooting like a motherfucker! I think I just heard Lil' Dray let the 'K' off too."

"Fuck is you doing then?" D.W. asked moving past him. "Come on."

"I ain't strap." Billy Lo admitted knowing from experience the damage them 'Fire Balls' could cause. "I was only coming to holler at one of you niggas."

"A'ight then. Stay here but call Diamond." Mumbles barked taking off. He was already pulling his hammer before he even came off Baker Street behind D.W. He instantly saw a red bandanna wearing nigga with long dreadlocks crawling around near a bent-up Beamer that had smashed into a house and went to work.

"Help." The dude pleaded as Mumbles walked up and put two shots in his red flag. Mumbles looked around as D.W. made sure the other two Bloods were dead. The streets were all but still empty, but he knew it wouldn't be for much longer.

"Shit!" D.W. fired getting Mumbles attention.

Mumbles looked up the block and saw something that broke his heart and damn near made his knees buckle. Charm was on the ground holding the lifeless, blood-covered body of his little sister.

"We got to go Dug." D.W. mustered enough strength to speak. "Mumbles!" D.W. stepped in front of him with a little more bass in his voice. "We got to bounce Dug."

Mumbles knew that he was right. Now wasn't the time to help Charm. He had to help himself. The sound of police sirens was quickly closing in, and people were starting to exit their safe havens. So, it was time to get out of sight.

"Come on man, we out." Mumbles grabbed D.W., and they took off running.

Chapter 20

City Officials were going off, and the Governor was demanding answers. A seven-year-old little girl murdered by a 'Stray Bullet' in a gang and gun-battle was too much. All kind of people were coming forward, and names were being dropped like bad artists from a record label. This wasn't one of those situations where life would just simply go on. People would not just heal, and the world would not just forget. The media covered the entire funeral service from start to finish.

Little Tiffany was laid to rest in a beautiful mini pink casket and everybody, who was somebody, stopped by to pay their respects. Within forty-eight hours it was learned that the other three dead suspects and the one still believed to be at large were all a part of the notorious Tree Top Piru, Blood gang who lived by their own set of rules, when Mumbles and them names started to surface as men of interest. Peaches did a live interview and assured the city that all, but one of the guys responsible for her daughter's death were dead. Which left the News to pose the question "If the shooters in question were 'Hoodlums or Heroes?'"

"We got to get to the bottom of this one fast." Detective Gibson said as she climbed back into the car. She and Baker had just left Tiffany Cola's mother house. "The Mayor's all over the captain's ass."

"I know." Detective Baker replied thinking more about the hurt in Little Tiffany's mother's eyes. It seemed like every couple of years some reckless wannabe gangster managed to hit the wrong person. "But, fuck the mayor. He's ain't going to do nothing but, put on a show for the public and sit his fat behind a desk. I wanna close this one for the family. Did you see how broken up she was?"

"I don't even want to think about it." Gibson started the car. "I know it's not much but, at least they did name that square right off North Avenue after her so nobody can ever forget."

"Yeah but that's not enough." Baker paused for a second then continued. "Whatever happened to the good ole' days when a motherfucker walked up and made? Sure, they got the right guy?"

"I don't know," Gibson replied honestly taking a deep breath. She knew from most of her arrest that there weren't too many real gangsters left. "It ain't no order in the streets no more. Guys are just opening fire anywhere now. It's like they don't care."

"They don't." Baker retorted. "Most of them be acting out of emotions. Blinded by their own rage. By the time the shooting stops they done shot both women, and children ending up in an asshole full of shit."

"You're right about that, but I bet you this. Somebody's gonna pay for this one. One way or another."

"They always do," Baker added. That was the one thing that he still admired about the game. No crimes against innocent women and children went unpunished. "On this side or the other."

******

"Are you okay baby?" Lakeria came up and kissed Billy Lo on his bare shoulder as he stared blindly into the mirror in deep thought.

"Huh? Oh, umm, yeah baby. I'm good." Billy Lo turned around and pulled her into his arms. It had been three days since he'd asked for her hand in marriage and he still couldn't believe that she actually said yes! He'd brought tears to her eyes when he got down on one knee and produced a unique ten karat, diamond covered engagement ring. "I just got a few things on my mind."

"Well, I'm here if you need to talk okay." She softly kissed him again before wrapping her arms around him and holding him tight.

"Thanks." Billy Lo held her tight. It was moments like these that made him realize just how lucky he was. He truly cherished what they shared and promised himself that he'd   always do whatever it took to make sure that Lakeria knew that she was not only beautiful but also special.

"Well, let me get in this shower so I can get to work."

Billy Lo wanted to talk to Lakeria about what was on his mind. About the sins, he was about to commit but, how could he? She would never understand. They had grown up in two different worlds. Lakeria came from a world where education was King, and he came from a world where survival was the only thing that mattered. A world where anything went. A world that labeled you either a predator or its prey. It was times like these that made him truly Miss Lotti.

"Okay, I'll see you later baby."

Billy Lo went to scoop Mumbles and Charm up as planned. Tonight, was the night that the Puppet Masters behind Little Tiffany's death would answer for their sins. It had taken a minute, but, Billy Lo had finally got the heads of the Tree Top Piru right where he wanted them.

******

"You sure you ready to do this Lil' nigga?" Mumbles looked back at Charm when they pulled into the 'Town House Motel' Parking Lot in a stolen truck. "This ain't no P-G-thirteen shit."

"Well give me my parental guidance then because I'm ready to get off into some horror shit!" Charm replied. Death had a funny way of affecting people. Whereas for Peaches, it made her want to do better. It had only managed to make Charm worst.

"A'ight." Mumbles turned back around. "Make the call Dug."

Billy Lo picked up the phone and dialed Africa's number to let her know that he was in place. After this move, Billy Lo planned to call it quits and do right by Lakeria. Fuck all the retirement money and everything else. The shit with Little Tiffany just kept eating away at him, and he couldn't help but blame himself. That was the only reason he'd let Mumbles talk him into bringing Charm along to revenge his little sister's death.

"Now what?" Charm questioned anxiously when Billy Lo ended the call.

"We wait." Billy Lo glanced back. He'd planned and planned and planned for this one. He had to because a good man in prison had once told him that 'those who failed to plan, planned to fail.'

"What's the room number?" Mumbles asked.

"Lucky seven." Billy Lo spit and everybody fell into their own thoughts.

"Let's rock and roll." Billy Lo spoke up after they'd waited for more than an hour after Africa had entered the room with Hyena and Jungle, the two Blood niggas responsible for ordering the hit that caused Little Tiffany's death. It had taken Billy Lo two days, a shopping spree, and a couple hours of X-rated sex to get Africa to go through with the move.

When Billy Lo, Mumbles, and Charm entered the room Africa was being pressed down into Hyena's chest as she rode him crying while Jungle was squatted like a frog behind her hitting her in the ass. So they used the element of surprise to their advantage and jumped all over Jungle and Hyena before they even knew what hit them.

Billy Lo knocked Jungle to the floor and started pistol whipping him, as Mumbles and Charm tossed Africa out of the way and quickly took care of Hyena.

Billy Lo ordered Africa to go sit outside in the truck as she hand-cuffed and gagged a 'tone drunk' Jungle. Mumbles handed Charm the duck-tape and started hog-tying Hyena. After both Hyena and Jungle were secure Billy Lo turned up the volume on the bullshit ass motel television and told Charm that it was his show.

For the next twenty minutes, Billy Lo and Mumbles sat back and watched as Charm's little blood-thirsty ass carried out his own form of pain, pleasure, and punishment on Hyena and Jungle. First, he beat them with the Crow-Bar he'd pulled out of Mumbles bag of tools and got them to admit that they had sent the hit as retaliation for the 'Red Maple' robbery and murders.

"Where's the other nigga at that had something to do with my sister's death?" Charm barked at Hyena. "Did he really flee back to The West Coast?"

"That's what the cops said, but the homies know better." Hyena spits blood and smiled.

"Where he at nigga?" Charm brought the Crow-Bar up and asked again.

"He's dead." Hyena replied. "That's on Blood, the homies ate him for that shit."

Charm stared at Hyena until he was satisfied he was telling the truth. Then looked at Billy Lo and Mumbles. "Help me turn these niggas over."

Once Charm had Hyena and Jungle on their side, and back he started repeatedly strewing a 25lb Dent-Puller into their ribs and stomachs and snatching out guts, blood, and chunks of meat.

Billy Lo kept turning his head to keep from throwing up. The child's play was over. Charm's little ass was a monster. Jungle was the first to go, his body could no longer take the trauma. Charm had beaten a bald spot into the side of his head and dreads were all over the motel room.

"A'ight baby boy. The show must close." Mumbles finally said. "Go ahead and finish this nigga off so we can get the fuck up outta here."

Charm nodded and slammed the Crow-Bar into Hyena's neck so hard that it went completely through and hit the floor.

"A'ight now, go ahead to the truck so me and Billy Lo can wipe this bitch down real quick."

Billy Lo and Mumbles wiped the room down and snatched all the sheets of the bed. Then they both used the pillows from the bed to muffle the sound of gunshots as they kneeled and shot both Hyena and Jungle in the head twice. They wanted to be sure that the deed was done. They needed to make sure that it was D. O.A. when the bodies were discovered. They didn't need this shit coming back to haunt them again.

Satisfied with their work they made sure the coast was clear then quickly moved for the truck.

Mumbles drove over to where Billy Lo had parked his car, in a secluded area near Dru Hill Park. Then watched as Billy Lo blew Africa's brains all over the inside seats and windows of the truck. Before removing a jug of gasoline from his car and soaking her body and the inside of the truck down like Mumbles said.

"Take notes baby boy." Mumbles spoke softly as they watched Billy Lo toss a lit match inside the truck. "Betrayal can never be rewarded with honor."

Billy Lo stood there watching the fire long enough to hear Africa's body crackling then he made his way over to the waiting car so that they could get the hell out of there.

Chapter 21

As always the 'Baltimore Day' yearly Cookout and Celebration' event kicked off on Friday and had Dru Hill Park packed with people out to enjoy themselves. There were celebrity basketball and football games going on. Kevin Liles and 92.Q was sponsoring the 'Rock Off Boys' in a live freestyle battle. Every rap group from 'Charm City to The Fresh of The Blue Bird' had shown up to accept the challenge. However, it was the milkshakes that brought all the boys to the park. It didn't matter if they were payers, players, or gangsters. They all wanted a taste of power.

Billy Lo entered the park on the Baltimore City Zoo side. Diamond had said that everybody would meet up around near Park Pool. If it hadn't been for the fact that Lakeria had jury duty and the fact that he'd given Diamond his word Billy Lo wouldn't have even shown up. He knew that it was time to start falling back. The game was bullshit.

As Billy Lo, moved slowly along with traffic, he peeped out the scenery. There were women everywhere. Milk-Shakes of all shapes, colors, and sizes. Walking around in booty shorts, body suits, red bottoms, open-toe stilettos, and anything else that showed off enough skin to drive a nigga crazy with lust. When Billy Lo finally came around near the pool, he spotted Lil' Dray and Charm fucking with a group of homemade yellow scarfs, tank-top, and mini-skirt wearing bitches with blonde hair on Ninja Motorcycles and pulled over.

*****

Black parked and entered the park on foot. The bumper to bumper traffic was just too much, and he didn't want to waste an hour on a ten-minute walk. Besides, he could also enjoy the sights. Black looked up at the sound of Dirt Bikes and saw like forty of them 12 O'clock Boys' cutting between cars on their Wild out Wheelie' shit. He recognized Lil' Ache, Get-A-Long, K.B., Little Net and a few other crazy niggas on 120 KX's and smiled. As he thought about how they had wild the pigs out a couple of weeks earlier and brought down a Ghetto Bird during a high-speed police chase that started after they decided to pay some fat chicks to hold the Mondawmin Mall doors open so that they could ride the dirt bikes through doing all kind of tricks and shit.

Black acknowledge everyone he knew as he made his way up the hill. Summer was officially here and 8-Day' was in full effect. Some of the baddest female crews in the city were out. Black saw bitches from the 38 Posse, T.A.B.U. Crew and The Knock 'Em' Down click. He even peeped the D.C. nigga Bucky Fields with a bunch of his Hell Razor Honey bitches and made a mental note to put his men on point that they were lurking.

Black walked up on Lil' Dray, and them shagging and gave them some love. He could not help but trip off to Billy Lo standing there with his shirt off, showing off his penitentiary cuts and tatts.

"Where's Diamond at?" Black questioned. He needed to holler at him for real. The nigga had really started acting like a bitch since he called it quits a few weeks ago and it was time to play on his greed.

"He ain't show up yet." Billy Lo replied.

D.W. pulled up on the grass and jumped out of a rented Pearl White Lincoln Navigator with a neon-green Super-Soaker 4000 water-gun full of red cherry juice. For all the little dummies that wanted to come out to the park and turn their noses up at niggas.

Bodymore Murderland

"Nigga, what the fuck is you up to?" Lil' Dray asked shaking his head as D.W. started removing Hennessy and Wine Coolers from the back of the truck.

"Don't start no shit.

Nigga I'm just trying to chill. Blow some piff, drink a little Hen-Rock, and get some pussy." D.W. spoke with a grin. "I can't lie, I hope I see that bad lil' red bitch with the white Benz from up Park Heights that fuck with that fat, black, ugly ass, little dick nigga."

"Nigga, you better leave my home girl alone." Billy Lo laughed, "Don't hate the player slim, hate the game."

"Nah, Nah Dug. I'ma put some flavor in her Lil' attitude. What's her name again, Timeeka right?"

"Nah, Timeeka is my man Seed's wife." Billy Lo said understanding how D.W. could get them mixed up. "But you definitely don't want to fuck with her. Shorty a nut, plus you'll have to kill Seed." He added then continued. "You're talking about Kim-Girl."

"Yeah well, I'm looking for lil' Kim-Girl's pretty ass." D.W. said pumping the Super Soaker ready to start some shit.

Mumbles was riding around going crazy. A little stupid ass dummie he had been dumb enough to fuck had just dropped the 'baby' bombshell on him, and he didn't know if he should believe the bitch or not. Because when he asked about her boyfriend, she started talking that 'I been fucking him for years now and he ain't shooting nothing but blanks' bull shit.

"Maybe I should just kill the bitch, huh girl?" Mumbles reached over and rubbed Cocaine's head and the full blooded, all white red-nosed pit bull barked.

"Yeah, I guess you're right, but I gotta make sure she does the right thing. Mumbles knew he didn't have the heart to kill a woman who might be carrying his seed; even if it wasn't Cat. Heaven knows he would be wrong, and Cat would never forgive him. That's only 'if' she ain't kill his ass.

"What the fuck am I gonna tell Cat, if this bitch doesn't go through with this abortion?" Mumbles questioned himself out loud. "Damn I should've never fucked that jealous ass, lying bitch raw."

There was nothing in the world that Mumbles loved more than Cat. She was his heart and soul. His rib and she'd always been there; even when nobody else was. Mumbles pounded the steering wheel more mad at himself than anything. He couldn't figure out how he had allowed a no good, snake ass bitch to put him in a position that might cost him more than he could stand to lose. He knew that now, no matter what happened. It was time to get his shit together.

So, after he made sure that the Lil' chick got the abortion. He was done, he wasn't flirting any more.

******

"So, what's on your mind?" Diamond asked Black when they stepped off to the side although he knew the answer.

"Man, I need you to come through for us one more time."

"I told y'all no slim. I'm not fucking with that shit man. I'm through. Y'all got to find another connect."

"Man, we been running around like crazy trying to get on," Black assured him. He couldn't believe that this was the same nigga that he used to send blow and shit to down the Jessup. Everything Mumbles had said was starting to become crystal clear. Diamond really didn't give a fuck about nobody but himself. "We ain't have no luck. That's why I need you to do this for me."

"Yo, I told you I'm through shorty."

"That's crazy," Black said and considered his next move. "I guess the finder's fee got to go back in niggas pockets."

"What finder's fee?" Diamond's whole demeanor changed as his greed kicked in. Free money was always good money to him, and any nigga who said different didn't know money. "How much money you lil' niggas got?"

"A hundred twenty-five grand." Black replied, "We put everything we had together. I even got Peanut to spot me a few stacks, so I was gonna slide you fifteen for making the move."

"Nigga! Why you ain't been say that?" Diamond asked but never gave Black a chance to answer. "Partners supposed to always put their cards on the table."

"So, we all good?" Black asked and thought about the crew's motto.

"We all good baby boy." Diamond smiled. "Give me about a week."

"Bet," Black put on a fake smile and looked at Diamond with sickness. He couldn't wait to hip Mumbles and them to the fact that they had been right all along, and see if they still wanted to swing Diamond a move.

"A'ight. Let's get back over here, and party before the police start breaking this shit up and shutting the park down."

Chapter 22

"A'ight I'll just swing past tomorrow then," Black replied and hung up the phone on Diamond before looking over at Lil' Dray. "Y'all niggas got less than twelve hours till show time."

"Then let me call Mumbles and D.W.'s dirty ass right now."

After Black had told Mumbles and them about how his cousin was carrying it, they decided to come up with another plan and show Diamond that the strongest cards were the ones that hadn't been played yet.

"You sure you wanna do this?" Lil' Dray questioned as he placed the cell phone to his ear and waited for D.W. to answer. "I mean, that nigga is still your cousin."

"Fuck that greedy ass nigga and them Muslims." Black fired. He was ready to get off into some gangster shit." You know our motto Dug."

"Ain't no question."

"Ain't nothing all good, when we all broke?" They spoke in unison and busted out laughing.

******

As always, the call came with directions.

"Take the money and go to the Enterprise Car Rental place on Fulton Avenue. There will be a black Sedan reserved under your name. Drive Downtown to the E-S-P-N-Zone's Parking Lot and park the car in D-twenty. Be sure to leave the money and key in the car under the front seat. Then take a thirty-minute hike, take in the sights, get yourself something, to eat or whatever. When you return take the Sedan parked in D-twenty-one and bounce. The key will be in the glove compartment. The package will be where it always is…"

Bodymore Murderland

Diamond hung up the phone, grabbed the bag of money and headed out the door to make the quick drop and pick up.

******

"We taking these bitches at the light!" Mumbles said to Lil' Dray pulling his mask down. It was time to show Diamond that anybody could get it. "I got the driver."

"A'ight." Lil' Dray replied. No more needed to be said. Lil' Dray, Mumbles, and D.W. had followed Diamond downtown from the rental spot and watched him with the patience of a high school teacher. When he got out of the rental car empty handed they made a group decision to stay with the money and sure as shit, ten minutes after Diamond had walked off an identical car pulled up, and two young looking Muslim chumps got out and climbed right into Diamond's rental and pulled off.

D.W. followed the car until it was in an isolated area before swerving in front of it. Mumbles and Lil' Dray wasted no time jumping out and handling their business. Mumbles shot the driver four times before he even knew what was happening and although his partner soon figured out what was going on, he never had a chance.

"*GET THE MONEY!* Mumbles yelled and kept an eye out as Lil' Dray snatched the back door of the Sedan open after breaking the window out with his gun and pulling the lock.

"Got it!" Lil' Dray fired pulling the bag from under the front passenger seat, holding it up.

"A'ight' let's go!" Mumbles ordered jumping back in the car.

Lil' Dray hopped in, and D.W. quickly hit the gas and took off leaving the two Muslims slumped over the steering wheel and seats in their own blood. They were gone in sixty seconds.

196

"We cross my cousin out over a brick or two/ and for that hundred stacks, we got the Muslims too." Black rapped over the Meek Mills 'Dreams and Nightmares' CD smiling as he tossed the duffel bag full of drugs he'd just gotten from his cousin on the table next to the money. "Now that's how you put that work in nigga. I didn't even have to pull my gun."

"Nah, nigga. I'm the one that put that work in." Mumbles assured him aiming his hands as if he had a gun. "I hit that Muslim four times in the dome." Everybody started laughing. They had all met back up at Black's house to wait on Diamond and discuss their next move.

"Both of you niggas crazy. Where Diamond?" Lil Dray asked curiously.

"Oh! he gone." Black replied. "He just gave me the bag and bounced."

"Sweet." Mumbles nodded.

"Yo, I can't believe we pulled that shit off. That nigga dumb as shit." Black said. "He makes a nigga miss that robbery shit."

"Nigga, all you got to do is line 'em' up, and you know we're gonna lay 'em' down." D.W. spat, and Black knew that he wasn't lying. The crew had always been down to come up by any means necessary.

"Let's see what we can do with the blow first," Black said. "But if all else fails, you niggas know what's next."

******

"Somebody explain to me again how is it that two brothers are ambushed and robbed out of one hundred grand in the middle of Downtown, and nobody knows anything?" The raspy voice of Walaa echoed throughout the room and bounced off the walls, but nobody replied. They all knew how the old Imam could be. "You got twenty-four hours to bring me either the head or the balls of the kuffars responsible for embarrassing this community Samad."

"I'm on it, Ock. I swear by Allah I'ma..."

Walaa brought his powerful fist down on the thick oath table cutting Samad off. He knew success had enemies, but nobody embarrassed the community. *NOBODY*. "You fucking clean this shit up, Samad. You hear me? You clean it up...or you take the fall, Ock."

"Sure, thing Walaa." Samad knew he couldn't argue with the Imam because although he was a just man, who would sacrifice ten kuffars to protect one Muslim brother he also demanded respect. So, Samad kept his thoughts to himself and walked out.

Samad made his way out to the waiting car and climbed in. His mind was all over the place. The hit had been too well orchestrated. It had been carried out with a touch of professionalism. It had to be a message from one of the gangstas. They had put outta business or slighted and hadn't even realized it.

"Hey, Ock." Jabbar peeped in the rear-view mirror before pulling off and continuing. "Me and the brothers were thinking we should work this thing backward."

"I think it's a good idea too, Ock." Mosi spoke up knowing that if the Imam ordered that Samad be disciplined, he was sure to get some lashes too. "It's probably just some young street punk from another chapter looking to make a name for himself."

Samad thought for a second. He had a twenty-four-hour window to get the Imam something solid, so he needed to use every resource and asset he had.

"Here's what we do Jabbar, I want you to put a tail on the last five people we did business with. Mosi, I want you to put some money on the streets and see what you can find out. If a little kid buys a dime bag of heroin, I wanna know about it." Samad said hoping that they could come up with something.

"That sounds like the way to get the job done." Jabbar adjusted the mirror as he came to the Key Bridge exit.

"I sure hope so," Samad said trying to remain optimistic. "Because if not, may Allah have mercy on my soul."

******

Billy Lo was busy planning and preparing for the upcoming birth of his daughter. It was crazy how he had slaughtered men in the streets and stood off against some of the most thorough gangsters to ever walk the Maryland Prison System. Yet, the reality of being a father scared him half to death. Just knowing that no matter what happened someone depended on him day and night was enough to rattle his cage. There were no days off, no quitting, and no timeouts. That was really something to think about.

It was true when they said that children changed everything. He and Lakeria had been fighting over names. Billy Lo wanted the name Ta'nyah, A'myiah or De'Bre'anna, but Lakeria wasn't having it. She wanted something simple like Latonya, Jasmine, or Victoria. Something without a thousand hyphens.

The wedding planning started coming along good once he decided to stay out of it and just let Lakeria and her mother handle everything. It would be a small wedding, twenty to thirty guests. Mainly Lakeria's friends and family, because the only two people Billy Lo planned to invite, were Diamond and his wife, Khadijah. Everything else was on Lakeria. The only planning Billy Lo wanted a part of was the Bachelor Party and Honeymoon.

Chapter 23

"Diamond." Walaa repeated trying to place the name. "Is he a kuffer?"

"Nah, Ock, I am talking about my uncle's friend." Samad replied. "The one that just came home. The one that I introduced to you last Friday after Ju'mah."

Walaa had been sitting in his Al-Haqq Masjid study reading the Baltimore Sun News Paper when Samad came in and brought him the latest news.

"I thought you said his name was Yusef?" Walaa remembered the light skinned brother Samad was referring too."

"It is. He just go by Diamond."

"Now you think he had something to do with the two brothers getting killed?" Walaa watched as Samad nodded. "And how did you hook up with this brother again?"

"I was trying to do my uncle a favor." Samad said knowing how tight Walaa and Shabazz were.

"Look how far that got you. This Kuffer lover may have turned around and not only taken your drugs, but also allowed the shedding of sacred Muslim blood. That means he has no honor and no respect." Walaa silently rose to his feet and walked over to the window. "You know, Ock, I remember a time when there were rules we lived by. You didn't just kill anybody, but that was the good ole days. Before all these hardened drugs, gangs, and loss of manners started making everybody crazy."

Samad knew that Walaa didn't want a response. He wanted results, because he always valued a good example over good advice any day.

"I don't know what Shabazz was thinking bringing this brother into our fold, but it's obvious he has no respect. And where there is no respect, there can be no order." Walaa turned to face him. "Do you understand what I am saying to you Ock?"

"Yeah." Samad shook his head.

"Good, because I don't wanna have to say it again." Walaa made his way around the desk and opened the door. "As-salaam, Alaikum, Ock."

"Wa alaikum as-salaam." Samad got up and walked out.

******

Diamond entered the Half Mile night club and followed Mosi to the back. He was still trying to figure out what the hell this meeting could be about. He prayed to Allah that the money hadn't been counterfeit or something. He would kill his cousin and them if that was the case.

"What's up, Ock?" Samad said, excitedly the second he walked into the room. "Glad you could make it. Take a seat, have a drink." Samad pushed a bottle of Patron across the table.

"Thanks." Diamond said taking a seat and pouring himself a drink as he tried to remain calm. Something wasn't right. He had been in enough Lion's Den to know that, but like an extraordinarily good poker player Samad's face gave away nothing. So, he just played it cool. "What's good, Ock?" Diamond asked after pouring himself a shot and sipping from his glass.

"I won't even bullshit with you, Ock. We got a problem." Samad looked Diamond straight in the eyes sternly. "I mean honestly, Ock, I got the go ahead to just crush you, but I believe in hearing a man out."

"Hold up, Samad." Diamond's heart started pounding as he looked around. "What are you talking about, Ock? If the money was short it had to be a mistake." Diamond added as his legs started to shake. Here he was in the back of a night club, surrounded by muslims who could smell fear.

Samad released a sincere laugh and looked from Diamond to Jabbar. "What he trying to be funny, Ock…Listen Diamond. The brothers never made it back to the mosque with that hundred grand of yours. Now either you were in on the take, or you just got a case of bad luck. Either way, you're stuck with the ball, Ock."

"Samad, I swear by Allah that whatever happened ain't have nothing to do with me." Diamond spoke truthfully.

"The thing is though Ock, your folks did. They're talking about it all over town. And you're the one that brought them kuffers to me, ock."

"What?" Diamond couldn't believe his ears. He had told Black and them that they weren't dealing with no basic muslims. He had told them that they were too well polished to fuck with. He had told them that they had police, politicians, and gangsters in their pocket. Now, these fools had gone and done some crazy shit that was probably about to get all of them killed. "Samad, I swear…"

"Save it, Ock. I don't think that you were directly involved. But, the only way you're walking outta here is if you play ball." Samad knew he had to give before he could take.

"What do I gotta do?" Diamond wasn't going down for Black and them, not this time. Them niggas had played him.

"Tell me everything you can about this robbery and the little kids who pulled it off." Samad replied and leaned back in his chair.

"I swear Samad, I don't know nothing."

Samad smiled and waved his finger at Diamond before speaking. "Tell me you weren't involved. Tell me you won't cooperate, but don't sit here in my face and tell me that you don't know nothing. That's disrespect."

"I mean um! What you wanna know?"

"How about we start with a proper introduction." Samad replied. "Tell me who these kids are."

"Okay, well ummm...you got Mumbles and Lil' Dray they be doing a lot of crazy stuff on their own. I bet it was one of them. D.W. just a follower. He will do anything them little suckers tell him to do. My little cousin Black the only one with some sense, but he was home all day, so I know that he wasn't with it because..." Diamond went on to tell Samad everything he knew or could think of as he tried to read him, but Samad was good at concealing his feelings.

"And what about the dude Billy Lo? He's the mastermind right?"

"Nah, Billy Lo don't even be messing around with Mumbles and them. He fell back the same time I did. He got a child on the way, Ock, so I know he wasn't with it either. Like I said, it had to be Mumbles, Lil' Dray, and D.W. I bet money on it. Them little suckers always starting some shit." Diamond thought for a second. He had to do something that would assure he still walked out of there alive.

"If you want me to I'll crush all them lil' niggas, Ock. I don't fuck with them like that anyway. All these lil' kids fucked up in the head out here today anyway. They be thinking they ready, like a nigga won't split their wigs. It's them pills."

"I appreciate the offer, but I think you need to sit this one out, Ock." Samad got up and strolled behind Diamond.

"So, what do you want me to do?" Diamond asked nervously as he prayed this wasn't the end of the road for him.

"Just keep your mouth shut, sit tight, and let me take it from here." Samad said patting him on the shoulder still impossible to read.

******

"License and Registration please." The police officer spoke after approaching the driver's side window.

"What seems to be the problem officer?" D.W. tried to sound proper as the cop and his partner shined lights all in the car from both sides. He couldn't figure out why they'd pulled him over. He had just walked out of 7-11 after grabbing a bite to eat.

"Routine investigation Sir." The cop replied as D.W. handed him his credentials. "We had a two-eleven a couple of blocks over and your car kind of fits the description of the getaway vehicle."

"Oh!" D.W. relaxed. It was too much bullshit going on with the police in the city.

"Just give me a second to run your name and plates through the system and then you can be on your way." The cop said before walking back to his patrol car.

"You make sure you stay put buddy." The cop on the passenger side said before shining the flashlight in D.W.'s face again and following his partner.

"I am very sorry Mr. White, but we're gonna need you to take a ride over to the scene for an in-person I.D." The cops said walking back up on the car with his hand on the butt of his gun. "I am sure it's just a simple mix up, but you have to understand that with your record it's just--"

"Yeah man, whatever." D.W. fired taking off his seatbelt before climbing out of the car. He had already been smart enough to slip his revolver down in between the seat and armrest. "Let's just get this shit over and down with."

"Could you turn around and put your hands up on the hood so that I can pat you down?" The cop asked taking a step back as D.W. started to comply.

******

"Man, who the fuck is it?" Lil' Dray barked hitting the blunt, walking over to the door.

"Domino's Pizza!"

"*Domino's Pizza?*" Lil' Dray repeated unlocking the front door to look the delivery guy up and down. "What's up?"

"Someone order a large Pepperoni Pizza with extra Cheese?"

"Not me." Lil' Dray turned to look at Mumbles lounging on the couch. "You ordered a pizza nigga?"

"Nah, but I damn sure want some." Mumbles stopped talking to Cat for a moment to reply. He had the munchies like shit. "Go ahead and grab that joint. I got half." Mumbles spit then turned his attention back to Cat. "Now what you say? You in there watching Boomerang? You probably in there being nasty too." Mumbles laughed. "Yes, you is. Every time you watch that damn sex scene you don't know how to act. Remember that time I caught you finger pop--"

"*HOLD UP NIGGA! WHAT'S UP?*" Lil' Dray barked.

Mumbles heard a scuffle and looked up just as the first of two deafening explosions rocked the house. He quickly dropped the phone and dove behind the couch and went for his gun all in one motion.

Lil' Dray didn't know what the fuck was going on when the delivery guy handed him the Pizza and pulled out a gun, but his killer instincts and battle tested reflexes made him slam the Pizza box into the nigga's face and try to get the fuck out of the way.

When Lil' Dray fell, Mumbles came up and let the fleeing delivery guy have the whole clip as Lil' Dray scrambled into the house. Mumbles heard a car burning rubber and broke back in the house just as Tina came flying down the stairs cursing and carrying on.

"I know y'all niggas not shooting in my damn house! My fucking son upstairs. I swear to god Andre if--" Tina stopped in mid-sentence and immediately ran over to Lil' Dray screaming when she saw all the blood. "Oh my God Andre! What the hell happen Mumbles?" Tina looked at Mumbles. "What the fuck you do!"

"*TINA! TINA!*" Lil 'Dray yelled grabbing her. "Bitch calm down and shut the fuck up for a second. Mumbles ain't do shit. "

"Yo, we gotta go!" Mumbles ran over and shut the front door. Tina was breathing all hard, looking crazy, and Mumbles was ready to get the fuck away from her fast.

"Listen. When the police get here, you ain't see shit a'ight?" Lil' Dray looked at Tina. "You hear what the fuck I'm saying? You ain't see shit. You heard shots, came down stairs and saw the door open. Don't say nothing else..."

Tina just shook her head in agreement.

"And call Cat back for me. Let her know that I'm okay." Mumbles said, and they were gone out the back door before Tina could even think about replying.

******

Billy Lo's cell phone had been ringing off the chain all night. D.W. was missing, somebody Mumbles, suspected Bloods. Had fire-bombed Black's crib, since that was their M.O. and Lil' Dray had been shot. And although Mumbles felt like it wasn't that bad he knew something was up and was ready to get busy because Cat had seen some suspicious looking men outside the house. Billy Lo told

him to be cool until he talked to D.W. and Diamond. They
promised to hook up in the morning and hung up.

When daylight broke Billy Lo put in a quick workout and hit
the shower. He planned to get with Mumbles after he took Lakeria
to her two o'clock doctor's appointment. He tried to call Diamond
again, but he still wasn't answering his phone. Billy Lo wasn't
feeling that at all.

"Baby run down to the corner store and grab me an orange
juice real quick pleaseeee." Lakeria begged as they came out of the
house. "We can stop at the Quickie Mart on the way to the clinic."

"Come on baby. The store right down the street." Lakeria put
on her prettiest puppy face. "Pretty please."

"Take these keys with your spoiled ass." Billy Lo tossed her the
keys to his truck so she could sit in the truck while he ran down to
the store. "Oh, you not going to help me get in." Lakeria teased.

"My bad." Billy Lo replied and walked Lakeria over to the
truck before opening the passenger side door to help her inside.
"There you go beautifully."

"Thank you, baby." Lakeria blushed as Billy Lo gave her a
quick kiss on the lips and closed the door.

Billy Lo ran down to the store and picked up two Tropicana
12oz Orange Juice before making his way to the register. Billy Lo
had just stepped out of the store and started back up the street
when a loud explosion rocked the block and sent him flying as
pieces of twisted metal and debris flew all over the place.

Billy Lo got up holding his head, trying to shake the daze off.
His ears were ringing and he could barely see anything as he
stumbled back towards the house. When he finally realized, what
had happened all he could do was run towards the wreckage.

"*NOOOO!*" Billy Lo screamed as bystanders fought to keep
him out of the burning truck. "*GET THE FUCK OFF ME!
LAKERIA! LAKERIA!*

Chapter 24

It took Billy Lo and them about two weeks to figure out who was responsible for all the sudden drama, and meet up. Shit had gotten out of control. D.W's unrecognizable, tortured body rolled from a moving van onto Gold Street. Black lost everything, and the word was that the police wanted to question Lil' Dray and Mumbles. However, Billy Lo had suffered the greatest lost. His future wife and unborn child had been killed by a radio rigged plastic explosive.

Billy Lo cried for three days straight. It felt like somebody had ripped his heart right out of his chest. Every time he pictured Lakeria 's face he lost another piece of his soul. At first, he wanted to just murk everybody. Lil' Dray, Black, D.W., everybody, even Diamond because he knew that somehow, someway, it was their fuck ups that had cost him the last woman in the world he truly gave a damn about.

Billy Lo didn't know if he should follow his heart or his head. It was like choosing between two children. So, after careful consideration, Billy Lo decided to follow his head and not his blood monitor. But, one thing was for sure somebody was going to pay for the death of his future wife and unborn seed.

"You know it's gonna be like a death wish going up against these motherfuckers?" Diamond said. "I mean, these niggas got all kinds of authorities in their pockets and they outnumber us ten to one."

"That's the consequences of being a man. If it were easy, everybody would be doing it." Billy Lo replied. Besides, we got the ups. We can hit any of their known locations at any time, but they can't protect all of them all the time."

"Come on slim; you know that shit don't win wars." Diamond stared at Billy Lo knowing how well acquainted he was with the evils of war.

"Man, who gives a fuck?" Black retorted with thick veins running up and down his neck. He was starting to realize that his cousin was nothing more than an articulated sucker with a serious bluff game. "Them whore drew first blood."

"Yeah, but if y'all lil' niggas didn't rob them then this--"

"Nigga you just shook!" Mumbles fired cutting him off. "Fuck them pussies. They bleed just like us. So, we're gonna show them how two-sided war can be."

"That's y'all lil' niggas problem now. Always wanting to go back and forth." Diamond shook his head. I ain't trying to see how two-sided war is. I'm trying to be on the side that wins. I fight to cheat death, not meet it."

"Yeah well, you got to be willing to put your life on the line first, if you want to beat death." Mumbles looked at Diamond's cowardly hearted ass in disgust. "Other than that, that shit just sound slick."

"Look, man, I don't give a fuck about none of that shit!" Billy Lo interjected. "I want revenge. Them bitches violated." Billy Lo added. He couldn't believe that Diamond was acting like he wanted him to just swallow his pride. "You can pick and choose your battles all you want. But this shit about honor. Fuck victory!"

"Come on slim, I know it's about principle for you." Diamond assured Billy Lo. "I was just saying niggas really need to think about this shit."

"I don't know where your head at right now." Billy Lo eyed Diamond curiously. "But don't ever make it seem like you're asking me to do something that you know you wouldn't do if Khadijah's name was on Lakeria's headstone. You're either with me or against me."

Diamond stood there staring at Billy Lo. He knew that the line had just officially been drawn. So, he made a commitment he hoped he'd live to keep. "You know I'm with you all the way slim. We family, let's take them motherfuckers to war."

"That's what I like to hear." Billy Lo nodded. He was dying to see what would happen when an unstoppable force went against an unmovable object.

"Load up the Titanic; then nigga let's ride." Lil ' Dray pulled his gun.

"All abroad!" D.W. seconded following suit.

"Slow down gangster." Billy Lo gestured with his hands. "First we study, then we strike it.

******

"Hey!" Detective Baker strolled into the Police Department 's Homicide Unit coffee room to find Gibson staring at the large white rectangle shaped paper that damn near covered the entire wall. A daily reminder of both the opened and closed homicides around the city throughout the year.

"Hey!" Baker came again. "Snap out of it!"

Gibson looked up and slowly released a smile. "Sorry." She said. "I was just lost in my own thoughts, so how did it go?"

"Sarge wants us to squeeze Chapple's girl a little more and try to get Pair's girl in for questioning."

"Tell Sarge to try and go talk to her," Gibson said as thoughts of the last attempt to interview Michael Pair's girlfriend came to mind. "The girl's too loyal. Do you remember what it was like the last time?"

"Yeah, like pulling teeth that never came out," Baker replied. They had to give Pair credit for one thing. He had groomed his girlfriend and groomed her good. "I told Sarge there was no use, but he wants to get as much info on this thing as possible."

Everybody knew that something was up. First a shoot-out in Chapple's living room. Then White's tortured body is dumped in the heart of West Baltimore. Not to mention the two-alarm fire at Green's place. Somebody was definitely gunning for her boys.

"We need to fine a weak link." Gibson got up. "Let's get word over to the city lock up. There's always some tough-guy gangster looking to cut a deal. In the meantime, let's swing back pass the hospital and see if our boy 's still unconscious."

******

D.W. was finally conscious, but he was so doped up on painkillers that he didn't know what was going on or truly understand where he was at. However, he was sure that he was under arrest because he was cuffed to the bed and in bad shape, he also knew that he had been tortured.

He remembered his teeth being pulled out, his toes being crushed and being beaten with bats and brass knuckles. He had passed out so many times from the blunt force trauma and loss of blood that he could not even remember if he ever gave his torturers the information they were after.

D.W. felt a presence in his midst and although he couldn't open his eyes, he knew it was unwanted company because the energy felt evil. He hoped it wasn't his time. Hs started praying to God that the grim reaper wasn't in the room.

"You don't look so good White. We told you that tough guy act would end up getting you in trouble."

Bodymore Murderland

D.W. heard the female voice and instantly knew who had entered the room, but the detectives had wasted their time because even in his current state there was no way in the world they would ever get him to violate the code of the streets. Muslim beef, was still beef, and all beef got settled in the streets.

"Why am I cuffed?" D.W. decided to ignore the *tough guy statement.*

"Because we found what was in your vacant car." Gibson replied and D.W. wondered if she was smiling or not. "And you're still on probation."

Chapter 25

The first thing Billy Lo and them did was hit anything or anyone they knew or felt like the Muslims were attached to. They robbed Muslim shops and night clubs. They beat and strong-armed oil and innocent men, and even shook down a few drug dealers they knew that the Muslims were supplying. Billy Lo figured that even if they were wrong, the Muslims would still get the message that times had changed, and since nobody was untouchable during war. The laws were silent.

Diamond had told them that Samad was a major fan of horse racing and loved to bet big. So, it was no surprise that when Billy Lo found out that Samad had large stakes invested in a four time 'Kentucky Derby' winner by the name Night Train, who would be competing in the 141st Pamlico Rack Track Preakness that he tried to set something up. However, it was today's move that they planned to show the Muslims their teeth and let them know that they had their hands full fucking with them and that street shit.

Billy Lo was standing just outside the gates of the Baltimore Orioles 'Camden Yard' Baseball Stadium at the mobile vending-machine they had stolen after killing the owner and using a nail-gun to hide his body inside a vacant garage. The Orioles/ Yankee's game was over, and the loud crowd was pouring out of the stadium into the city streets.

"That's our guy holding the little boy's hand with the Orioles Cap and big Flag." Billy Lo mumbled through his miniature Mascot-like orange and black Orioles Bird's head to Black as he started pushing the vending machine through the crowd.

"I'm ready." Black said but wasn't sure if Billy Lo heard him.

"ICE CREAM! ICE CREAM! GET YOUR ICE CREAM!"
Billy Lo ignored anyone who tried stop him for ice cream.

"Hey!" Samad barked slapping the top of the vending cart to
get the stupid bird's attention when he cut them off. "Watch where
you're going! You almost hit my son."

"Oh my bad, it's just so crowded out here." Billy Lo
apologized. "I'll tell you what, how about I give him a free ice
cream?"

"Can I Abu?" Samad's son questioned.

Samad wasn't in the mood to argue with his son. He had just
lost a fortune fucking with the bum ass Orioles. "Go ahead. Don't
give him too much, though."

"What's it gonna be little man?" Billy Lo unhooked the clamp
on the freezer door.

"Strawberry!" The little boy said excitedly.

"One strawberry cone coming up." Billy Lo looked over to
make sure that Black and them were in position and ready before
opening the freezer door, reaching inside, and pulling out an
extended clip Tec with the infrared-beam on it.

Jabbar saw the move first and quickly did the math. "IT'S A
HIT, OCK!" He yelled moving to protect Samad as the equation
came to him.

Billy Lo let the Tec rip, but the huge bird head was jive
throwing him off. Lil' Dray came out of the fleeing crowd with it
on his mind just as Mumbles and Black moved in to pin the driver
down. However, the driver had other plans, and since Samad
couldn't get to him, he did something that nobody expected.
Instead of leaving the car to protect Samad. He used the car to run
down anything in his path to go get him.

Samad was laid over top of his son when Adnan came out of
the car firing his pistol professionally. He saw one of the would-be

killers go down as the police closed in and made his way over to Samad.

Billy Lo and them took off running for Black's cousin's Ebony car that Diamond was driving as Adnan and a pretty banged up Jabbar got Samad, his son, and Mosi inside the car and pulled off in the midst of all the confusion.

Walaa was up on the roof attending to his pigeons when Tariq interrupted him with the bad news. The Imam had listened patiently as Tariq rumbled on and on about the hit on Samad, one of his most faithful Muslim brothers. Walaa was by representation a man slow to anger. He had to be, that's what made him such a great leader. But, this recent blunt disrespect had clearly shortened his fuse. Mosi had been his most trusted security detail amongst the community before he had given him over to Samad. Now they were both gone. Two loyal and thorough Muslims, all because of some stinking kuffers.

Walaa called for a 'Murder Meeting' in twenty four hours and summoned some of the city's most ruthless killers and renowned Muslims. He was about to turn the streets of Baltimore into a killing zone.

"…And call down Jessup and tell the brothers that I want Shabazz on the phone in ten minutes!" Walaa ordered calmly, as he continued to feed his birds.

******

Detectives Baker and Gibson were roaming the city streets checking for leads in the White case when the call for back-up came over the radio. Shots fired outside of the Baltimore Orioles Baseball Stadium. Several people had been injured. There had been a running police gun battle and two 10-7's (out of service) at the scene. Baltimore at its finest. One officer looking to get his five minutes of fame. Claimed to have been hit, but the paramedics quickly put an end to that.

"If it's true that the two victims inside the car were in fact Muslims then we might be looking at one of religion-wars where everybody is struggling for power." Baker laughed not sure if he believed all the media hype about the so-called Baltimore-based Islamic Gang.

"This thing has gang-war written all over it," Gibson replied looking around. "Just look at how tacky it was. A Muslim Gang? Give me a break. They'd be much more seasoned, than this more prudent. They would have never opened fire in a crowd of civilians like this. Let alone a public place in broad daylight."

Baker nodded, what Gibson was saying made a lot of sense. "I think our shooters were after someone else."

"Okay, let's assume that your right and our victims weren't the intended targets. It was still a well-planned hit gone bad. So, where does that leave us?" Baker questioned.

"Odds are these guys won't live to see breakfast."

"So, we're looking to see a couple more bodies before midnight?" Baker thought about the possibility of a few more bodies on the department's hands. "I hope they don't fall in our district."

"Oh, I don't think we gotta worry about that," Gibson assured him. "These are Muslims we're talking about. If they're truly involved the bodies will fall, but they'll probably come across our desk as missing persons because we'll never find them. Think about how many of these dudes are former Gangstas."

******

"I'm just saying slim. I'm not trying to die or go back to prison for somebody else's fuck ups." Diamond said before leaning down to do another line. It had been a week since the baseball stadium shooting, and he had been ducking Billy Lo and them out for real. "Niggas got me driving getaway cars and going at Muslims and shit, Ock."

"Yeah, but family is family slim." Joe Louis replied as Diamond sat up straight and tilted his head back so that the heroin could rush straight to his brain. Truthfully, Joe Louis could care less about the Muslim beef. Niggas were acting like Gangstas, so they deserved to be treated like Gangstas. But, Diamond kept feeding him lines, so he kept giving him advice. "If they ride, you got to ride. That's how it go."

"True, but them little niggas on some crazy shit." Diamond used the card to separate two more lines for him and Joe Louis. "They running all down in Baby Mecca, robbing night clubs and stuff."

"Now that's my kind of shit!" Joe Louis seemed to perk up. He lived for that drama. "How much they been getting them chumps for?"

"It depends. Ten here, fifteen there. One time they got them for--"

Diamond never got a chance to finish because Joe Louis's front door came flying off the hinges. A split second before Baltimore City's Armed Thugs came storming through the door waving guns.

"BALTIMORE CITY POLICE DEPARTMENT! DON'T NOBODY MOVE!"

Diamond and Joe Louis did exactly what the officers said to do, but that didn't stop them from getting slammed on the floor and choked out on some UFC type shit before being handcuffed.

Bodymore Murderland

"Man, what the fuck is going on?" Joe Louis demanded as the police picked a hand-cuffed Diamond up on off the floor.

"Don't worry Mr. Louis we're not here for you, *this time.*" The Lieutenant smiled, "We got a body warrant for Mr. Brinkley."

"What?" Diamond barked. "Man, I ain't do shit!"

"Tell it to the judge." The Lieutenant replied. "Read him his rights."

"Yusef Brinkley, you are under arrest for two counts of first-degree murder. You have the right to remain silent. You have the right to an attorney. Anything you say and do can and will be used against you in the court of..."

Diamond's mind went blink as he was being forced into the back of a police car. He couldn't even think straight. Had the police just said *murder?* Khadijah was going to kill him. She didn't have another bid in her.

In no time, Diamond arrived at the gold mirrored Police Headquarter Downtown and was quickly escorted to the sixth floor and left inside a small interrogation room. Diamond knew the routine. It had been the same thing twenty-five years ago. The same tricks and techniques. Let a nigga sweat, toss around a few crime scene photos, claim to have the case in a bag, run the good cop, bad cop game, and threaten a motherfucker with a thousand years in prison. But, Diamond would do what he always did. Look at the detectives like they were crazy and requested a lawyer. Because he knew that to be a true gangster you had to start strong and finish stronger.

"Good afternoon Mr. Brinkley." A manly looking bitch entered the room followed by another dude who placed a stack of papers on the table. "I am Detective Venus Malone, and this is my partner Detective Dean Waters."

"What's up?"

"First, can I get you anything?" Detective Malone asked.

"Yeah." Diamond leaned back in his chair. "A lawyer."

"You know what?" The male detective chump quickly moved around the table to Diamond's side. "You're going to show my partner some respect motherfucker!"

"Man, I just asked for a lawyer." Diamond tilted back just a bit before answering because the detective's breath smelled like stale tobacco, strong coffee, old donuts, and ass.

"Ease up Waters." The boy looking bitch intervened as if she might understand what Diamond had to endure. "Look, Mr. Brinkley; I know that you're a vet. I know that you're familiar with how the systems works, so I won't even try to sit here and play on your intelligence." Detective Malone started collecting the evidence off the table. "I'll tell you this though. We got your wife Khadijah down the hall in another room."

"*What!*" Diamond shot up in his seat. "Fuck you mean, you got my wife?"

"Oh, nobody told you what this is all about?" Detective Malone stopped and looked at Diamond. She saw something register in his eyes, but couldn't be sure if it was fear or amusement.

"Shorty don't play games with me. What the fuck is my wife doing down here?" Diamond demanded to know ready to go off.

"She's being charged with two counts of accessory to commit murder." The male chump spoke up. Diamond almost lost his breath. He didn't know what the fuck was going on.

But there was no way he was letting his wife go to prison for some shit she knew absolutely nothing about. What kind of man would he be if he did some weak shit like that? Honestly, it wouldn't have even mattered if she did know something. It was his job as not only as a husband but as a man to protect her.

"Man, somebody tell me what the fuck is going on."

Bodymore Murderland

"Okay Brinkley, this is the short version." Detective Malone took her seat again once she realized that she had Diamond's attention. "We got at least five witnesses that can put you near or at the Owings Mills, Book, and Cafe shooting with your wife, who we believe drove you away from the scene. However, I don't think that's enough to convince a jury that you pulled the trigger."

Diamond smiled. He knew he could take them in the trial. "That's because I didn't do it."

"Hold on, let me finish." Detective Malone said. "Now we have also managed to come up with an old nineteen ninety-four prison incident report involving you and one of our victims in a stabbing in which you were transferred to the Maryland University Shock Trauma Center for treatment."

"But I got to tell you, Mr. Brinkley; our strongest evidence is the gentleman who is willing to testify that you not only told him about the murders but that you turned around and sold him this." Detective Malone opened a large manila envelope and dumped an evidence bag with a gun in it out on the table.

"Bingo!" Detective Shitty breath added his two cents when Diamond got a good look at the familiar looking .357 Magnum.

"That bitch ass nigga" Diamond mumbled under his breath. He knew exactly where they had gotten the burner from now. His old running partner Monty down Murphy Homes. He had sold it to him for eight fifties of that '1058 blow. Along with his 9 millimeter.

"Okay, so what the fuck y'all want?" Diamond shook his head. He could not believe Monty's bitch ass. After all, the work he had put in now he was snitching. Now he knew why Monty's Baby Mama. ain't speak. What the fuck could she say now that she knew her King was weak?

"Maybe we should be the ones asking you that Mr. Brinkley." Detective Malone replied. "So, what is it that you want Mr. Brinkley?"

"I want the charges against my wife dropped."

"And what are you willing to give up in exchange for your wife's freedom? Mr. Brinkley because we know that there was either someone else with you, or you had another weapon."

Diamond took a deep breath and thought for a moment. He knew what had to be done. So, he swallowed his pride and spoke, "Me…I'll give you me."

Chapter 26

While Mumbles, Black and Lil' Dray laid low at the house Billy Lo's fiancée, Lakeria had planned to sell after all the remodeling was done, going over their next plan of attack. Billy Lo made his way into the city to secure a few lawyers for the storm he knew was coming and to see what was going on.

The Police Department had managed to locate a bleary surveillance video of the Camden Yards shooting, and the news was playing it over and over again in hopes of getting a break on the identity of any of the shooters. There was also a $100,000 reward being offered for any information leading to the arrest and conviction of any of the people involved.

Billy Lo swung pass Charm's spot and yelled at Joe Louis for a few before shooting back out to the house. The streets were definitely talking. Pouring fuel on the coals of conflict and feeding the flames of falsehood that could one day cause pain. It was like people just didn't give a fuck about the destruction caused by their damaging whispers and untrustworthy gossip.

"First you wanna poison racing horses and rob night clubs and shit. Now you just wanna straight go down in Baby Mecca like cowboys." Billy Lo almost laughed because it was kind of funny.

"I like it." Mumbles said siding with Lil' Dray. "Hit them bitches in their own backyard for real. Let 'em' know we ain't slowing down."

"We did make a hell of a first impression didn't we man?" Black smiled thinking about how they caught the Muslim chumps, off-guard with the element of surprise. "What you think, we can't pull it off Dug?"

"Nah, I'm not saying that." Billy Lo assured them. He was more worried about getting out then going in. "I just think we need to consider all the pros and cons first. The main one being that Baby Mecca is only a few blocks away from the Police Station."

"Yeah, Dug right about that." Black rubbed his chin as if to reconsider his murder-map. He'd forgotten all about the Main Police Department. "Maybe you or Diamond should go holler at Herbert and see what he can tell us about response time and stuff."

"Oh yeah, I forgot to tell you Diamond locked up." Billy Lo replied.

"That's why a nigga ain't been able to catch up with him."

"*What, locked up?*" Black repeated confused. "When all this happen?"

"Thursday." Billy Lo got up from the couch. He had to use the bathroom. "Police ran up in Joe shit and grabbed him on two bodies. At least that's what Joe told me. He said they had a warrant and everything. "

"Damn," Black mumbled as Billy Lo headed for the stairs. "You definitely gotta yell at Herbert now."

******

"I want y'all to rock all the little punks. We need to send a clear message." Walaa addressed the room full of well known, seasoned killers he had summoned to clean up his little problem. There were 'The Bates Brothers, Azziz and Abdul Hawk, Skinny Rashid Salih, and Samee Davenport. Then there was two of East Baltimore's most wanted and feared Big Al Griffin, a heavy-weight built gangsta with cherubic features and his right hand man, Donta 'E-Don' Walker, a crooked-eyed, lil' Wayne looking nutcase. And finally, there was the Imam's very own Adnan.

Bodymore Murderland

"I want the streets to understand that disrespect will not be tolerated against this community. Take all the brothers you need and use whatever tactics necessary. Walaa chose his words carefully knowing very well that the values of a leader was what shaped his soldier's characters and ultimately defined their actions. "They shed sacred blood, so don't show them little wanna-be gangsters no mercy."

When the tier officer told Diamond and his cell buddy that they would be coming out after dinner he jumped up and put the cheap ass; state issued toothbrush in his mouth. The doors could not open quick enough. The Doc House (D.O.C.) had been locked down for a bullshit ass escapes when Diamond came over from Central Bookings last week, and his cell buddy had been whining day in and day out. If he wasn't complaining about the food, he was crying about the cold ass showers or the five-minute phone calls or the gang dudes.

The nigga had something to say about everything. Diamond felt suffocated. He wished he could've stayed over the Bookings because there was a better chance that he might slip up and catch Monty.

Diamond stepped out on the tier with the rest of the Parole Violators waiting for a Law or Revocation Hearing and shook his head. He couldn't believe he'd allowed his ego to get him back in a box. It had to be karma. Or maybe it was just plain old stupidity. Whatever the case Diamond knew he had to find a way up out of this shit.

"Okay, Listen up gentlemen. If I call your name, please step forward and grab your mail." The fine little tier officer said and started shuffling through the first stack of mail. "Devon Hagens, Lemon Bullock, Flowers, Bagley…" When Diamond heard the fourth name, he instantly started looking for black ass Randy from the old pen and smiled when he saw him walking through the crowd to get his mail. The last time they had bumped into each other had been when he went with Billy Lo to get Lakeria's name tattooed around his ring finger downtown.

"Black Randy!" Diamond yelled as Black Randy checked out his envelope.

Black Randy looked up and smirked when he saw who was calling him. "Oh shit! My nigga Diamond. What's up slim?"

"Ain't too much; you know me." Diamond replied giving him some love as he came over. "Fuck is you doing over here? I just saw you downtown."

"My baby mother fucked around and got me hemmed up on a domestic beef." Black Randy leaned back and put his foot up on the rail. "Bitch crazy slim. She knows I can't stand no V.O.P. I got warrants all over North Carolina and V.A."

"Damn slim. How long you been over this joint?"

"Like three weeks. This spot some trash too slim. You can't even get no visits. The only good thing about this spot is that it's a bunch of bad bitches over here." Black Randy looked around. "So, what the fuck happened with you?"

"Man, these bitches just snatched me on two bodies."

"Damn slim, two bodies." Black Randy shook his head. "I hope you make out on that shit."

"Yeah, me too." Diamond paused for a second. "You remember Marvin Blocker from the pen don't you?"

"Hell, yeah Monty. Y'all niggas use to be together every day before you got jammed up and went in the Super Max."

"His bitch ass the one telling on me. Yo told them folks that I sold him the murder weapon."

"Fuck no!" Black Randy said like he couldn't believe it because he knew like Diamond knew that there was a profound difference between a witness who has no vested interest in criminal activity and a snitch who benefits greatly. "That nigga's father probably rolling over in his grave."

"Probably so," Diamond repeated. "That's why I was trying to get these peoples to let me ride this shit out over the bookings so that I could catch up with that nigga."

"You don't know where that nigga at?"

"Nah, but I'ma definitely find out." Diamond assured him. "I just got to get on the horn."

"Well, you of all people know how I get down. Black Randy gave Diamond that look. "You find out where that bitch at and I'll make it happen, but yo, you know that shit is not going to be free."

"I ain't looking for no favors." Diamond knew that the days of getting niggas touched for G.P. (general principle) was almost non-existent. It didn't matter if the nigga told on Allah or raped the Virgin Mary if the money wasn't right, or a major nigga ain't give the call it wasn't happening. "You find a nigga to do it, and I'll put the money wherever you want it at. "

"You gonna have to kick out half up front."

"How much we talking?"

"A cool stack." Black Randy replied knowing how cheap the price of life was in prison. "That'll give me enough to be straight and look out for a few of my lil' comrades."

"Bet." Diamond nodded. "Give me a few days to catch up with my man."

******

The next morning Diamond had to run around like crazy. First, he went down to medical to take his intake physical, which would have been cool had he not had to sit in the waiting area for two hours listening to a bunch of fools trading war stories. Then as soon as he got back up to the 7th floor, the tier officer informed him that he had to go back downstairs to classification to see his Case Manager, who turned out to be a bad little dime piece name Shena Poteat that he knew from back in the day.

Diamond couldn't help but tell her that he was still sweet on her after she said she would do what she could to keep him from going back down Jessup to 'The Cut.'

Diamond shot back up to the 7th floor and put the phone in a Cobra clutch.

It was time to remind Monty that the jungles were still the jungle 'be it steel or concrete,' and all the rules still applied.

Chapter 27

The news was bad, but not surprising. Diamond had confessed to a double murder beef to save his wife, and Tina was cooperating with the police. At first Lil' Dray didn't want to believe it. Because he knew that she knew better. He had schooled her but, Lil' Dray knew that Herbert was reliable. He wouldn't just lie. Herbert had too much to lose to play games. Not only was he crooked, but he had been supplying them with all types of police equipment and information he'd been getting from other members of his, who worked in law enforcement.

"Mumbles, you, Lil' Dray, and Black stay outside. Me and Joe are going in."

Billy Lo looked around the room, while Lil' Dray and them had been hiding out and gathering information to put them in a position of power. The Muslims had been making their presence felt. First, a bunch of their workers was snatched off the streets and beaten. Then one of Mumbles brother's bodies was found rolled up inside some carpet in an alley just off Gold Street, and now Tina was missing. "Once the fireworks start y'all let them bitches have it!"

"Let's rock and roll then," Black said moving for the door. It was time to strike back for Mumbles brother. "Let's show these suckers what time it is."

"Let's do it." Billy Lo seconded as he followed Black's lead. He knew that the Muslims hated anyone or anything that they saw as a threat to the normal order of their operation.

By the time, they arrived in Baby Mecca night had fallen. Billy Lo and Joe Louis left the car running and walked into the restaurant looking for trouble. Billy Lo didn't like to involve innocent people in street affairs, but it was getting hard to stand by certain vows in a game that was constantly changing and most of the time had no rules.

"Good evening gentlemen. May I help you?"

"Yeah, go in the back and tell who's ever in charge that you got a guy out here thinking about shooting the place up." Billy Lo replied with an evil grin that made the Host run off as if he understood that contemplating was always a prelude to commission. "Let's take a table in the back." Billy Lo added and walked on through like he owned the joint as the rest of the staff looked at him like he was crazy.

Seconds after Billy Lo and Joe Louis found a table and took a seat they were approached by two well-dressed Muslims.

"What seems to be the problem?" The bigger of the two spoke up cracking his knuckles. "Hey! Hey! I am talking to you, Ock!"

Billy Lo just continued to smirk. Fools never sensed danger. They never considered who they were dealing with, never considered that most of the time the strong assumed the position of weakness. Instead, fools tried to use aggression, size, and other forms of intimidation to create this illusion of strength. Today it wouldn't work.

"You find something funny, Ock?" The big guy advanced like he was about to snatch Billy Lo up from the table, but Joe Louis came up and hit him with a six-inch hook that forced him to do a half somersault flip over a chair.

The other Muslim went for his gun, but Billy Lo already had the drop on him and didn't blink once before opening his whole head up with his heat and causing pure panic.

As soon as Billy Lo and Joe Louis started moving for the doors amid all the chaos, two more chumps in suits came out of the kitchen firing like 'Mad Men' and both Billy Lo and Joe Louis were forced to grab fleeing customers for protection and fired back.

Bodymore Murderland

Outside Lil' Dray heard the sounds of gunshots and saw several important looking men exiting a side door and didn't think twice before opening fire with double handed action. A few Muslims fired back, but he still managed to cut two of them down before he was knocked off his bike with the impact of a horse kick.

Lil' Dray crawled back over to his Ninja thankful that he had listened to Billy Lo and worn the vest. It still felt like his ribs or something was broken though because his breath was only coming in short spurts. However, his adrenaline and the thought of jail kept him pushing until he got back on the bike under a hail of bullets and took off.

******

Billy Lo came through the door just as sparks flew and glass exploded. He still had the bitch as a shield, "LET'S GO!" He screamed holding the door open for Joe Louis with his leg.

Joe Louis was cutting through tables and firing wildly while Billy Lo continued to dump on the two Muslims. They slowed down but didn't stop as Joe Louis slung his human shield to the floor and made a fast break for the door.

"Please." The bitch Billy Lo was holding pleaded, struggling to get free.

"Bitch!" Billy Lo choked her harder just as Joe Louis fell at his feet. One look told him it was over. With no time to waste Billy Lo opened fire again and started dragging the bitch towards the car.

******

Black tapped Mumbles on the leg to let him know to follow the fast fleeing black Lincoln Continental. Black was strapped to

230

Delmont M. Player

Mumbles with a leather belt. Once they hit the expressway
Mumbles kicked the gears and started cutting through the cars so he
could come up on the Lincoln from the driver's side.

"Hit the driver first!" Mumbles yelled over his shoulder as they
came right up on the window. Black quickly aimed the pistol-grip
20 Gauge Mossberg 500 at the window and squeezed off twice. The
window turned into a fireball, and a few buck-shots tore through
Black's leg.

"Shit!" Black cried and aimed at the back window before firing
again. "Yo, it's armored!"

"Hit the wheels!" Mumbles ordered. "Hit the wheels!"

The driver of the car tried to crush Black and Mumbles
between two cars before Black could let off again. The move forced
Mumbles to swerve and skin half his leg on the expressway lane-
divider, so rather than try his hand again, Mumbles switched gears
and crossed lanes, disappearing into traffic.

Chapter 28

"You mean to tell me that somebody let some kuffars take a shot at me?" Walaa questioned, slamming his hand into the table as the thoughts of police still crawling all over Baby Mecca and the Masjid flashed in his mind. "When did these kuffars get crazy? When did their balls get so big? Somebody's putting batteries in these little kid's backs. They aren't that smart, nor disciplined to pull off what they did without help. I want everybody to look into the possibility that they're greater forces at work. Probably a Shayk.

"But whatever or whoever it is. I want it stopped now! You hear me?" Walaa looked around the room slowly. "There's no way I am letting no fucking kids get out on me period."

Everybody got up and started moving. The Imam had spoken and no more needed to be said. Mumbles and them had gotten the only shot they would get. There would be no more classic 'Meeting Engagements' wherein two opposing forces, only vaguely aware of each other's presence, suddenly finding themselves face to face on an unprepared battlefield. No, the next time the Muslims laid eyes on Billy Lo and them it was 'Ball game."

Walaa stopped Adnan and asked him to hang back until everyone was gone, then he spoke freely. "Listen Ock, these little friends of Shabazz's done murdered multiple brothers. That can't stand, Ock. There's no way that we can let that stand."

"I know." Adnan looked into the hardened eyes of a man who'd seen it all, and it was one of the only times that ever witnessed a softness.

232

Delmont M. Player

"And then the stuff with Samad gotta be handled, Ock. He can't make it back in front of that Grand Jury." Walaa said shaking his head. He could not believe that Samad would go out like that. But word from a few people on their payroll was that Samad was taking Federal Prosecutors as far back as the 1970s Bank Secrecy Act, when their bank friends and other financial institutions were required to report any transactions of more than ten grand in the U.S. Treasury Department, but didn't. That was back before all the Terrorism, before Muslims were hated so much, and back when Al-Haqq Masjid heads did things differently.

"I am all over it, Ock." Adnan felt bad about having to crush another Muslim brother, but Samad had always been the 'Megalomaniac' type anyway. "Inshaalah, I'll have it handled in a few days."

"A yo, that sound like some shit straight out of a movie." The fat dude standing next to Diamond said as everybody stood around watching the six o'clock News. Diamond couldn't believe what he was hearing. Somebody had to be talking. Diamond stood there glued to the television as the news reporter continued to talk about everything from the shoot-out at Lil' Dray's house to the Lakeria's car-bombing. The FBI, DEA, ATF and other local agencies were all working together to bring all those involved in what they were calling an ongoing rival gang power struggle' to justice.

When the reporter went to another story Diamond walked off in his own thoughts. He knew that shit was about to get ugly. After walking a hole in the floor, Diamond went over and looked out the 7th-floor window and sighed. It never failed to amaze him how no matter what happened life always went on. The world continued to move.

******

Bodymore Murderland

Detectives were running around going crazy. The Police Chief was demanding answers and arrests, and nobody had slept in days because careers were on the line. It was election time, and the Mayor would do anything to please the public. Even if it meant firing good detectives and transferring half of the police force.

"We got to figure out exactly who was with Joe Louis first," Gibson said to no one in particular although it was at least ten detectives sitting around the table that was littered with open case files, notes, coffee mugs, styrofoam cartons of stale cheese steak and fries congealed with cold grease and donuts.

"The Feds can't be giving us everything." Another detective spoke up. "I mean it just doesn't make sense."

"Were we able to get any hits on DNA and prints?"

"Won't know for a few weeks. The labs are working over time, but we're talking about a couple of thousand samples."

"Okay, let's consider for a minute that the information the Feds gave us is good. Who is this guy Billy?" Gibson asked a questioned that brought everyone to silence. And for a moment the only thing that could be heard was the sounds of the usual office activity. The distant sounds of light whispers, copy-machine, and phones.

"Why don't we start with the things we do know and work from there?" Baker replied breaking the silence. "We know that Green's cousin was recently arrested for double homicide in Joe Louis's house. We know that White was tortured. We know that Chapple's girlfriend is either missing or with him. We know about Pair's…"

The detectives sat there for the next two hours and compared notes and everything else they could think of. They even stared at photos of all the victims they thought maybe linked to the case because despite popular belief 'dead men did talk.' You just had to get a little closer to hear them.

It was just after 9 P.M. when a phone call brought good news. DNA testing from a seven-month-old home-invasion murder/rape case over in South Baltimore had just linked White to it. So, Gibson and Baker cut the meeting short and drove straight over to the University of Maryland to give White the good news.

******

"You're in over your head this time White. Not only did you shit heads kill four people, but y'all also managed to kill an FBI Informant." Gibson smiled at D.W. "That's right. Preacher...a-k-a Allen Smallwood was a paid informant."

"You know what that means right White?" Baker couldn't help but add his two cents. "That means you're going to be looking at the Lethal Injection."

D.W. just laid there with a dumb ass look on his face as if he knew that he was fucked. Gibson and Baker had already booked him on a two-year-old homicide from a Pratt Street Jewelry Store. For the gun he had been stupid enough to hold onto.

"You can lay there and play tough all you want White, but I assure you that when this thing is over, you'll being sitting on Death Row begging to give up some information."

******

"That's for the nigga Joe Louis." Black poured out some Jack Daniels. "Yo was a fucking old gangster! He was loyal as shit too! That's a lot more than I can say for most of these old niggas."

"You right about that." Mumbles replied looking off into the sky as he rubbed Cocaine's head before leaning over to pick at the scabs on his wounded leg when they started to itch.

"Man, stop fucking with that nasty ass shit!" Black barked looking at the damage the buck-shots had left behind a week ago. "That shit going to end up getting infected watch."

"Shit keep itching." Mumbles continued picking.

"Yo, I can't stop thinking about that shit with Diamond. How the fuck is he gonna play us like that?" Black asked never really expecting an answer. "After all the shit, I did for that nigga when he was down."

"Wait til we get a chance to talk to D.W. ourselves." Mumbles replied wanting to avoid the topic that had everybody on edge. D.W. had told Tiara that Diamond had given them up to the Muslims. Billy Lo didn't believe it. Despite the fact that Black and Lil' Dray made a good case. As far as Mumbles, he was undecided because he knew that the Muslims would say anything to get D.W. to talk after the way they had been giving them hell. "You know how females be getting shit mixed up."

"Come on Dug; you can't tell me that that shit doesn't make a lot of sense. Think about it." Black paused. "How they get on us? How the fuck they find out where nigga's laid their heads? I bet that's probably why that nigga didn't want us to get at them whores in the first place. His bitch ass was playing the fifty the whole time. Snake ass nigga. He lucky he locked back up cause I would push his shit back myself. Straight like that, family or no family."

"Let's just deal with this other shit first." Mumbles said more concerned with keeping his life than taking Diamond's at the moment.

Black and Mumbles didn't pay the trash truck coming down the alley much attention until the trash men hopped off the bumper to grab the trash cans from the yard and Cocaine started barking, but by then it was too late, they were looking down the barrels of Sawed-Off Shot-Guns and the only thing Mumbles was thinking was that he should've listened to cat and took his dumb ass back down her crazy ass aunt Pooh's house.

The first blast hit Mumbles and flipped him and his chair clean over. Black froze up for a second when he saw his childhood best friend and brother in arms head burst. Cocaine went leaping over the fence to attack Mumbles shooter. When the shooter's partner took a second to get Cocaine off him before she could lock on his neck, Black made a run for it.

"Ahhhhh!" Was all Black could get out as two pumpkin-balls ripped through his back and knocked him across the kitchen floor as he cut through the back door.

******

Lil' Dray had just dozed off when the sounds of gunfire started ringing off. So, he jumped up, grabbed his tone, and took off, taking the steps two and three at a time.

When Lil' Dray arrived at the kitchen, he saw Black laid out across the kitchen floor near the table and gripped his tone tighter as he rushed out the back door. There was a dude attempting to help another bloody chump onto the steel bed of the trash truck. Lil' Dray brought his hammer up and opened fire as he tried to walk them down.

The bloody chump fell to the ground and the other dude dove into the mouth as the truck took off. Lil' Dray quickly jumped the fence and continued to dump on the trunk before turning back to finish the bloody chump off with no remorse.

When Lil' Dray jumped back over the fence to get low, he spotted Mumbles and Cocaine and almost collapsed. However, the thought of retaliation kept him on his feet. Lil' Dray hit the front door and took off. The safe house wasn't safe no more.

A few blocks over Lil' Dray located the car they kept for situations like this and sat there for a minute letting the tears roll. He had just lost his last two brothers in arms, and now he was all alone.

"You bitches gonna pay." Lil' Dray vowed thinking about the Muslims as he put the car in drive. "I swear you bitches gonna pay."

Chapter 29

"We know somebody's holding out on us." Baker said looking over the information he had gathered from the city's narcotic unit and the State Police Intelligence Division." We just need to find out why."

"No! We need to find out who." Gibson retorted thinking about all the statewide raids that had been taking place lately. "And I already have a few ideas too."

The last month had been crazy, first DNA linked White to another unsolved murder/rape case. Then the only witness in the Brinkley case gets stabbed within inches of his life. and now some two-bit FBI Agent kept trying to contact Gibson because the bodies that turned up at what the FBI believed to be a safe house shoot-out that left more questions than answers. But, the craziest thing was the fact that the Federal Government had gone to great lengths to assure that nothing about the investigations or victims would be leaked to the press until everything was wrapped up and an arrest was made.

"Good. Then we can start there." Baker said looking up.

The police were kicking doors in left and right, and the only reason that Lil' Dray had decided to show his face was because he needed to get up with Billy Lo and see if Herbert had found out anything about Black and Mumbles. The News wasn't saying shit, and he knew that he could only avoid Cat and Peanut for so long before they got to tripping.

Lil' Dray spotted Billy Lo the moment he walked into the crowded 'Lake Trout.' It was the reason he chose to meet up there. The place was always packed, and you could see everything going on around you outside due to the glass windows. Besides, Lil' Dray couldn't think of a safer place for one of Maryland's Most Wanted to hideout then in plain sight at the most famous fish spot in Baltimore, which just so happened to be right next door to the North/Western Police Station.

"What's up Dug?" Lil' Dray asked giving Billy Lo some love.

"I'm taking it easy slim." Billy Lo replied quickly surveying his surroundings. "So, what's on your mind?"

"Revenge." Lil' Dray spoke from the heart before him, and Billy Lo went on to discuss a few options and views. Lil' Dray wanted to strike immediately, but Billy Lo felt like they needed to wait.

"It's too hot right now. Everybody on edge, let's wait until shit cools down." Billy Lo paused to give Lil' Dray a moment to consider what he said before continuing. "Herbert said they're going crazy downtown. Waiting for any of us to slip up. They got surveillance and shit set up all over the city."

After a while, Lil' Dray agreed with Billy Lo. Revenge was still revenge, be it now or later. So, they would let the dust settle for a little bit and then roll on the Muslims again.

"Just don't go getting cold feet on me Dug." Lil' Dray said.

"Never that, I always pay my debts."

Billy Lo gave Lil' Dray a nice piece of cash to hold him over and vanished after they made plans to answer Lil' Dray's call for revenge when he returned from out of town.

******

"Man, it'll never be like that again." Diamond continued to shave his head. He and his cell buddy were having a discussion about the change of times. "The late eighties and early nineties were the shit! Everything was jumping. Dudes were getting money; it was less hating and less snitching."

"You ain't lying about that." Diamond's cell buddy agreed. "Plus, if a dude didn't like you for whatever reason. Y'all could scrap head up and keep it moving like men with no hard feelings because more niggas respected the fact that you fought, rather than how you fought."

"Yeah… shit ain't like that no more. A lot of these jokers don't even want to fight." Diamond shook his head. "I remember a time when you couldn't even hang out if you couldn't hold your own, or you didn't at least fight. Now you got suckers being treated like men. I know females more thorough than half these lames."

"Me too, but yo, remember how slick broads use to be back then?"

"Nigga what! Finger-Waves, Buns, Shirley Temples, Bamboo-Earrings with the names. I can go on and on slim." Diamond stopped shaving and waved his hand before dipping the razor into the plugged-up sink water again to remove the soap and hair. "Women were just more into looking good back then."

"Yeah, I don't know what the fuck wrong with these bitches today. I mean, I respect the fact that a lot of them more thorough than these niggas but damn you ain't got to dress like it. That's why I'm glad that my old lady a throw-back. She was born in eighty-four, but she got an old soul. Shorty a rider. That's my reflection. The female version of me. "

"Then you got lucky because ain't a whole lot of them left." Diamond assured him. That was why he cherished Khadijah so much. She was a part of a rare breed. She had stood beside him when most females wouldn't, and for that, it was nothing that he wouldn't do for her.

"But ain't no sense in driving ourselves crazy about that shit slim." Diamond's cell buddy added and Diamond knew he was right. Times had changed, but that didn't stop Diamond from thinking back to when shit was more authentic. The women, the dudes, the game, everything. You could not just fake it to make it because you had to carry your own weight and earn your own bones. "Too many dudes go untested, so you know they ain't cut like that for real, and these broads don't know shit about being loyal because the dudes that supposed to teach them weak their motherfucking selves."

All Diamond could do was nod in agreement because his cell buddy was definitely right.

******

"Yo, who got the tier?" Diamond asked after he got finished making his evening Salat. He was trying to figure out if he had enough time to use the bathroom before the guard opened the cell door and he had to feed-up the tier for dinner.

"Your girl." His cell replied smiling.

"My wife at home slim. I keep telling you that." Diamond said knowing that his cell buddy was referring to the regular tier officer Ms. Green. A fine lil' slim, plain-Jane cutie with bubbly eyes and a nice ass. Diamond was jive sweet on her, but would never admit it. Especially to his half-slick ass cell buddy. The nigga talked a good game, but for real the nigga couldn't hold water.

After feeling up and messing with Ms. Green for a minute Diamond went down to the bottom tier to holler at Black Randy about their little situation. They had to come to some kind of understanding because they would both probably be leaving soon. Black Randy had taken a cop for eighteen months, and Diamond's Revocation Hearing was in the morning.

"Allah knows best." Diamond said when Black Randy asked him how he thought he would make out in the morning. "I'm at his mercy slim. Inshallah, all goes well."

"I heard that." Black Randy laughed. He believed in controlling his own destiny. "I hope you make out on that other thing too. Monty definitely got your message."

"Let's just hope he took it, cause a nigga ain't got another bid in him."

"I feel you slim."

"Ah nigga, you don't feel me." Diamond shook his head and smiled. "You done been back three/four times. You better stop putting your hands on them, women."

"A lot of times when you're addicted to something you tend to abuse it in one form or another." Black Randy said sincerely, and Diamond knew that was the truth.

Chapter 30

By the time, Billy Lo got back in town, shit had gone from bad to worst. Diamond's wife Khadijah had been shot to death on her way to work, bits and pieces of D.W.'s twenty-five, page statement had made the front page of the Baltimore Sun Newspaper and Billy Lo, himself was now as wanted as Black and them had been.

Then there were the sealed indictments that were about to come down, so Billy Lo knew that shit was about to hit the fan and with the laws of the jungle being so fucked up he knew that a lot of niggas would go for self.

After a few days, Billy Lo located Diamond down the 'Cut' and got the scoop on a lot of shit. He could tell that the death of his wife had crushed him because all he kept saying was that he wished they had stuck to the original plan, but Billy Lo felt like there was no sense in crying over spilled milk. He wanted to ask Diamond about the shit D.W. had been pumping to Tiara about him and the Muslims, but decided that a rat's word wasn't worth shit. Besides, like the old Bible Proverbs goes, he who walks with integrity walks securely, and he who perverts his ways shall become known'.

"Dug, you know I'ma move on them chumps again, so you might as well get Shabazz now." Billy Lo said knowing that there were no friends in wars. Only family. Billy Lo listened to Diamond's reply and smiled. Any excuse not to put that work in. It was a cold world and a friend to all was a friend to none. But Billy Lo didn't make the rules he just lived by them. Diamond had a better chance at seeing a dog catch his own tail then he did at not being expandable to the Muslims.

Delmont M. Player

"All I'm saying is that you better do him before he do you. Don't let that old nigga rock you to sleep slim."

Billy Lo hung up after promising to find out about the nigga Monty that was telling on Diamond. The last thing the lawyer had told Diamond about Monty was that he was down the Super Max losing his mind. He could barely walk since his Achilles heels had been cut after Black Randy's comrades beat and stabbed him over the jail.

It was amazing what a person's own thoughts could do to him. Billy Lo knew from doing hole-time in prison that it took a strong motherfucker to live with their own thoughts twenty four hours a day once the demons started to eat away at him and the cell walls closed in.

******

"Boy, you ain't ready yet?" A sexy little chocolate C.O. asked walking up in front of D.W.'s administrative lock-up cell to get him for a visit. "You said five minutes."

"Here I come now," D.W. replied grabbing the rest of the paperwork he had for Tiara.

"McCall! McCall!" D.W.'s neighbor called out. "I know you hear me yo!"

"Brigham, I ain't paying you no mind.

"You don't want nothing." She fired but still looked.

D.W. slowed his roll a little bit. He knew what time it was. Poochie was busting shorty's head and he damn sure wasn't about to walk into the line of fire.

"Keep on. I'ma write your little dick ass up."

D.W. smiled. He knew that Poochie didn't give a fuck. The nigga had just butchered his cell buddy and chopped up a guard over some missing family photos and would put the dick on any female. Especially the ones that came running down there all day to get it. Some of the guards had D.W. ready to jump out there, the way they were on it. Standing there until Poochie nutted and shit.

"Damn! I love your lil' phat ass, McCall." Poochie fired like he had just gotten finished making love to her. "I swear to God!"

Shorty shook her head and looked at D.W. "Again, you got five seconds to come on, or you gonna miss your Lil' visit cause I'm gone." She said anxiously.

"I'm ready. I'm ready." D.W. hurried up and cuffed up so she could get the door popped. He had been in the jail for a few weeks now on A-Section. The only tier over Steel Side with only two cells. It was located right across from intake and housed the most dangerous inmates. Niggas like Dennis Wise, Lil Phil Cook, Marcus 'Moon' Alexander, Anthony Jones, Joe Dancer, and old gangster Turk motherfuckers who put in work both in and out of prison. But every so often dudes like D.W. ended up taking up bed space for what could be considered their own protection and or simply having high profile cases.

D.W. saw niggas looking at him and whispering as the guard escorted him to the visiting area. He knew that they were probably talking bad about him. Calling him a rat and some more shit, but he wasn't concerned about nobody but the niggas he loved and respected. Fuck the rest of them lames. They ain't know his story. Half of em' had taken the Lil' Sun News Paper article and ran with it. But who had he told on other than himself? That's exactly why he was taking all his paperwork up to Tiara so niggas could see for themselves who was really telling on who.

The funny part about it was that half of the dudes that had something to say were suckers he would rob or slap the shit out of on the streets. The other half were chumps him, or his men had carried in one form or another. Niggas who ain't know nothing about facing certain death.

When D.W. got inside the visiting booth and saw Tiara looking all good with her big ole' belly, he couldn't do anything but smile. She was the reason why he had played shit like he did. He wanted to be able to watch his seed grow up even if it was from behind the bars. So, anybody who didn't understand that, or like it could suck his dick.

"Hey, gorgeous," D.W. spoke picking up the phone and looking at his baby mother, who like so many black women had become used to bearing the burden of her man's misfortune.

"Hey." Tiara smiled. "I miss you."

"I miss you too baby," D.W. said wholeheartedly. "Did you ever get a chance to catch up with Lil' Dray for me?"

"Yeah, I told his brother. He said he is going to grab the paperwork tomorrow. Oh, and I gave the guard your court clothes too."

"Thanks, baby. You always come through.

******

After circling the block a few times to make sure things were on the up and up Lil' Dray parked right in front of Charm's house and got out with his Glock .40 at the ready. He had already made up his mind that if the police ran down on him. He was shooting it out. As far as he was concerned, he didn't have anything else to lose.

The door came open as Lil' Dray approached and a familiar looking dude stepped out shining. It took Lil' Dray a moment to recognize exactly who he was looking at. "Keystone?" He said to be sure. When Keystone smiled Lil' Dray, just nodded at the shapely dressed con artist. "I see you Dug. What you hit the lottery or something?"

"Nah, I wish." Keystone laughed just as Peaches came out of the house glowing. "Just came into a little scratch."

"Hello, stranger." Peaches said. "Long time no see."

"How you been doing Miss Peaches?" Lil' Dray questioned checking her out. "Fine. God is good." Peaches replied.

"I heard that." Lil' Dray looked her up and down again. She truly looked good. She had picked up some weight and all that.

"Well, if you don't mind, we're running a little late for church." Peaches said as Keystone took her hand to guide her down the steps. "Calvin and them are inside."

"A'ight thanks. You take care." Lil' Dray stepped to the side to let them pass.

"You too." Peaches said.

"Hey! Keystone!" Lil' Dray waited for him to turn around. Let me get ten dollars."

"If you need it, you got it home slice." Keystone replied laughing as he unlocked the car door for Peaches before going in his pocket.

"Nah man, I'm just messing with you." Lil' Dray put his hands up and dipped on into the house.

Inside the house, Charm and Billy Lo were sitting at the table waiting for him. They had a lot to talk about.

"What's up nigga?" Charm asked getting up and giving Lil' Dray some love. "It took you long enough."

"I had to make sure shit was cool." Lil' Dray looked over at Billy Lo.

"What's up with you Dug?"

"I'm waiting on you to explain to me what you told Charm." Billy Lo fired. "I know you ain't trying to defend what that rat did."

"Defend a rat?" Lil' Dray looked at Charm for understanding. "I ain't defending no fucking body."

"Then what's all this shit about D.W. not being fucked up?" Billy Lo questioned with his face twisted up. "I read the News Paper."

"And I read the actual statement." Lil' Dray stared at Billy Lo jive disappointed. He could not believe that Billy Lo thought that he would protect no rat. "Now don't get me wrong. Yo was definitely out of order with all the dry-snitching shit, but he ain't the one that told on us."

"So, what you saying?" Billy Lo looked at him like he was crazy. He didn't care if D.W. was trying to save himself or his mother. Snitching was snitching. And he had violated to the highest degree. "Who gave us up?"

"See for yourself." Lil' Dray replied pulling the papers out of his back pocket and tossing them across the table. "That straight out of D.W.'s discovery."

Lil' Dray watched as Billy Lo picked up the papers so he and Charm could read them. He knew that the blow he had just dealt would hurt more than any physical one. A lot of so-called 'real niggas' knew or found out a nigga they fucked with was squealing and continued to deal with them, but Lil' Dray honestly didn't think that Billy Lo was one of them.

"I can't believe this bitch ass nigga!" Billy Lo kept saying over and over again as he read Diamond's statement to the police. The nigga had told everything. Even shit he wasn't even home to witness. Billy Lo felt sick to his stomach. This wasn't just another nigga turning his trigger finger to a witness finger. This was his man. His big brother. Now he knew that Diamond wasn't the most thorough nigga playing the game, but he never thought that he would become a fucking rat.

Bodymore Murderland

"That's crazy yo." Charm remembered something Mumbles had told him about 'always valuing his honor over his heart,' because love could be deceiving and make you vulnerable. "That nigga better not call here no more."

Billy Lo just sat there staring at the 'niggas won't believe I'm doing this statement' to the detectives and thought back to all the times Diamond had tried to justify dealing with a rat after claiming to hate them. All the ambiguous views and weak shit he shook off as just another form of prison maturity.

"I guess it's true what they say then." Lil' Dray got up to leave. "Prison has a way of breaking niggas. They go in walking tall and come out crawling."

"Not all of them." Billy Lo assured him. "We got to find a way to reach on the other side of that gun-tower and show Diamond's bitch ass that what he thinks is a loophole out of the game is actually the noose that will hang him for his sins against it."

"Well as you can see, we can't use Herbert no more. Hey put yo' all in the mix too." Lil' Dray shook his head.

"Yeah well, we gotta come up with something."

"You go ahead and do you." Lil' Dray said. The niggas he trusted were all dead. "I'ma do my own thing for now on."

Billy Lo stared at Lil' Dray kind of insulted but only nodded.

*****

"So, have you heard from Billy Lo, Ock?" Shabazz questioned Diamond as they sat outside in the yard on the bleachers enjoying the weather, feeding the birds.

"Yeah." Diamond had thought about lying, but for some reason, he knew it was a rhetorical question. "Charm gave him my number, and he got at me last night."

250

"Remind me. Charm is the little guy y'all been grooming right?"

"Yeah, the one who's little sister got killed."

"Right." Shabazz tossed a few pieces of bread up on the concrete landing near the windows. "Now, did you do what I asked?"

"It was my first time talking to him in a minute, so I didn't want to come off sounding crazy. Shorty sharp. He would've picked right up on that."

Diamond knew that Billy Lo had the mind of a chess master so every move that he made would've to be a calculated one because rather Billy Lo was on offense or defense he read everything like a master before making his next move. "Just give me some time."

"Don't take too long Ock."

"Oh nah, I'm on it." Diamond knew he had to do something. Simply getting Billy Lo locked up wasn't an option. The little nigga went too hard to have him running around the system as an enemy. So, Diamond had to put together a plan that would turn one of Billy Lo's greatest strengths against him. "Shorty Loyal." By using Billy Lo's loyalty to bring him to his Muslim brothers, he would kill two threats with one death. He trusted me. So, all I got to do is tell him shit cool."

If Diamond's plan worked, it would get Billy Lo completely out of the way. So, that he wouldn't even have to be concerned with him retaliating after he testified and it would further prove to the brothers that he hadn't had anything to do with the robbery and murders that jumped off.

The only other thing Diamond had to do was forget all the shit he had said to the Feds about Shabazz and the Community. He wasn't even worried about his little cousin and them. Black and Mumbles were dead, D.W. was basically about to be washed up and as far as Lil' Dray went. He could easily get touched if push came to shove and he came in the system acting like he really wanted some work. Because there would still be a lot of soldiers, who stood by his side even after the paperwork came out.

"You know the thing I like about the birds Ock?" Shabazz asked but never gave Diamond a chance to respond. "They stick together no matter the weather. When one goes astray, they never look back. That's a powerful thing, Ock. A good friend of mines once told me that we are no different than the birds. So, as long as we stick together we can't lose. Even when we face trouble."

"It's only when greed guides us that we lose. Because greed is the sin that leads to death. Greed is the weakness that allows the cat to capture us. Because no one is there to watch our backs, and the cat can leap out of nowhere, but when we all eat together as one the cat can't win because we can see him lurking and the second he leaps we all fly off in different directions and leave him in confusion. That Ock is how you trick the cat every time. By eating together and never letting greed get the best of us."

Diamond looked at Shabazz's hard face as he continued to feed the birds.   He didn't know what to say or if he should say anything at all. So, he just kept his peace and continued to watch him feed the birds.

Chapter 31

"So, how do you wanna play this detective?" Detective Baker questioned Malone staring at the new problem laying across the concrete floor.

"It's your call. You're the lead on this case."

Detective Malone tried to think for a moment. "I say we cover it up. At least for now."

Detective Gibson spoke up. "I mean, the ball's already rolling. And besides Brinkley's already in too deep."

"Yeah but, we gotta consider the law also." Detective Malone reminded them. "This could easily turn into an ugly 'Brady Violation' down the line."

"You're kidding yourself detective if you think Brinkley's going to live long enough to appeal his case." Gibson knew that no matter what happened, win, lose or draw. Within a few months, the Muslims would start cleaning house, if they hadn't already begun. "These are still Gangsters we are dealing with here."

"I agree." Baker walked over and squatted down next to the cold corpse of their key witness. "There's no way he's walking away from this. None of these kids are. Just look what they did to Samad Knight and he was *Muslim*. I'd be surprised if we found any more bodies. You see how Chapple's girl just disappeared."

"I just want to make sure everybody gets what they want." Detective Malone said. "Close my case, let the Feds get the Muslims on some Terrorist Act, and you guys can finally get to nail Chapple and White to the Cross."

"In that case, all you got to do is keep Brinkley from saying that he's getting a deal for cooperating while he's on the stand and your job is done."

"Sounds good to me," Baker added. "Your ass is covered. The department's ass is covered. And everybody gets their man. Mission complete. Let some big shot lawyer do all the digging. Ain't that what they get paid for?"

"I just don't want nothing to come back to bite me in the ass later. Remember what happened in the Jodie Hill case when detectives bent the rules to get the greater evil?" Malone stated more than questioned looking up at the light fixture to where the apparent suicide had begun and ended. "I want to retire with my pension intact. Not be forced out by some innocent project assholes."

"Look, you had a witness. And that witness regardless of his motives got you a confession and allowed us to level other criminal charges against several suspects. Case closed." Baker said trying to get Detective Malone to understand that the Brinkley case was much bigger than some wannabe gangster name Marvin Blocker who decided to hang himself in a jail cell. "What judge do you really know that will side against you?"

"I have to agree with Baker," Gibson said. "No judge in their right mind would see that as foul play, and Brinkley wanted to talk. Think about it, his wife's dead, so he can't continue to use that as an excuse no more. What's his lawyer going to say about that?"

Detective Malone knew that a lot of guys got tired of honoring some street code that they no longer respected themselves, but that wasn't what concerned her.

"Okay, let's just play it by ear for now. That way we can stay out in front of it." Malone replied. "But, I'ma still run a small article on Blocker's suicide in the police blotter. We can't hide that. It's public information."

"Yeah, but there's also no law that bounds us to do a lawyer's job." Gibson retorted. "All we have to do is make it available."

"Exactly." Malone smiled. That was her reason for running the small article. "That's why if they don't ask, we don't tell."

******

Lil' Dray wasn't bullshitting when he said he was ready to put in some work. Patience had never been one of his strong suits, and after the shit, with Diamond and D.W. there was no way he was trusting nobody except family.

After the sit-down with Billy Lo, all Lil' Dray did was make moves and plans that centered around striking the Muslims, because there was no way in the world he was going to let them get away with leaving, his brothers stretched out like that. He was too thirsty for blood, and they had already proven that those bitches bled and died just like them. So, if them bitches couldn't finish him. Then they'd better be prepared to run like hell because he was coming full force.

Lil' Dray knew he'd need some help, but since he couldn't imagine getting it in with anybody except family. He decided to link-up with his cousins Pierre and Little Clyde, because drama and gunplay were right up them niggas alley, and they had both stood up under all kinds of problems and pressure.

"Another one bites the dust." Pierre fired referring to D.W. as Lil' Dray brought him and Little Clyde up to speed.

"Damn, yo put in all that work for nothing." Little Clyde added.

Lil' Dray just shook his head. Pierre and Little Clyde were right. D.W was once a respected, even feared nigga. Known to squeeze first and ask questions last. Now he was just another so-called gangster that bitched-up when it was time to face the fire.

"Yeah, you know it ain't how you start, but rather how you finish that count in this game," Pierre stated knowing that his big cousins knew like he did that when it came to a nigga's character, Rep, or name in the streets your faults were added up first. "But, fuck all that. Let's get back to this other shit. Now, what were you saying about the car stuff?"

"Nah." Lil' Dray replied looking at Little Clyde. "I was asking Cuzzo if he was still nice with that car shit."

"What?" Little Clyde grinned and pulled out a flat-head screwdriver. "Ain't nothing change nigga."

"Then we gonna need something big enough to lay across the back seats."

"Say no more." Little Clyde nodded.

******

"Stop trying to run!" Billy Lo barked slapping the Lil' red-bone gangster bitch he'd been fucking and staying with from time to time since he came back from out of town across the ass before rearranging the pillow that laid under her stomach. "I thought you were a gangster?"

"Mmmmh..." She moaned as Billy Lo pushed his dick back inside her tight little pussy. "I am, but your dick big as shit!"

"I got you though." Billy Lo slapped her ass again and watched it wiggle as he held her by the waist and tried to go balls deep again.

"Ssss..." She grabbed the sheets, bit the pillow, and curled her back in trying to control Billy Lo's deepness because he was tearing her little ass up.

Billy Lo continued to fuck her hard until he saw her cum coating his dick like thick cake icing then he laid back and let her suck his dick until his eyes disappeared up in his head, his toes curled, and he nutted all down her throat.

"I bet your ass hungry now." She said rolling out of bed after swallowing his cum.

"You know I am." Billy Lo smiled and fell back into a pillow.

"I'ma go make us something to eat." She said wiping her mouth and face off with a damped cloth before tossing it on Billy Lo's chest.

Billy Lo watched her walk out of the room throwing her little ass as he wiped his dick and nuts off. She reminded him so much of Lotti's crazy ass.

******

After Shaneeka had left the house, Billy Lo tried to contact Lil' Dray again with no luck. He guessed Lil' Dray was still on some kid shit and hoped that he ain't do no dumb shit before he could catch up with him because he had a plan that would kill all the bullshit. Something like a peace offering.

Billy Lo's phone rung, but he refused to answer it once he saw who was calling. He was too mad at the moment and didn't want to say anything that could stop him from playing Diamond out of position and walking him right into his 'Rat Trap.' Plus, Billy Lo realized that Diamond's phone could be tapped, so he had to limit his conversation.

Billy Lo knew that what he'd planned was a hell of a move, but he also knew that it would work because them Muslim niggas had always been the 'Business before blood' type. Blood brought unnecessary heat and unwanted attention. And that was very bad for business.

Shabazz had told Diamond that Walaa was a man of sound judgment and fairness. A man who was always for peace and order first, but Billy Lo wasn't stupid. He knew that there was no way he could sit down with The Imam without some backing or insurance. So, he picked up the phone and tried Lil' Dray's number again.

******

Lil' Dray and Pierre laid in total darkness as Little Clyde drove the stolen Dodge Charger into Baby Mecca. It was time to put all the planning and plotting to use. Little Clyde and Pierre had been clocking one of the Muslim's little hang out spots all week to see how the Muslims came and went. Now it was time to let their nuts hang. Lil' Dray was nervous as shit. Every time Little Clyde stopped at a light or Pierre whispered something silly he would tighten the grip on the two twin Glock .40's that laid flat across his chest because he thought it was time to put in work. When he felt the car come to a complete stop and heard the car door open his gut told him exactly what time it was.

"This it right here Cuzzo," Pierre mumbled anxiously. "Watch how hard I go on these niggas, I'ma drag."

"Shush!" Lil' Dray fired. He just knew motherfuckers could hear him. "Be quiet nigga!"

"Hey, you gotta move that, Ock."

Lil' Dray elbowed Pierre. He could hear a Muslim dude approaching the car. This was exactly why he hadn't let Little Clyde bring his chopper, because he wanted to get right on these niggas. He wanted to walk them niggas down one at a time and issue head shots.

"You deaf or something, Ock? I said you can't park here nigga!" The Muslim dude slapped or hit the trunk making Lil' Dray jump and almost squeeze off. "Move this shit!

"Just give me a second homie." Little Clyde pleaded. "I got some Prayer Rugs in the trunk for dirt cheap."

Lil Dray clinched his teeth and his nostrils flared in anticipation for what was about to come next when he heard the lock on the trunk pop.

"I got multiple colors too homie…" Little Clyde was saying as he opened the trunk. "My man said y'all be buying this type of…"

The Muslim dude looked down just in time for Lil' Dray to knock the whole bottom part of his mouth off and from that moment on it was 'work call.'

Little Clyde spun around and started firing. Pierre sat up and started dumping on all the Muslims who were too old or too fat to run and tried to take cover behind a now flipped over card table. Lil' Dray climbed out of the trunk, shot the Muslim on the ground again, and then started cutting Muslims down. Glass was shattering, poker chips and card were flying, and people were screaming. They had never witnessed nothing like this in Baby Mecca.

"LET'S GO! LET'S GO!" Pierre yelled when the Muslims were no longer moving. "Them niggas done."

Lil' Dray hopped back in the trunk and laid down beside Pierre. "Come on Cuzzo! Close the trunk!"

"F-B-I! FREEZE!"

Little Clyde and Pierre had never realized that the FBI had the Muslim shop under constant surveillance. Lil' Dray and Pierre laid there looking Little Clyde straight in the eyes as he let go of the trunk.

"I ain't going to jail Cuzzo." Lil 'Dray mumbled peeping over the rim of the trunk as FBI Agents closed in with their guns drawn.

"Easy now. Just drop the weapon and turn around slowly."

Bodymore Murderland

"Chapple! You and the other guy stay put and toss the guns!" Another FBI Agent yelled.

Little Clyde looked at Pierre and Lil' Dray and made a break for it. The FBI Agents immediately took aim and let off. Lil' Dray knew that Little Clyde had to be down when agents started calling for him to toss his weapon again. Lil' Dray knew that he and Pierre had two options, but for him, prison wasn't either one.

"What you gonna do Cuzzo?" Pierre asked looking over at him.

"I'm down for whatever."

"Then let's give these bitches what they want." Lil' Dray said throwing his hand over the lip of the trunk firing wildly, striking one of the agents in the face and throat with a cop killer.

Lil' Dray knew that they had to get out of there, but the agents rattled the Charger with what felt like a one-hundred rounds and kept them pent down.

"Y'ALL NIGGAS GET THE FUCK OUTTA HERE CUZZO!"

Lil' Dray heard Little Clyde holler from the other side of the metal shell just before shots rung out again. "Go Cuzzo, get outta here." Lil' Dray ordered, but Pierre didn't answer. "Cuzzo! Cuzzo!"

When Lil' Dray realized that Pierre was gone, shot with bullets that were meant for him. He grabbed Pierre guns and aired them out. Then took that opportunity to roll out of the trunk and scramble around the Charger as at least four bullets cut into his flesh.

Lil' Dray banged back until one Glock was empty and the other one jammed.

Lil' Dray could hear more police cars sliding to a stop close by. He knew they were closing in. He looked over for Little Clyde, but he too was already gone. Fuck it! He thought when he heard police footsteps approaching the Dodge Charger from both ends. They had already dusted his cousins.

"LET ME SEE YOUR HANDS CHAPPLE! LET ME SEE YOUR HANDS!"

"Fuck you bitch!" Lil' Dray barked unjamming his Glock.40. "Y'all will never take me alive!" He added before sticking the Glock.40 around the side of the car and squeezing the trigger with every ounce of strength he had left as agents moved in to let him have it.

As Lil' Dray laid there dying in a pool of his own blood, he smiled because he knew that there wasn't no more niggas like him or his cousin.

Chapter 32

"I just can't do this shit no more Donald. I'm tired of lying and being phony. The baby's not yours, and there's no way I'm going to wait around for you to do a life sentence. I've already been dealing with my baby father anyway. And they talking about you was raping women and shit."

Tiara's words kept echoing over and over again in D.W.'s head. He was losing everything that mattered. First his freedom, then his brothers and now his family. D.W. got up off the bunk and punched the wall. He knew that Tiara was right. He had treated her like shit when he was home, but he wasn't on no new shit because he was locked-up. Tiara was truly the only woman he ever loved, even though he hadn't always shown it, and the thought of losing her was almost too much.

"*Fuck!*" D.W. fired out of frustration. His mother had told him a thousand times. "Take good care of your woman, and she'll always take good care of you." Now he wished he would've listened.

"Damn yo, a nigga trying to sleep." D.W.'s cell buddy exhaled deeply like he had an attitude, rolled over, and mumbled something D.W. couldn't really make out.

"What your P-C ass say?" D.W. demanded looking over at the bunk daring his cell buddy to say something slick, so he could snatch him out of bed and beat his ass. "Yeah nigga, that's what the fuck I thought!"

D.W. had constantly been feeling like he had something to prove since arriving at the Penitentiary Annex in Jessup, Maryland

and requesting Protective Custody more out of sense than fear. He knew that he'd done a lot of dirt in the streets, slumped a lot of good men, and with all the hot shit being tossed around niggas may feel like he was fair game. Even suckers, who would normally mind their manners might try something slick.

D.W. knew that he couldn't do a life bid on P.C. No matter how much of a gladiator's school the Annex was rumored to be. One thing for sure and two things for certain. Joining a gang or religious following wasn't an option. Especially since he hadn't even listened to his parents when he was on the streets. That would be like an insult.

D.W. felt like if he just laid-low for a while and let niggas forget all about him. He would eventually be able to show his face in General Population. Because he wasn't about to turn into one of them wild ass P.C. niggas that snitched on men, talked shit to gangsters and sold death to killers because they couldn't get to him. There was no greater death sentence in prison then being an Indian who all the Cowboys were after.

******

Diamond talked to Billy Lo, and everything was set. It seemed like Billy Lo had been reading his mind. He wanted to have a sit-down with the brothers, and he refused to sit down with anybody but *'Walaa'* himself. Billy Lo also said that the meeting had to be held in a secluded, but public place at a time and location of his choice. Diamond assured him that would be no problem, but told him that he would have to get back with him about meeting 'The Imam.'

Diamond smiled as Billy Lo explained what he wanted to do. He wanted to tap-out, he'd had enough. Diamond had told them that they couldn't go up against the Muslims and win. Now he had lost everything worth living, dying, and fighting for. "Don't even worry about that slim. I got you. Just give me a few hours to run it pass Shabazz and line something up." Diamond continued to smile. Now Billy Lo was the one in the trick-bag.

When Diamond hung up with Billy Lo. He immediately went and ran everything down to Shabazz. Twisting the truth just enough to make it appear like it was his powers and not Billy Lo's plans that brought shit together.

"You did good Ock." Shabazz patted him on the back. "Go ahead and set up the meeting, but make sure you tell that little nigga that he better come alone."

"Done." Diamond nodded his head. He felt like a true chess player, and he was about to make Billy Lo a pawn in his game.

******

Billy Lo had a lot on his mind as he drove towards the meeting that had been arranged by Him, Diamond, and Shabazz. So, much had changed in one year. Billy Lo had lost his family and gained someone else's foes. And the one dude that he'd trusted the most. The one motherfucker that he'd come to admire and respect turned out to be a fucking rat and snake.

Billy Lo watched as the clouds dropped and created a thick fog in the morning sky. When the light rain started to fall, he prayed to God to watch over him because he knew that he was about to toy with death. But, just in case God was too busy he had recruited Zimbabwe and one of his men to hold him down.

Billy Lo parked his rental, grabbed Walaa's gift and got out of the car to make his way over to his former boss's trailer office. He disregarded the '**Be back later**' sign and knocked on the door before smirking and looking around the busy construction site. It all made sense now. Diamond had been playing him for the Muslim from the start. His gut had made him wonder how Diamond knew about the construction job, but he'd written it off as nothing because Diamond was his big brother.

"Come on in!" Someone called out.

Billy Lo turned the knob and put on his poker face as he entered the square room with a small desk and long couch. "Evening gentleman." Billy Lo said as he was approached and roughly patted down by a large Muslim.

"He's clean Ock." The big Muslim assured Walaa taking the bag out of Billy Lo's hand before shoving him towards the desk.

"Welcome." Walaa said as the big Muslim joker dumped the contents of Billy Lo's bag out on the couch.

"You must be Walaa?" Billy Lo said sticking his hand out.

"The one and only." Walaa replied disregarding Billy Lo's hand as he leaned back in the recliner. A sign of disrespect.

Billy Lo studied his face before looking around to size up the situation he'd just walked into. But, it showed nothing, except maybe the true facade of a Poker Player. Billy Lo tried to read the little guy standing off to the left of Walaa, but again got nothing.

"You know you got some big balls Ock, but I like that. It shows potential. And potential can be very powerful." Walaa said. "So, tell me, why are we here?"

"I've come to make a peace offering."

"The kuffar behind most of my troubles has come to offer me peace." The Imam couldn't help but laugh. "You gotta love these kuffars? Let me ask you something Ock. How is it that you can offer me something that you don't have the power to give?"

Billy Lo stared at the unreadable Imam for a second and figured that he wanted to remain in control. "Well, not peace. More like a gift. A solution to all of our Government problems."

"And what is it that you want for this ummm…gift of yours?"

"A clean slate." Billy Lo got to the point of the meeting. "I want to be able to walk away from this alive."

Walaa took a long look at Billy Lo before he spoke. "And when do I get this little gift of yours?"

"You already have some of it." Billy Lo gestured towards the papers spread all over the couch. "The rest is stashed some place safe."

The big Joker who had searched Billy Lo quickly gathered the papers back together and handed them to Walaa.

"And just where did you get this information?" Zayne Dela' monte questioned flipping through the papers. "I notice that there's a list of names here, but how do I know if it's authentic?"

"I can't reveal my sources, but I'll tell you this. Everything I gave you is the real deal. And you can check it by the case numbers."

"I like you Ock; I really do," Walaa said handing the papers back to the big Joker. "But unfortunately, this gift of yours is no good to me because I already possess it."

Billy Lo sat there stuck on stupid as Walaa smiled and got to his feet, as a car horn went off outside a few times.

"Your rides here Ock." The little Muslim said peeping out the window. "Well, I guess that concludes our business." Walaa, grabbed his coat off the back of the recliner and made his way around the desk.

"I wish we could've met under batter circumstances Ock. Maybe you would've been a Muslim." Walaa smiled again and headed for the door. "But look on the bright side, I never leave dangling threads, so Yusef's sins won't go unpunished."

"Now let's really find out what you know." The big Muslim joker, spoke up slipping on some leather gloves as the little one followed Walaa to the door and locked it behind him.

"This is my favorite part." The little Muslim dude said staring at Billy Lo from the other end of the trailer. "I enjoy crushing kuffars."

Billy Lo sensed danger and rushed the Muslim Joker, but two heavy blows put him on his back a second before the leather glove covered hand tighten around his throat and lifted him up in mid-air. "You ready to tell me what else you know?"

"Fuck...you." Billy Lo managed to say before spitting blood in the Muslim Joker's face. "Suck my dick."

"This is gonna be fun." The big Joker wiped his face and looked over at his partner before slamming his fist into Billy Lo's face again. "You like that tough guy? Let's see how much pain you can take."

Billy Lo almost blacked out when the big Muslim Joker tossed him across the room into the wall.

"Ahhhh...!" Billy Lo moaned and rolled over clutching his arm. "You better kill me nigga."

"Come on, don't tell me you're hurt already. I'm just getting started." The big Joker walked up towering over top of Billy Lo just as someone knocked on the trailer's door. The big Joker kicked Billy Lo in the ribs with his sharp size thirteens then signaled for his partner to get the door.

"Hold up a second." The little Muslim dude barked slipping his .22 back into his waistband before approaching the door. "I said hold up! Damn!" He fired when somebody knocked again.

When the little dude cracked the door, two ski-mask wearing goons in trench-coats forced their way inside with guns.

"Hey!" The big Joker took one step forward when one of the gunmen slammed the butt of his gun into the center of his partner's forehead and put him out cold.

Bodymore Murderland

"Come on big boy." The short one barked aiming his gun at the big Joker like he was dying to kill something. "Try me, so I can slump your big ass up in here."

Billy Lo struggles to get to his feet and shake the dizziness off. It was a good thing he never 'trusted nothing' and always 'expected anything,' because it had just, more or less, saved his life.

"Fuck took you niggas so long?" Billy Lo asked looking from Little Dinky to Zimbabwe.

"You said twenty minutes," Zimbabwe replied.

"Fuck!" Billy Lo touched his swollen face before kneeing the big Joker in his nuts. "Punk motherfucker. Get the gun off that little bitch over there too!"

Zimbabwe leaned down and snatched the .22 out of the little Muslim dude's dip and tossed it to Billy Lo.

"Little Dinky, make sure were still straight outside." Billy Lo gestured towards the windows.

"We good slim." Little Dinky peeped out the window at all the construction workers going on about their business. "Ain't nobody paying us no mind."

"A'ight." Billy Lo picked up a book of matches off the desk and struck them before tossing them on the couch. Then he kicked the trash can over in the corner and lit that up too.

The big Muslim Joker laughed. "You think setting little fires gonna help you? You're not getting away with this."

"I just did." Billy Lo smiled before shooting the big Joker in the head six times and walking out with Little Dinky and Zimbabwe by his side as the fire started running up the wall to create an evil of its own.

Chapter 33

"Hey, I just got a tip on Izzard!" Baker came rushing into the coffee room pulling on his coat. "He's holed up at some female's house in East Baltimore!"

Gibson damn near spilled her coffee getting up and snatching her coat. This was the break they had been waiting on for weeks.

"What do we know so far?" Gibson questioned moving quickly with Baker towards the elevators.

"Not much but, the caller was sure that Izzard's staying with his cousin Shaneeka Kitt just off Loch Raven Boulevard in the 500 block of Stonewood Road," Baker replied looking at his notes, before pressing the elevator button again. "He recognized him from the news."

"I'll have a couple of marked-cars meets us over there." Gibson pulled out her radio.

"You make sure they don't move until we get there because I wanna be the one who slaps the cuffs on this asshole." Baker hit the elevator buttons again. "Come on, come on, come on, got damn it!"

"Got you," Gibson said calling it in.

On the drive over to Stonewood Road, both detectives were quiet. Lost in their own thoughts. They didn't talk until everybody met up in the White Tower Parking Lot a half mile away from Izzard's location.

"Okay, team one will take the back. You, you, and you will cover the front with me and Detective Baker. Teams three and four will secure the front and back perimeters." Gibson spoke strapping on her bulletproof vest. "If things go south remain in position until more back-up arrives. Is that understood?"

"Yes Ma'am." The officers said in unison.

"Good because this guy is considered to be armed and extremely dangerous. And we know that they're not about holding court in the streets."

"Now let's gear up and go get this asshole." Baker spat moving for the car. "And make sure that badges are visible. That way if anybody just so happens to have to shoot this motherfucker They're covered."

"Team two your up first. Your E-T-A should be ten seconds ahead of us. Teams three and four will stay on my bumper and bring up the rear. Understood?" Gibson took one more look around until she was satisfied. "Okay, let's go nail this son of a bitch."

The drive to Shaneeka Kitt's home lasted every bit of five minutes. Gibson communicated with all the teams over the radio. The 'go ahead' came after team two was in position. Baker had been so focused on the raid that he almost ran an elderly lady down when he brought the Crown Victoria onto Stonewood doing about 60mph.

"Go! Go! Go!" Gibson barked into the radio before jumping from the car and running towards the house with several other officers.

"Baltimore City Police Department!" One officer yelled and sent Shaneeka's front door flying with the hit of a heavy, steel log before Baker and them stormed in making demands.

"Nobody move! Freeze! We got a runner!"

Gibson was the first to spot Izzard heading for the back door with his gun drawn. *"He's got a weapon!"*

Delmont M. Player

Baker came through the door ready to 'shoot to kill just as another officer tackled Izzard to the kitchen floor and wrestled him into a pair of cuffs with the help of Gibson. "Secure the rest of the house!" He ordered.

Shaneeka Kitt was found upstairs in the shower, and a thorough search of the basement produced another male hiding under an old furnace, and just like everybody else inside the house, he claimed to have never met or even heard of anybody with the name Anthony Izzard.

"Our guy was definitely here." Baker pulled Gibson to the side and showed her the Police Scanner that had been in an upstairs bedroom. "She's lying."

"Well, there's no law against that," Gibson said knowing that most people lied by nature, especially women.

"Damn, I wanted to nail this asshole!" Baker looked over at Shaneeka Kitt, wrapped in a towel, sitting on the couch hand-cuffed and wished he could charge her for harboring a fugitive or something. He never understood what good women saw in bad boys.

"We'll get him," Gibson said. "But, for now, we'll just run these two downtown, for gun possession and resist and see if we get a hit off their prints."

******

"My bad homie." Diamond bumped into the tier-runner as he came onto the tier to holler at Shabazz. "You know if Shabazz down there?"

"I ain't even sure homie." The dude replied and continued off the tier.

"Shabazz." Diamond walked up and peeped in Shabazz's cell. "Yeah, Ock." Shabazz looked up with a smile.

"What's good?" The make-shift curtain was already pulled back, and Shabazz was sitting on his bed counting postage stamps, so Diamond stepped in.

"Ain't too much. Trying to make sure this money straight."

"What's up? Everything good?" Diamond asked concerned.

"Yeah, I just had some words with the tier-runner about a couple of dollars that's all," Shabazz replied pushing about one-hundred stamps across the bed to him. "Here. Make sure that kid straight for the weekend. "

"I got 'em'."

"So, have you heard anything from our friend?"

"Nah, not yet, but he'll probably get at me soon."

"Make sure you let me know when he does."

"You know I got you." Diamond assured him. "I'm just waiting for that nigga to call."

******

Billy Lo felt fucked up about the way Zimbabwe and Little Dinky got jammed up. He had wanted to tell them what time it was when the call for the raid came across the police scanner, but there wasn't enough time. He and Shaneeka had been tangled up in bed, and they were all the way down the basement. Billy Lo couldn't do anything but shake his head as he watched the police escort Zimbabwe and Little Dinky from Shaneeka's crib because he had gotten them caught up in his shit.

Billy Lo knew it was time to do something. The city was too small, and the cops were closing in. The detectives had looked him right in the eyes, and he thought he was caught. For some reason, despite how good he felt like he was hidden. He just knew the detectives had him. Especially when them bitches came right up on him, but they kept moving. Which was good for everybody involved. Because had they would've spotted him; they would've had to call in the judge and jury because he was holding court in the streets. Going back to prison was out of the question.

Once the police were gone, Billy Lo knew that he had to get the fuck out of East Baltimore. He paid Shaneeka for her front door and drove around until he found a twenty-one dollar Motel spot that accepted cash over in South Baltimore off Washington Boulevard. After he got some sleep and cleared his head, he called the only person he felt like he could trust. Charm. Herbert had already said that he would only help him one more time because Diamond had made him hot and he wasn't about to jeopardized his family, freedom, or career over somebody else's bullshit.

Chapter 34

"So, what are you planning to do?" Charm questioned Billy Lo as they sat inside the small Motel room where he'd just delivered a few guns.

Billy Lo looked up from cleaning one of the three guns that laid across the sheet less bed to where Charm was standing near the door and spoke. "I'll hit em' where it will hurt the most."

Charm nodded as if he understood, but Billy Lo knew he didn't. "So, what do you need me to do?"

Billy Lo thought for a second. He had already taken care of everything. Recovered his whole stash, smashed Zimbabwe's baby mother off for him, and Little Dinky and hooked up with Herbert's scared ass. "Learn from our mistakes, and always remember that 'being a gangster is more than just an imagination. It's a mindset, a way of life. Honor your elders, protect all women and children, and respect the innocence at all cost. Charm a true gangster's focus is money, but money without honor and respect in this line of work is a death sentence."

"I heard that." Charm nodded.

Billy Lo got to his feet and gave Charm a pound and brotherly hug. "I appreciate you coming through for me soldier, but I want you to go ahead and get up out of here, so you don't get caught up."

"So that's it huh?"

"Yeah, like I said. Come Friday I'm gone no matter what." Billy Lo replied without going into details. "I done did my homework. Now it's time to take these niggas to the streets."

Delmont M. Player

******

The smack had him stick, frozen, sitting on his bunk high as a kite. Shabazz had just blessed him with something that was taking like a twenty before dinner and promised to touch him again by lock time, so Diamond went straight to the cell and put a couple 50's up in his system, but something wasn't right. The smack had instantly numbed him and made his nose start to bleed.

"Damn that rat-poison fucked that nigga up. Check to see if his ass dead."

Diamond looked up to see two lil' dudes he always saw running around the jail starting shit standing over him. He hadn't even heard them niggas enter the cell. "Man, do y'all Lil' motherfuckers know who I am?" Diamond questioned with a smile.

"You mean, who you was?" One of the Lil' dudes replied with a smirk of his own. He couldn't believe that Diamond was still breathing. "Dug, we gotta finish this nigga off."

"Oh, I got him." The second Lil' dude said pulling out a large jail-house shake. "Just get all his shit."

Although he could barely move or talk. Diamond saw the shit-covered knife Shabazz always carried and knew what time it was. He had not survived 24/25 years amongst the wolves being stupid. Shabazz had rocked him to sleep, and he knew that if the blade didn't kill him, the toxins from the feces surely would. *'Damn!'* He thought wishing he had listened to Billy Lo.

"Yeah bitch, it's judgment day." The Lil' dude fired slamming the shit-covered knife into Diamond's chest. "Hot ass nigga!" He slammed the knife into Diamond's neck this time. "You thought you got away didn't you bitch? You thought that shit wasn't going to catch up to you huh? Nah bitch, nah…"

Diamond thought about a story in the Bible where Satan tried to tempt Jesus into selling his soul when he was tired, hungry, and in need. He had offered him the kingdom, and all the worldly satisfaction that came with it just like the police had offered him a way out and all the help that came with it. But, unlike Diamond, Jesus had been smart enough to keep his faith and honor his conviction to God because he knew that shortcuts were dangerous.

They may seem, at the moment, to offer a road free from sufferance and responsibility, but in the end, the pain they carry was always much worse than anything one could imagine.

"This is for Fly Feet!" The Lil' dude barked hitting him again. "And this one is from Shabazz bitch!" The Lil' dude slowly pushed the blade up in between Diamond's ribs until it got to the handle and gave a final twist. "He said your services are no longer needed."

******

"Well, that didn't work," Baker said as they exited the prison. "I guess White wants to hold on to whatever little dignity he has left."

Baker and Gibson had just left the Penitentiary Annex trying to get White to give up anything he knew about Izzard. Something that could help them track his ass down.

"I don't think that's it." Gibson retorted opening the car door. "He probably just doesn't know anything. He's in protective custody. By all counts in the streets, he's a snitch. Who's going to tell him something? He fell from grace."

"Well, there's still Friday." Baker ducked into the car behind Gibson.

"You think that motherfucker's information is legit?" Gibson asked.

"It better be. At lease for his sake." Baker replied knowing that if Izzard did not show up, then he would personally see to it that their source was not only charged with obstructing but a conspiracy. "Or Internal Affairs will be the least of his worries."

Chapter 35

Friday morning seemed to come faster than Billy Lo expected and the weather was crazy. Billy Lo left the Motel around dawn. He wanted to be ten steps ahead of his prey because he knew that the early bird always got the worm. After doing all his homework, Billy Lo had come up with a murder plan that would silence all the critics who thought the Muslims was untouchable and send a message to the underworld that 'anybody could get it.'

Billy Lo checked his watch. He knew that The Imam arrived at Masjid early on Fridays because of Juman. Which was good in his mind because it would give him time to put his work in, get back to the Motel to grab his shit and catch his 2:15 P.M. bus before it departed from the station.

Billy Lo checked his clip for the umpteenth time. He had wanted to use the new AK-47 that he'd gotten Charm to pick up from his man to ball Walaa and his whole security team up, but ever since the last attempt he knew that he had to get up close and personal if he wanted to knock Walaa off for real and for good.

That was the reason for the silencer, but if all else failed and he was forced to run up on Walaa's armored-car again, he had loaded the clip with Black Rhino Shells to ensure success.

Billy Lo saw the dark gray clouds moving in, checked his watch again, and waited. Walaa would be pulling up any minute now.

"Anything on that little kuffar?" Walaa asked from the back seat of the black, tinted window Jaguar as they drove through Baby Mecca towards Al-Haqq. He wanted to be able to get in early and goover his Khutbah like always.

"Nah Ock, but if what the Young Brother says checks out. Then we should be hearing something in a couple of hours."

Tariq took his eyes off the road for a second to look into the rearview mirror.

Wales nodded. He did not talk a lot of business in public. Especially with the type of technology the feds were using nowadays.

When they arrived at the Mosque, it was all but empty outside. There were only a few brothers who had shown up early. Tariq exited the Jag and stood guard as a brother came out of the Masjid approaching Walaa's door with an umbrella. Walaa climbed out of the car adjusting his Jallabiya before quickly greeting a few brothers and ducking inside as Tariq and another brother remained outside.

The inside of the Al-Haqq Masjid was laid out like the basic Mosque throughout the city. Qu'ran's, Prayer Rugs, and oils could easily be found in one of the small offices near the back. Walaa removed his shoes and moved to the front to get a quick salat in before he started going over his Khutbah. He of all people knew how important Friday Prayers were in Islam. Allah was said to stand the Angels at the door of the Masjid and write down the names of all the people who entered.

"Allahu Akbar. Subhanak Allahumma wa bi-hamdika." Walaa opened the lines of communication with allah by stating that 'Allah is the Greatest, Pure and glorified are You, O'Allah. "Wa tabarakas muks wa ta' ala jadduka, wa la alaaha…"

"As-salaam Alaikum." Billy Lo greeted one of the only three brothers besides Walaa who weren't making Salat when he entered the Mosque. He had already been inside a few times, even attending service once, so he knew the layout. Billy Lo smiled to himself as the Muslim with the two little boys watched him like a hawk. Probably wondering why he hadn't removed his shoes. Billy Lo knew that people were going to say a lot of crazy things about him after today. But he didn't give a fuck. The Muslim rules did not apply to him. He lived by the street code and street laws, and as far as he was concerned niggas had touched his family, so all bets were off.

Billy Lo paused for a moment to watch Walaa prostrate. He wondered how the hell the devil himself could walk into Allah's house and not catch fire. Then he eased his heat out and closed the distance between he and Walaa.

Walaa had just finished seeking refuge with Allah from Satan, the accursed when he felt Billy Lo's presence and opened his eyes to look over his shoulder. "You really ain't got no respect, Ock? This is a Mosque." Walaa spotted the gun, but maintained his composure.

"And I've come to deliver the message." Billy Lo quickly took another look at the Muslim guy and the two little boys to see if their eyes were still on him, but honestly it didn't matter because there was no turning back. The time had come for Walaa to answer for his sins against Billy Lo's family. "Game over Ock."

Never one to rattle easy and always determined to suffer in the name of Allah gracefully, Walaa didn't flinch when Billy Lo raised the gun. He simply said, "Allah knows best." Then he turned back around and continued to offer prayer.

Billy Lo let him prostrate again before pulling the trigger twice issuing two headshots. Walaa remained in prostration as the blood poured slowly from his head. He even died with dignity.

The sound of the muffled gun-shots echoed throughout the small Mosque and got the other two Muslims attention, so Billy Lo stuffed the gun back in his dip and headed for the exit.

"As-Salaam Alaikum." Billy Lo greeted one of the brothers on his way out, but he just looked at Billy Lo like he was insane and back up to let him on by.

"Nobody come outside for five minutes." Billy Lo stopped and added before going out the door. He hoped that he wouldn't have to crush nobody else.

"You aren't staying for service, Ock?" Tariq asked the older Muslim brother as he exited the Mosque, but he just waved him off and kept on walking.

"That old nigga crazy Ock. He did the same thing last week." The other Muslim brother said to Tariq shaking his head.

Billy Lo made it to the car just as the father came running out of the Mosque speaking in Arabic. So he hopped in the car, started it up, and tried to pull off before the Muslims got on him, but he wasn't that lucky. Tariq and the other Muslims stepped out into the middle of the street and opened fire on him. Billy Lo ducked down and gunned the car towards them as the windows shattered and bullets rocked the car. He turned the corner under heavy gun fire and disappeared down the block. It was definitely time to get out of town.

Billy Lo headed for the Motel as he wondered how the hell the Muslims were going to explain to the community that they had allowed The Imam to get shot twice in the head as he prayed for forgiveness by a non-believer.

"WHAT THE FUCK!" Billy Lo instantly knew something was wrong the moment he opened the Motel room door. The whole place had been ransacked. The night-stand and small dresser draws were snatched out. The bed had been flipped over, and the clothes in his traveling suitcase were all over the room. Somebody had been looking for something. Then it hit him. Oh shit!

Billy Lo pulled out his gun and ran for the small bathroom praying that the only nigga he trusted hadn't double-crossed him. *Bitch!* Billy Lo locked up at the open vent and knew without looking that his money was gone. He looked at his watch. "Damn!" he mumbled. There was no way that he could find Charm and still catch his bus. So, he had two choices. Hunt Charm's little cruddy ass down and bury him, or take what little money he had on him and run. He chose the latter, but he definitely planned to come back for Charm's little punk ass later.

Billy Lo's blood was boiling as he stuffed what cash he had in the suitcase and checked his ticket. It took everything in him not to say fuck it and go after Charm. He even thought about stopping pass Peaches house and pushing her shit back too, but he was from the old school where women and children were always 'off limits'

Plus, he knew that the city was crawling with police by now and his freedom tasted a little bit better than revenge at the moment. He wiped the room down and switched disguises before leaving the Motel. He had one more move to make, and one more road to cross.

******

Do you really think he's going to show? Baker looked at his watch.

"The ticket's still good for an hour," Gibson replied. "Besides this is his last chance to get out of the city clean."

Baker prayed that Gibson was right because after word had come about The Al-Haqq Shooting, it didn't seem like Izzard was making any plans to leave. He seemed like he was taking care of unfinished business. "Let's hope he thinks so."

"Oh, he's coming," Gibson assured him. She would bet money on it. She could feel it in her gut as she watched passengers aboard the Greyhound. Everything she knew about Izzard said that he was calculated. He's probably just stalling for time. "And when he gets here...we take him in, or we take him down."

Delmont M. Player

******

Billy Lo made it to the Bus Station twenty minutes before his bus was to depart and decided to wait inside. News of the fallen Imam was spreading like wildfire and talk of their on-going feud was already being linked to his death. So, Billy Lo wasn't surprised when his name and face flashed across the screen. He put his head down and sat his ass down.

ALL PASSENGERS FOR THE 430 TO NEW YORK, NEED TO BOARD THE BUS NOW. IT WILL BE DEPARTING IN FIVE MINUTES! I REPEAT ALL PASSENGERS FOR THE 430 TO NEW YORK NEED TO BOARD THE BUS NOW!

Billy Lo's mind was still on Charm when the announcer came over the loudspeaker. He grabbed his suitcase and made his way out of the bus terminal. All he had to do was make it to his cousin Tiffany's house up in Staten Island, and he knew that he would be good. She wasn't the only family he had up top but, she was by far the most thorough.

Billy Lo almost shitted on himself when he saw Detectives Gibson and Baker loading the luggage as he approached the bus. He wanted to turn back, but he knew that it was too late. The station had to be flooded with cops. So, he played it cool and stepped straight to them as thoughts of having to come back to kill another motherfucker for crossing him instantly came to mind.

"Good afternoon Ma' am. Let me get that for you." Baker said reaching for the suitcase.

"Thank you, sweetheart." Billy Lo put on his best grandma voice and handed the detective his suitcase. Then he smiled and kept on moving with the crowd towards the door glad that he hadn't let the left-hand know exactly what the right-hand planned to do when he supplied the bus ticket.

"Right this way Ma'am." The bus driver gestured as Billy Lo came up to him. Detective Baker's mind was racing. Something about the elderly woman struck him as odd. Then it hit him. Baker's brain started working before his body did. The old lady had been on Shaneeka Kitt's block during the raid. He had almost ran her down in the street.

"Izzard's the lady!" Baker fired finally moving towards the front of the crowd.

"What?" Gibson was confused.

"The old lady is IZZARD!" Baker went for his gun just as the first shot went off. He saw the elderly woman go down as the bus driver stepped over top of her and fired again.

Gibson drew her weapon and yelled for people to take cover as other officers came from everywhere.

"DROP IT!" Baker aimed his gun at the bus driver. But, he only looked up, screamed "Allahu Akbar!" And starting firing. He shot the bus driver in the back and chest and knocking him off his feet before quickly advancing to kick his gun out of reach. If he weren't dead, he would be soon.

OFFICER DOWN! OFFICER DOWN! Baker spent around to see Gibson laying on the ground bleeding like crazy and almost lost it.

"What are you just standing there for?" Baker questioned rushing to Gibson's aid. "Get her a fucking ambulance NOW!"

Chapter 36

"Man, why don't you just let me and Frank handle this shit? Deli looked over at me as we sat outside of the University of Maryland Hospital in Downtown Baltimore several days after the Bus Station showdown that left a detective bitch banged up, a Muslim dead, and Billy Lo hooked to a Life Support Machine under constant guard.

"Nah Dug, I started this shit, so I got to finish it," I replied checking my gun one more time before stuffing it into my dip. It wasn't that I didn't have faith in Deli and Frank's ability to get the job done. I had seen their work when we all got jammed up for spanking the bitch ass nigga Shawn with my cousin Slate for touching his sister. I trusted them niggas with my life and freedom. They were some of the first niggas I turned to when Mumbles first put me on my feet. But, this shit was not only the price of independence. It was personal, so I wanted to make sure there were no mistakes personally.

"You just keep this bitch running and ready to go.

"A'ight then nigga. Let's get this shit over with." Frank fired from the back seat opening the door.

"Let's make it happen." I climbed from the car with Frank and left the door cracked before walking into the hospital. Times were changing, and it was time for these old niggas to 'get down or lay down.'

Me and Frank made it to the elevators and rode in silence both lost in our own thoughts. The Muslims had approached me with a deal that I couldn't refuse. All I had to do was finish the job on Billy Lo, so the choice was easy.

Bodymore Murderland

First of all, I'd already crossed the nigga anyway when I got Frank to watch me and Deli's back while we searched Billy Lo's Motel Room after he left. Then the nigga was really the reason why my little sister got killed.

When me and Frank got off the elevator on the ninth floor, I saw the Intense Care Unit sign and peeped around the corner pass the Nurse's Station. There were two Security Guards posted up outside of what I assumed to be Billy Lo's room.

"The guards still there," I said turning back around to face Frank and confirm what we already knew. "So, what I' ma do is go all the way around to the other end. When you see, me coming, run up on the police and tell 'em' something crazy."

"Huh?" Frank looked at me like I had lost my mind. "What the fuck am I supposed to tell 'em?"

"I don't know. Anything. Tell 'em' a nigga waving a gun around in the waiting room or some shit. Just get them away from Billy Lo's door."

"Then what?" Frank asked.

"What you think crazy?" Now I was the one staring at him like he had lost his mind. "Meet me back at the car."

"Bet." Frank gave me a quick pound and hug. "One."

"One," I repeated. "And don't forget to keep your head down, so the camera won't pick your face up."

"A 'ight." Monk nodded, and it was show time.

I took the long way to the ninth floor, passing both the waiting room and Vending Machine Area. I passed a smiling Doctor and fine, big-boned, caramel-complexioned RN, who probably thought that I was another baby-faced kid visiting a sick relative.

When I made it to the other end of the hallway, I peeped out and quickly signaled to Frank. The guards were outside of Billy Lo's room joking. I watched as Frank ran pass the Nurse's Station screaming and carrying on until the guards stopped him. After a brief discussion, the guards took off running behind Frank. Once they turned the corner, I pulled the closest fire alarm and headed for Billy Lo's room.

The halls instantly filled with patients, family members, and personnel as an announcer started telling everybody to remain calm and move towards the closest exit over the hospital speakers. I moved quickly down the crowded hall looking for the right number.

"7...6...4...3...got it!"

I entered Billy Lo's room and closed the door. Billy Lo was chained to the bed with all kind of tubes and shit attached to his body. He looked up as I walked over to the bed and removed the chrome snub-nose .38 from my dip. I wondered how he felt now with me standing over top of him. I stood there until I was certain that he could see through the bullshit ass disguise then I raised the .38 and shot him once in the chest and twice in the head to be sure the deed was done.

Once Billy Lo's blood and brains spilled out over the hospital bed whites, I, stuffed the smoking tone back in my dip and got the fuck out of there fast.

*****

"GO! GO!" I ordered jumping back in the car as police and firemen came from everywhere. Get the fuck out of here before we get boxed in.

"Did you handle that nigga?" Deli questioned putting the car into drive.

"Nigga just drive!" Frank barked anxiously looking around.

"Let's just say that all conquerors must one day be conquered," I replied picking up the wet cloth off the back seat to wipe my face knowing that no more needed to be said. As Deli turned the music on and let Hell Rell's *'For The of Hell of It'* continue bumping...

"*I can't lie/ always wanted to be a gangster. Since a shorty/ always wanted to be a gangster. Watched TV/ always rooted for the gangster. I can't lie...*"

To be continued...

ABOUT THE AUTHOR

In 1999, after being wrongfully convicted of 1ˢᵗ degree murder and handgun violation, Delmont M. Player was sentenced to life plus, and shipped off to one of the most dangerous prisons in the State of Maryland as a young, angry, hard-headed kid, who could barely read or write. However, he refused to break or submit to what was considered the prison norms 'mentally, physically, or spiritually. So after years of earning the respect of his peers and captors on all the manly levels, Delmont decided to try something new.

Today, Delmont is a self-educated man of God and youth mentor fighting for his freedom. He has penned several books, completed numerous 'Self-Help' programs, obtained his High School Diploma, received VT Computer Technology College training, and built a family based production company called 'Players Over Everything', to continue his family's dynasty.

FOR MORE INFORMATION...
Write or Log onto:
Delmont M. Player #286573/#1775708
North Branch Correctional Institution
14100 Mcmullen Hwy., S.W.
Cumberland, Maryland 21502
Delmontplayer62147066@voiceforinmates.com
Poeproductionzz@gmail.com
Like him on facebook @DelmontMicheal or follow him on IG:
@1_1coolplay88

Bodymore Murderland

Made in the USA
Columbia, SC
08 August 2017